The
Patriot Guard

Ameythist Moreland

DEDICATION

This book is dedicated to my great grandmother, Carol, for
showing me that superheroes truly do exist.

ACKNOWLEDGMENTS

A special thanks goes out to my husband, Kyle, for listening to all of my late night ramblings and for giving me some of my best ideas. My wonderful editor, Caitlin Hall, deserves special recognition as well for being so amazing and helpful. If it weren't for her, this book would probably be unreadable. There are so many people to thank. This book would not have been possible without the love and support of my family. Thank you all for believing in me.

ONE

She's going to be late, Cale Pearson thinks as he glances around the staging area. *You would think after all of her hard work she would at least be on time to her own ceremony.*

He can tell people are starting to get anxious; they go live in less than ten minutes. Television crewmembers are rushing back and forth, unsure what they should be doing. The only ones oblivious to Parker's tardiness are the lighting engineers on the catwalk above, busy trying to get the spotlights angled *just* right on the stage. One of the workers is leaning too far over the edge, wobbling and making Cale nervous.

Don't make me save you...not today. It's Parker's day and the last thing she needs is "Patriot Prime" stepping on her toes.

He sighs.

Cale hates his name. Not "Cale," but his hero name, "Patriot Prime." He almost laughed in their faces when the members of the Tribunal named him, only catching at the last second they were being serious. He puts on a good front, though, whenever he is in character— puffs out his chest, pulls his shoulders back, and walks tall, looking down on people in what he hopes is a heroic manner. To him, it just feels condescending, but the crowds eat it up.

That's the whole point of this. The crowds, the people cheering and buying merchandise. Of course that's not the party line; the Tribunal tries to sell the Patriot Guard as being here to protect the citizens of New Edison, to inspire hope and pride. The program was started when the number of Variants began to skyrocket. People tend to get a bit nervous when genetically mutated populations begin to grow, especially when the mutations give them special abilities like breathing under water, controlling electricity, or even passing through walls.

Although, I still swear that one's a myth.

Variants have been noted all throughout history, but until recently they only popped up about once in every million people. In the last decade, they've become much more common—around one per every couple thousand people. The Patriot Guard is supposed to offer peace of mind, but deep down Cale feels that, to the Tribunal at least, the PG is more concerned with lining their wallets. He would never speak this aloud, though. General Linwood doesn't hide his distaste for Cale very well as it is—best not to give him something else to dislike.

From the very beginning of the Patriot Guard Project, Cale and General Linwood hadn't gotten along.

It's hard to believe it has been two years since they recruited me.

He had just come out of basic training when he was approached about joining a top-secret project. He was one of thirty recruits. There were other soldiers like him, but there were also policemen, secret service members, and even a world champion boxer.

The program started out by pushing everyone to their physical and mental limits. For two weeks straight, they were tested at all hours of the day: obstacle courses, logic tests, drills in the middle of the night, and on one occasion they hadn't even known they were being tested. The instructors had staged a terrorist attack to see how they would react, going so far as to put candidates they had already ruled out into comas so deep they appeared dead.

At the end of the two weeks, there were ten recruits left.

The final ten were given medical waivers to sign before they could continue in the project. Cale had tried to read through his, but it was over five hundred pages long and he didn't understand half of the legal jargon. He signed it anyway. He wanted to serve his country, and by that point it didn't really seem like he could refuse.

He and the other recruits were moved to a secret medical facility on the outskirts of New Edison. The injections were administered the day after they arrived.

The deaths began right away.

Dr. Maura Bellamy, top scientist of the genetic engineering field and a pioneer in nanobot technology, created the serum. It was supposed to be an advanced form of gene therapy, meant to give the recruits extreme strength, speed, and regeneration capabilities.

Four died within hours of being given the injection and two more deteriorated quickly over the following three days. The others took a bit longer. When it seemed the final four were stable and would survive, they began training, trying to develop and hone their new skills.

Only Cale, Ike Warf, John Spoke, and Walter Hask, the boxing champion, remained. They were meant to compete against one another, each vying to be number one. In every test, Cale came in second to Walter; Ike and John took turns beating one another for third.

Tempers started to shorten, and at first, everyone assumed it was due to the competitive nature of the testing.

They were wrong.

Ike and John were paired together for combatives, with everyone standing on the sidelines, waiting to see who would win. They were always neck-and-neck in the other tests, so people were eager to see who would be the victor. Some of the researchers even had a gambling pool going.

The test started normally; one would advance, one

would defend, and eventually someone would land a blow. But with each hit, the two men seemed to become a bit more unhinged, their rage becoming increasingly evident. Before long, they were snarling and tearing into one another.

The test manager called out "foul," and told them to cool it. When they didn't respond, he called out again, thinking they must not have heard him.

Cale wondered why he was the only one who could see that they were past hearing.

The manager stepped in to intervene just as Cale called out to warn him against it. It was too late; the poor man was torn to shreds. There was blood everywhere, and before anyone could decide what to do and how to stop them, they ripped one another apart.

After a moment of deafening silence, all hell broke loose.

Cale and Walter were separated and locked inside padded rooms. The researchers were afraid they would attack each other too.

It was discovered that Ike and John's levels of adrenaline and testosterone were through the roof at the time of their deaths, while their serotonin levels were at rock bottom.

After extensive tests were run on them, showing their hormone levels were within the norm, Cale and Walter were released from solitary confinement and set back to training. They were monitored closely for several weeks, and everything always came back normal on their tests.

Walter continued to beat Cale at every obstacle, and quickly became a favorite of General Linwood. Whenever the General would visit to inquire about the Patriot Guard Project's success, he and Walter bantered like old friends, all but ignoring Cale. For a while, this angered Cale, because damn it he worked hard too! Eventually he learned to ignore the two.

The Tribunal, the group responsible for all decisions

regarding the Patriot Guard, made up of General Sampson Linwood, Dr. Maura Bellamy, and Senator Andrew Scott, finally decided after a few months of training that it was time to unveil its new heroes. A meeting was called to discuss all of the arrangements.

Details were settled on quickly and everything ran smoothly until the issue of names was brought up. It was the first time Cale had ever seen the General and Walter at odds. General Linwood demanded Walter take an "appropriate" hero name, while Walter was determined to keep his boxing nickname because it was what people knew him by.

It didn't take long for a screaming match to ensue, both men jumping up from their chairs. Cale could tell Walter was starting to lose it; Walter kept twitching his head to the side and clenching his jaw. He snarled loudly and launched himself in the General's direction. A security officer, one of five that had been brought in after the Ike and John incident, stepped in front of him. Walter snapped his neck without even pausing in his steps.

General Linwood was forced to draw his handgun and shoot him. It took three bullets to bring Walter down, two to the chest and one to the head.

The remaining security officers converged on Cale and he soon found himself back in solitary. The autopsy results on Walter were the same as the others: high adrenaline and testosterone, with low serotonin.

Cale's levels continued to remain steady, even when faced with the numerous stress tests forced upon him by the Tribunal members. They were just being "thorough," they said.

Eventually, Cale was deemed safe and "graduated" the program. He was dubbed Patriot Prime and, much to General Linwood's dismay, named hero of New Edison. The other recruits were never mentioned; the Tribunal refused to let their deaths affect the city's view of Cale and the Patriot Project.

The public had been skeptical at first, but shortly after Cale had been revealed to the people, he became a true hero in their eyes. He rescued a group of students who had become trapped after a local elementary school suffered a partial collapse. Since then, people haven't been able to get enough of him.

That was where Parker came in.

The demands for Cale's attention and help were becoming too numerous. How could one person protect an entire city? It's not like he could prevent every mugging, car theft, or act of vandalism, even with his enhanced abilities.

He appealed to the Tribunal, trying to get them to see. Cale was so burnt out; he would be hero to no one unless he could get some rest.

He was told they would look into a solution.

The Tribunal decided that Patriot Prime needed a sidekick. It was also decided the best way to choose a sidekick was through a televised competition, a reality show, *Patriot Guard: Next Generation*. It would be a great publicity stunt, and a way for the public to really feel connected to the program. Any person eighteen or older could audition, though only twenty-five were chosen. Those chosen were, secretly and off-camera, given a new, safer, type of injection: a combination of super steroids and nanobots programmed to repair damage inflicted to the body.

After it became evident the new injection didn't have the problems of the old one, the competition began. The contestants were put through a sort of basic training, meant to teach them fundamental combat skills and weapons handling. After that, they were given tasks and missions to complete for points. Contestants were weeded out over a period of six months until only one remained.

Parker.

At first Cale had been certain the only reason Parker made the cut was because she was General Linwood's daughter; only two other females had made it and they had both been in the special forces. Parker didn't seem to have much of a background story other than being the General's daughter, which was, of course, what the show's producers focused on.

Cale had been angry about her presence. So many had died on the way to making this possible, and yet Parker just got to saunter in using her family connections. It was a disgrace.

Then, one day, he actually got to see her in action. She was amazing, even before the injection. She was much faster than anyone else, her reflexes lighting quick. She dominated any test they threw at her. Cale knew immediately that she would be the ultimate winner.

"Where the hell is that girl?" somebody growls.

Startled back to the present, Cale turns to see General Linwood looking angrier than usual, and again finds himself wondering how Linwood and Parker could be related. The General, with his blond hair and hard, angled features, is the exact opposite of Parker's brown locks and soft face. The only resemblance between the two is their matching chocolate eyes, though Cale has noticed in the past that, when she is in a good mood, Parker's eyes are a much lighter shade of honey. General Linwood is never in a good mood, so he isn't sure if that is a shared trait.

"I'm sure she's on her way, Sir. There is no way Parker would miss this," Cale assures the General.

"Well, thank you, Patriot Prime. I didn't realize your super powers now included clairvoyance."

Cale sighs heavily and turns away, heading towards his designated mark. All of the cameras are focused on a podium set up at center stage with the PG logo easily visible on the bright red backdrop.

"Somebody find her!" General Linwood orders. "This must start on time!"

What's the rush? Cale thinks. *Everyone already knows who the winner is. Today is just about swearing her in. How many people are tuned in on a Thursday morning anyway?*

~

Parker Linwood rushes down the hallway at top speed, gracefully dodging bystanders without a second thought, trying to make her way to the presentation staging area.

I'm going to be late!

Parker picks up her pace until the people she passes become nothing more than blurs of color. She is running so quickly that she completely misses the door to the staging area and, while skidding to a halt, grabs onto the shoulders of a stagehand, almost taking him to the ground with her.

"Sorry!" she offers over her shoulder as she makes her way back towards the door.

"Some hero," the guy mutters angrily as he turns back to his work.

"I'm here!" Parker announces as she bursts through the door.

The show's producer, Ellen Jeski, emerges from a small crowd of waiting people and gives her a stern look. Well, she at least *tries* to look stern. Her attitude is undercut by her completely nonthreatening size and appearance. Ellen is barely five feet tall and is completely overshadowed by Parker's five-foot-eight frame.

"We go live in four minutes!" Ellen enunciates, blond curls bouncing. "And where is the costume I approved?"

"You approved that?" Parker scoffs. "That's why I'm late. I did not work my ass of for six months so any hope of being taken seriously could be thrown out the window when I take the stage in underwear and thigh high boots!"

Parker had been appalled when she was given the costume they expected her to wear; blue leather boy shorts, thigh high black boots with a four-inch heel, a white bustier, and a red cape emblazoned with the black monogram "SS."

The Stolid Sentry, she mocks inwardly.

She made her way to the costume room of the studio, leaving behind a verbally abused stylist, and picked out her own outfit. Deciding that someone labeled "stolid" shouldn't dress so flamboyantly, Parker settled on a more subdued costume. She donned a pair of black skinny jeans, black buckled boots, a white long-sleeved top, black bulletproof vest, and as an afterthought decided to keep the red cape as it was the only thing with her emblem. She then made a pass through the prop department, grabbing a holster and two fake handguns.

I'll pick up real ones later.

From there, Parker had made a dash for the staging area.

"The public wants a show," Ellen tells her grabbing her arm and dragging her towards the stage.

"I thought the public wants a hero?" Parker counters.

"They want both," a commanding voice interrupts.

Parker stiffens automatically, recognizing its owner.

"General Linwood, perhaps you can talk some sense into your daughter?" Ellen asks plaintively.

Sampson Linwood marches over and looks Parker up and down appraisingly.

"Sorry, Ms. Jeski. I must admit I am glad that my daughter will not be parading around in her under-things."

Parker almost lets herself feel elated… *almost.*

"Although, you could have picked something a bit more patriotic, couldn't you, Parker?" he asks, condescendingly.

She is used to his double-edged compliments. They are always more insult than approval.

"Yes, father, I suppose I could have."

"We will have to fix this later. We are about to go live!" Ellen squeals, ushering everyone to their places.

Parker takes a deep breath as she approaches the stage. Her nerves are starting to get the best of her. In every moment leading up to now, she has been too busy to be nervous and hasn't had a chance to think about actually interacting with the public. Sure, she has been on everyone's TV for the last six months for the show, been interviewed for magazines and newspapers, but now she is getting ready to step from behind the cameras and into the direct line of judgmental gazes. It is with an overwhelming weight on her shoulders that Parker takes her place on stage, to the left of the podium.

She looks over to see Cale standing parallel to her. He gives her a reassuring smile and mouths *not fair,* indicating her costume. Despite her nerves, she finds herself smiling in response. She has to admit that she is much happier to be in her outfit than Cale's. He is wearing his normal hero garb: navy blue cargo pants, combat boots, a red, figure-hugging armored shirt with "PP", his initials, in white, and a thick utility belt held up by a large American flag belt buckle. The ensemble is topped off with a red domino mask and white cape.

The first time Parker had met Cale, he had been in this uniform, coming to visit the contestants on set. He stood on the sidelines watching them train. Everyone seemed too afraid to actually approach him and settled on whispering to one another that they couldn't believe it was actually *him.* Parker had no such qualms.

"I see what the ladies say are true," she'd said loudly, walking over to him.

His blue eyes tightened a bit, trying to decipher her intentions. She had to angle her face upwards to meet his gaze; he is at least 6'3".

"And what is it that they say?" he asked.

"That you have a large PP," Parker shrugged, and then unable to help herself, she burst out laughing.

Her comment seemed to catch him off guard, but he soon joined in her laughter.

"I'm Parker," she said extending her hand. "I intend on being your sidekick."

"Oh, really?" he reached out to shake her hand. "I'm guessing that means you already know that I'm Cale."

"Who doesn't know who you are? Your blonde hair, blue eyes, and perfect smile are on every other billboard in New Edison," she joked.

"Well aren't we cozy," General Linwood said harshly, coming up from behind Parker.

"Shouldn't you be training?" he asked her.

Before she could stumble through a response, Cale jumped in.

"Sorry, General. That was my fault. I shouldn't have interrupted the training session."

From that day, Parker and Cale formed a tentative friendship and eventually grew to be inseparable. They chatted whenever they had the chance, discussing the other candidates, combat tactics, and pretty much everything else. It was easy to see that Cale and Parker's father did not get along very well, which just gave them something else to bond over. On days when General Linwood was being especially atrocious, they would take turns speculating what caused his bad mood.

"Why is there so much more bran than raisins?" Cale mocked, trying to mimic the General's voice.

"No, no," Parker would snicker, then deepening her voice she would try, "what do you mean you used two percent milk in my coffee? Anything other than whole milk is unpatriotic!"

"Now I must go kick a puppy to release my frustrations!" Cale continued, and they would both lose it and start laughing uncontrollably.

More often than not, General Linwood would appear out of nowhere to break up their discussions with orders for Parker to get back to work.

Parker had tried to get to know the other contestants, but all of them had avoided her advances at friendship from the beginning, most of them assuming she was only there because of her father. It wasn't until they began competing and she wiped the floor with them that they decided to give her a chance, but by then Parker didn't want anything to do with them. They had made their decision, and now they had to deal with it.

None of the eliminated contestants are present for the ceremony, and Parker is glad. She is also glad to have Cale so close by, needing the support of a friend to make it through the event.

"We go live in thirty seconds!" Ellen shouts.

Senator Andrew Scott hurries to stand behind the podium. He is by far the most public friendly member of the Tribunal and therefore does most of the public speaking. Dr. Bellamy isn't much of a people person, preferring the solitude of her lab, and General Linwood is… well, General Linwood. He has a hard time not being rude and abrasive.

Senator Scott is an everyman: early 40s, graying brown hair, blue eyes, almost six feet tall, with a lean build and a politician's smile. He is the perfect person to be running the show.

"Three, two, one," Ellen counts down in a whisper.

The show's theme song starts and the red lights on the cameras turn on. Parker places a proud smile on her face as she sees the stage fill the monitor near one of the cameramen.

"Ladies and gentlemen of New Edison," Senator Scott begins, his face filling the monitor as the cameras zoom in. "Today is the day you have been waiting for! Today is the day you meet your new hero!"

He pauses dramatically.

"For the last six months you've watched her fight, sweat, and bleed to make it here. She has worked hard, and sacrificed so much to serve you… to protect you."

At this point on the monitor, the stage disappears and is replaced by a video montage of the challenges Parker faced throughout the competition. Afterwards, interviews start playing; her trainers, judges, Cale, and even her father all have something to say about her.

"She was always a determined little girl," General Linwood says in a clip.

"I honestly believe that Parker is the right choice, and that the Patriot Guard will be lucky to have her," Cale says, nodding, in the next.

Parker takes a deep breath, shakes out her arms, and rolls her neck in a circle, preparing for what she knows comes next.

"Back on you in three, two, one," Ellen signals.

"Outstanding," Senator Scott tells the cameras. "Now, finally, it's time to swear in our new hero. Miss Linwood, if you please?"

Parker walks slowly and surely over to join the Senator behind the podium. They turn to face each other, and begin.

"Please repeat after me," Senator Scott tells her. "I, Parker Linwood, solemnly swear…"

"I, Parker Linwood, solemnly swear…"

"To uphold the United States Government and to protect the citizens of New Edison to the best of my capabilities."

Parker repeats him.

"To follow the orders given to me by the Patriot Guard Tribunal," Senator Scott continues.

"To follow the orders given to me by the Patriot Guard Tribunal…"

"And to be a solid pillar of the community, always relied upon and never yielding."

After she repeats the final line of the oath, Senator Scott reaches out to place a black domino mask on her face, tying it just below her high ponytail. He then leads her over to where Cale stands; Cale takes Parker's hand and lifts it above their heads.

"Ladies and gentlemen, may I introduce the Stolid Sentry! The newest member of the Patriot Guard!" the Senator booms loudly. "Now—"

Whatever Senator Scott is preparing to say is drowned out by a crewmember calling everyone's attention. The monitor no longer has the stage on it, but instead a special news report.

"Three masked gunmen were seen rushing into the New Edison National Bank just moments ago," the newscaster reports, showcasing blurry footage from someone's cell phone. "Police have yet to reach the scene…"

"Welcome to the team," Cale tells Parker. "Looks like you're starting sooner than you planned."

TWO

You've got to be kidding me, Parker thinks as she follows Cale in rushing off the stage.

"The car is out back," he tells her over his shoulder.

"Parker!" General Linwood calls, rushing up to her. "You're going to need this, and please, be careful."

He pushes a small black case into her hands and gives her a quick, dismissive, nod. She wonders what is in the container but doesn't have time to waste by investigating. She turns away and hurries after Cale.

They find the car almost as soon as they exit the building.

"Nice," Parker comments appreciatively.

The car is a new Camero in flat black with chrome rims. On the hood, she just barely makes out the logo "SS" in glossy black.

"Is that—?" Parker starts, feeling a smile spread across her face.

Cale laughs.

"Yup. It's a present from the Tribunal. I'd let you drive, but I really think you'll need to unpack that box during the ride," he says, jumping behind the wheel.

Parker gives the car one more appreciative look, quickly climbs in, and then begins to unlatch the case.

"Hey—seatbelt," Cale chastises. "You're a role model now."

He turns the key in the ignition and pulls out of the

17

parking lot, urging the speedometer needle up as he hits the main road.

She sighs dramatically and clicks her safety belt in before anxiously returning her attention to the mysterious container. With careful fingers, she gently releases the clasps of the case. Inside, she finds two black .40 caliber pistols, the butts engraved with "Stolid Sentry."

She lets out a low whistle.

"Oh, yes. These will definitely come in handy."

Parker removes her prop guns from the holster and tosses them in the back seat, then lovingly sheaths her new custom pieces in their place.

"I'm getting all sorts of presents today," she comments, grabbing the doorframe as Cale takes a sharp corner.

He is going well over the speed limit, weaving in and out of the morning traffic with ease.

"On your left!" Parker advises.

Cale swerves out of the way seconds before a large truck veers into their lane.

"Good eye," he compliments.

"Wouldn't want you wrecking my car before I can even drive it."

The studio isn't far from the robbery scene, and they reach their destination in no time.

Cale makes a quick turn and pulls up in front of the bank; its stone face is the most impressive on the block, making it easy to spot. The bank is nestled tightly between two other buildings; it has one main door in front, with a stone staircase leading up to it.

Cale parks the car directly in front of the stairs, granting them quick access.

"Let's get in there, hero," he says, throwing the door open and rushing towards the steps.

Parker exits the car and chases after him, following Cale's suit at the bank entrance and drawing her gun. He peeks through the windows, craning his neck to get a look.

"I don't see them."

"Maybe they are in the back, with the safe," Parker suggests.

"Either way, this is our only way in. There is no other entrance. Keep your eyes open and weapon up."

Parker nods and follows Cale through the front door, staying crouched. Inside, there are at least two-dozen civilians lying face down, their hands resting on the backs of their heads. One of them, a young woman, hears Cale and Parker's entrance.

"Oh, thank God," she whispers, obviously relieved. "Patriot Prime is here."

The others, hearing her, all start mumbling and craning their necks to try to get a glance at him from their awkward positions on the floor.

Cale places his forefinger to his lips, silently shushing them, but it's too late.

"What's going on out there?" someone shouts from the back room.

The bank is fairly large and open; the room they are in is made of marble and is quite grand looking, with pillars spread throughout. Centered is the row of teller's windows, and behind that is the entrance to the back room that houses the vault and safety deposit boxes.

This is where the gunmen come from, filing out one after another. All three are wearing cliché black ski masks, and two are carrying bulging bags of cash in addition to their weapons.

"Well, well, look who's come to save the day–Patriot Prime and his new girlfriend. What's the matter, Prime? Couldn't handle it on your own?" the first gunman asks, his voice tinted with just a hint of an accent.

Parker almost rolls her eyes when she realizes he sounds like a movie mob boss.

He is the only one not carrying a sack of money, instead wielding a firearm in each hand. Despite his arrogant comment, he seems a bit nervous, his hands just slightly unsteady and eyes shifting around quickly, searching for an exit.

"I can handle just fine," Cale says coolly. "I brought her because I've grown bored with petty lowlifes like yourself and how easy you are to beat. I figured I'd give someone else a chance at the tedium."

The gunman just snorts and readjusts his aim, one gun on Cale and one on Parker.

"Now, now. No one has to get hurt," Parker offers. "Just put your weapons down, and come outside with us."

"Ain't happening, girly. We aren't leaving here without this money," the wannabe-mobster swears. "We worked too hard to just walk away."

"Nobody said anything about walking away," she tells him. "You're still going to jail. I just thought you'd be more comfortable in your tiny cell without a bunch of injuries to tend to."

"Someone is feeling cocky. That's good. It'll make you more fun to take down."

The three robbers stay in a tight formation, slowly walking around the counter.

"Have you not turned on a TV in the last six months?" Cale asks. "You really don't want to tick her off."

As the third robber comes around the counter, his foot catches, causing him to jerk forward. Both Cale and Parker whip their guns to face him. At the last second, Parker realizes this is the only opening the mouthy mobster needed.

"Down!" she shouts, just before he starts firing.

Parker drops and rolls behind the closest marble pillar, thankful that all of the civilians are off to the side of the room and out of the line of fire. She hears stone breaking as a bullet hits the pillar she is crouching behind. Cale is off to her side, also crouching behind a support column. He looks at her and gives her a signal for one of the combat tactics they have practiced numerous times.

She nods her head in agreement, and then stoops down to grab a chunk of the broken stone.

The room is quiet except for someone's muffled crying coming from where the civilians are grouped. The gunfire has ceased momentarily.

Parker uses this to her advantage and tosses the stone off to her side, away from Cale's location. The effect is immediate. From the number of bullets being fired at the decoy, Parker can tell that all three men have their attention directed to her left. She steps out to her right and Cale joins her, both taking aim at the robbers. Cale gets off a shot before the men realize what is happening and hits the third gunman. The second gunman, a big hulking fellow, drops to tend to his injured partner, but Parker knows it is too late. There is no coming back from where Cale shot him.

The first robber, completely ignoring his companions, opens fire on Cale. Before he even pulls the trigger, Parker can see the trajectory of his bullet. It is going to hit Cale right in the heart. Putting her advanced speed to the test, Parker launches herself at Cale. She manages to push him out the way of being shot in the heart, but the bullet still lodges into his right shoulder.

"Ah!" Cale cries out, hitting the ground.

Parker falls next to him and reaches out to examine his shoulder. The amount of blood makes it difficult to see the wound.

Parker vaguely recognizes mouthy mobster's voice shouting, urging his hulking partner to get up and leave their fallen friend. They use her distraction to their advantage and make a break for the front door.

"I'm fine," Cale pants, clamping a hand over his bleeding shoulder. "Go get them."

Parker gives him a brisk nod and takes off after the robbers.

"Someone call an ambulance!" she shouts to the civilians on her way out.

She races down the front stairs, frantically searching for a sign to tell her which direction the men went.

She hears an engine roar to life and twists around to see a man in a ski mask pulling out of a street parking spot, just a few yards from where Cale left the Camero.

He roasts the tires of his late-model SUV and takes off down the street.

Shit… the last thing I need on my first day, aside from my partner being shot, is this jerk running down an unsuspecting pedestrian.

Parker jumps into the waiting Camero, eager to catch up. The car purrs the instant she twists the key and she peels out after the robbers.

Luckily, by this time, everyone is already at work, so the city streets are much less congested than they had been earlier. It doesn't take long for her to catch up to the robbers' gas-guzzler. Her car was built for speed.

Parker loves going fast.

When she was a child, her father bought her a two-year-old male horse named Tempo. On weekends, he would drive her out to the country to the stables where Tempo was kept. She would get to spend the whole afternoon riding with her father. On days when he was in a particularly good mood, he would challenge Parker to a race. Those were some of the best days of her childhood: the wind rushing past her face, the adrenaline coursing through her, and the excitement often exploding from her in peals of laughter as she would pull ahead and take the lead.

After her mother passed way, her weekend trips to the country stopped abruptly. Her father sold Tempo and started to withdraw from Parker. She missed the exhilaration and speed, she missed her racehorse also, but mostly she missed her dad. She couldn't seem to bring him back to his old self, and there was no way to get Tempo back, so she settled for speed.

She would take her bike out and ride at the highest

speed she could manage. When that didn't work, she ripped the brake off of her bike, hoping that knowing she couldn't stop would add to the thrill. It did a little, but mostly it just got her into more crashes. When she hit high school, Parker started dating a senior with a motorcycle, though it didn't last long. He didn't like to let Parker drive.

One of her favorite perks of joining the second generation Patriot Project was her enhanced speed. While the injection seemed to give everyone a bit of an edge while running, it made Parker fly. She could run circles around everyone else. It was one of the things that put her in the lead, figuratively speaking, to win the competition.

The SUV in front of her banks a hard right. Parker follows easily, figuring the robbers are heading for the edge of town.

As if jurisdiction will stop me.

She presses the gas pedal to the floor, urging the Camero faster. The engine roars as she manages to get her car level with the SUV. She looks over to signal the robbers; Parker is going to ram them unless they pull over. As she starts to point at the other vehicle she notices something...

There is only one robber in the SUV.

Just as the realization settles over her, Parker hears a loud *click* from the backseat.

"Why don't you just slow on down a bit, and get behind the SUV, *hero*?" someone sneers from behind her, the unfamiliar voice suggesting she's dealing with the big, overly muscled robber.

Anger flashes through Parker as she does what he instructs.

How could I forget to check in the back?

She lets a slow breath out through gritted teeth as she watches her speedometer fall. Once behind the other vehicle, she gets a glimpse of the carjacker grinning at her in his rearview mirror.

"Just follow him," she's instructed, a gun digging into

the side of her neck.

Parker flicks her gaze to back to the mirror and feels a small, triumphant, smirk tugging at the corners of her mouth. Her carjacker is holding one of the guns she threw in the backseat, a prop gun.

"I don't take orders from criminals," she spits.

Using her full speed, Parker reaches beneath her for the metal bar that controls leg room. She releases the catch and throws her seat back as hard as she can into his knees. He cries out loudly in pain, but Parker ignores him and grabs at the controls on the side of her seat. She uses all of her weight to recline back, effectively pinning him. Twisting awkwardly, Parker punches the robber in the side of his head and knocks him out cold.

Without a second thought, she pulls herself back into place and speeds up to regain her close distance to the SUV. Ready to end this, Parker lines her car up just right, and smashes into the side of the other vehicle, causing it to spin into a light post. She slams on her breaks and stops near the crashed SUV.

"Sorry, baby," she whispers to the Camero, brushing the hood gently with her hand as she climbs out.

She quickly rounds her car and positions herself, gun in hand, right in front of the SUV's driver door.

Loud sirens alert her to the approaching police.

Smoke is pouring form under the hood of the robbers' vehicle, and broken glass litters the pavement. The driver's door swings open, and the first robber tumbles out coughing, and lands on his knees. He is cradling one arm tightly against his chest, and holding the other in the air, weaponless.

"Okay," he sputters, his accent thickening in his pain, "You got me."

Parker keeps her gun trained on him and advances cautiously. When she is certain he is no longer armed, she comes within arm's reach and stretches out to remove his ski mask.

He looks to be in his early-to mid-twenties, with red hair and blue eyes. She has the oddest feeling that she has seen him somewhere before, but cannot, for the life of her, recall where.

"Do I know you?" she asks him.

The robber just gives her a slight smirk and ignores her question.

Just then, the police reach the scene, and quickly rush in to handle the criminals. Two officers come up, take hold of the red-haired robber, and haul him to his feet, ready to cart him off.

"Wait," Parker interrupts. "I was questioning him."

"That's really not your area, Sentry. You catch them, and we handle the rest," one of the officers tells her.

Parker just sighs and nods.

"The other one is in the back of my car, unconscious," she says.

"Thank you, we'll handle it."

As she prepares to leave the scene, Parker is ambushed by scores of news teams, all trying to get her picture and a quote. She stands beside her car, which surprisingly has no signs of damage, and is peppered with questions.

"How do you like being a hero?"

"What brand are your jeans?"

"Is this what you expected when you won the competition?"

"Is Patriot Prime going to be alright?"

Parker holds up her hands to silence the small mob.

"My first day may have turned out a little more action-packed then I had anticipated, but if I have helped make the people of New Edison even a little safer, then it was well worth it. Now, if you will excuse me, I would really love to go check on my partner."

With that, she quickly climbs into her car and heads off to PG headquarters, knowing that's where they would have taken Cale.

~

Cale wakes up to the sound of soft beeping and hum of electric devices. He can instantly tell that he's lying in a hospital bed.

He slowly opens his eyes to check his surroundings and quickly recognizes that he is in one of the labs below the Patriot Guard headquarters. His memory is a little fuzzy; he tries to back track through what he can recall.

One of the robbers shot me... that bullet would have killed me if Parker hadn't pushed me out of the way, Cale remembers. *She went after the two remaining robbers, and then...* his mind is blank.

He must have passed out after she left.

Cale attempts to sit up in bed, but finds his hands restrained, cuffed to the rails.

What the hell?

Seeing a call button next to where his hands are resting, he grabs it and rings for help. He only has to wait a few moments.

Dr. Bellamy sweeps into the room and gives him a slight smile.

"Good, you're awake."

"Yes, and I'm handcuffed," he answers, wagging his wrist, causing the cuffs to clank against the bed rails.

"That was for safety purposes," she says. "You were thrashing around, striking out at my research assistants. You weren't yourself."

"I promise that I am myself now. Can you unchain me?"

Without pause, Dr. Bellamy pulls the key to his cuffs from her pocket and releases him.

"Everyone was a bit nervous," she tells him. "Your levels were... *off* while you were healing. Don't worry, they are back to normal now," she says catching the concern on his face.

"While I was healing? How is my shoulder now?" he asks.

"Take a look."

Cale sits up in bed and pulls his hospital gown down over his right shoulder. Where before there had been a bleeding hole, now there is only black scabbed wound.

"How long have I been here?" he asks.

"Oh… about thirty hours."

"What? It's healed that quickly?"

Dr. Bellamy only nods at him.

They knew the serum was supposed to give him faster regeneration capabilities, but they had never really put it to the test, other than a few minor cuts on his arms and whatever injuries resulted from training. The Doctor felt that anything more would have been inhumane.

There is a slight redness around the sore and Cale reaches out to touch it. His whole shoulder feels like it is on fire when his finger makes contact and he quickly pulls back.

"Careful," Dr. Bellamy chides, "it isn't completely healed yet. You don't want to reopen it."

They sit in silence for a moment, Bellamy studying the monitors attached to him and then making notes on his medical chart. Cale feels drained, despite his long "nap."

"Oh! What happened with the robbery? Is Parker alright?" he asks eagerly.

He is treated with a small laugh and a genuine smile.

It isn't often that Dr. Bellamy smiles, but when she does, Cale can't help but think she looks more like a retired super model than a scientist. She has a tall slender frame, extremely bright green eyes, and platinum blonde hair that is only just starting to sport a few grays, despite her age. Regardless of all of this, she still has a very approachable air to her, and gives off a motherly vibe. She is, by far, Cale's favorite member of the Tribunal.

"Parker was sensational. She's been all over the news,

and she actually handled the reporters quite well," she tells him.

"Good, I'm glad her first day wasn't a total disaster. Though, I'm sure the memory will be slightly marred by her partner almost getting himself killed."

Dr. Bellamy just shakes her head at him, an amused expression playing on her face.

There is a loud, demanding knock on the door to the lab. Before anyone can bid him to enter, General Linwood comes marching in.

"I heard you were awake," Linwood says, eyeing Cale.

"As you can see," he replies, his tone coming out a bit more sarcastically than he intends.

"How are you feeling?" Linwood asks, and Cale suspects it isn't because the General actually cares about his wellbeing.

"I'm doing good."

"Can you get out of bed? Are you able to walk?"

"I haven't tried yet," Cale starts.

"And I don't think it is a good idea," Dr. Bellamy rushes, glaring at General Linwood.

"Well the decision isn't up to you, Maura. We need him to go out on patrol as soon as possible. He needs to run interference and show the strength of the Patriot Guard," Linwood tells her, pompously.

"You must not have heard yourself clearly, Sampson. The reasons you just stated show it is clearly *my* decision. I am his doctor, and I am a member of the Tribunal, as well. I say no patrol."

"The Senator has already agreed with me. So, you find yourself outvoted, once again." General Linwood gives her a smile of malicious triumph and turns his attention back to Cale. "If you can walk, you are to be upstairs in an hour to meet Parker for patrol. It won't be a taxing evening; just taking a stroll through downtown to show the people you are alive and well. I trust you won't disappoint me."

Before Cale can say anything, the General turns on heel and quickly strides out of the lab.

"Cale, you don't have to go," Dr. Bellamy tells him.

"I should at least try," he says. "The Tribunal has spoken, and it is my duty to listen."

Slowly, Cale turns to lower his legs over the side of the bed, and then tries to ease himself into a standing position; he's slightly unsteady, but he manages.

"You look a bit wobbly," Dr. Bellamy comments.

"I'm just a little dehydrated and could use something to eat. I'm sure I'll be good enough to go on patrol after that," Cale assures her.

She doesn't quite look like she believes him, but must realize she isn't going to win, so she just nods.

"I'll have some dinner sent to you," the Doctor tells him, standing to leave. "Just don't push it. If healing causes your levels to spike, you really don't want to mess around with that."

Before Cale can think of an answer, Dr. Bellamy exits the lab, leaving him to his own fuzzy thoughts.

THREE

After he eats, Cale does indeed feel better. He walks a few laps around the lab, and though his shoulder still aches, he decides he is well enough to go on patrol. He rings his call button again, bringing in a random research assistant, who he sends to fetch him another costume. It doesn't take long for the researcher to bring him one; PG headquarters is full of spares.

Their wardrobe budget has got to be insane, Cale thinks as he dresses.

Once he is in uniform, Cale makes his way to the central elevators that will take him up to the main floor.

The Patriot Guard headquarters is located in the center of New Edison, and comprised of four levels; two stories above ground and two basement levels. The main floor contains several offices where PG personnel take phone calls about crime happening throughout the city, then file it in order of importance before deciding whether it is a matter that Patriot Prime should be involved in or not. There is also a living quarters area in the back where workers can crash out during particularly busy times.

The second story is for authorized personnel only, and the list of the authorized is rather short. The main feature of the second story is the War Room, where the Tribunal delivers most of its orders, but there is also another set of private rooms, where Cale has slept off his exhaustion on several occasions. The first basement level is a training arena for Cale, and now Parker, to hone their skills and develop new tactics. The second basement level is where Cale was brought after being shot, the PG private lab. It is here that Dr. Bellamy continues to work on and refine her serum.

Part of Cale hopes that she has completely abandoned her first serum, the one that made him who he is now. He doesn't want her retesting it, fearing the destruction it could bring. He had been quite skeptical about the *Patriot Guard: Second Generation* when he was first told of it. Of course, Cale was excited about having a partner, but he didn't like the idea of the Tribunal using a batch of unsuspecting civilians as guinea pigs. The competition had worked out though, which just went to prove that the Tribunal knew what was best, when it came down to it.

When Cale exits the elevator on the main floor, he finds Parker pacing anxiously in the lobby.

"I hear congratulations are in order. They say you showed up Patriot Prime and took down a ring of bank robbers single handedly," Cale says, sneaking up behind her.

"You know what they say," she replies, turning to face him, "a new generation means an improved model."

Cale laughs.

"How are you doing? They wouldn't let me down to see you."

"I'm doing pretty good. My shoulder looks like I got shot weeks ago, rather than hours. It's a little sore, but it would be a bit much to expect anything else."

"Are you sure you're okay to patrol?" she asks.

"This barely counts as a patrol, Parker. The General just wants me to be seen, to put to rest any speculation of my impending death."

"But if you really aren't feeling well enough, I could talk to him."

"No," he says, "I'm fine. That really won't be necessary. Let's just go do this."

Parker nods and follows him as he heads for the door.

Cale does not want Parker trying to talk to her father about him for a couple of reasons. Firstly, because having someone else appeal on his behalf would do nothing to gain favor with the General. Secondly, he doesn't want to put any more strain on the pair's relationship.

Aside from Parker's skill, Cale had noticed another piece of evidence that made it clear she wasn't chosen due to her family connection; Parker doesn't seem to get along any better with General Linwood than Cale does. Whenever the two are near each other, they are at odds. As soon as he sees her, the General barks out orders at Parker, and surprisingly, she immediately listens. If anyone else were to speak to her so disrespectfully, Parker would drop them before they had a chance to finish their sentence.

He isn't sure the source of their problems, but he definitely doesn't want to add to them. Cale suspects that part of the reason Parker joined the Patriot Guard program in the first place was to help close the rift between herself and her father. He would never bring this up, though. If she wants to talk about it, she knows she can come to Cale.

They decide there is no subtle way to draw attention to themselves, so Cale and Parker elect to be painfully obvious. As the sun sets, they head straight to downtown New Edison. It's a Saturday, so the place is packed. People are lined up in front of the theater, eager for the new show, while others come in and out of the local clubs.

Just as they are walking past the line of theater patrons, Cale stops and turns to address the crowd.

"Spoiler alert," he says loudly, "the good guys win."

Instantly the crowd is cheering, and calling out to them.

"We love you, Patriot Prime!" someone yells.

Cale waves good-naturedly before he and Parker continue strolling down the sidewalk. They pass quite a few people, all of them staring, snapping pictures on their phones, or offering praise and expressions of gratitude.

As they pass one of the nightclubs, a group of three girls in their mid-twenties exit, spotting them straight away.

"Sentry!" one of them calls, waving.

Cale and Parker stop as the girls approach them.

"Can we get a picture with you?" another asks.

Before Parker can respond, one of the trio pushes a camera into Cale's hands and the girls gather on either side of her.

"Everyone smile and say 'Justice,'" Cale tells them, then snaps the picture.

"Thank you," one of them says, turning to Parker. "By the way, your costume is awesome!"

Cale hands the camera back and the girls quickly take off, talking loudly.

"How do you handle that?" Parker asks him. "Was it strange for you too, to have people coming up to you like you are a celebrity?"

"You get used to it," Cale laughs. "It was especially strange for me, because at first, no one wanted anything to do with me, but after that elementary school collapsed, and I rescued those students, they wouldn't leave me alone. It was jarring to go from practical pariah one day, to icon the next."

"Yeah, I bet that was pretty disconcerting."

"Hey, I thought they were going to assign you another costume?" he asks, just now noticing what Parker is wearing.

Her outfit is almost identical to the one she wore at her ceremony, the only difference being that the bulletproof vest she's wearing is thinner, offering easier movement and stylish flair.

"Didn't you see the news? I'm a fashion sensation. Girls everywhere are cheering for a practically dressed badass female hero. The Tribunal didn't dare change my costume."

"Lucky you have all those two-faced feminists on your side. No one cares what *I'm* wearing, so long as they can see the outline of my awesome muscled chest."

"Hey! Not *all* feminists are two-faced," Parker says, but she can't control the laughter that follows. "Besides, you *do* have an awesomely muscled chest."

They continue to walk around downtown a bit longer, waving, taking pictures with people, and even signing autographs. She does a good job hiding her unease, but Cale can tell Parker is still uncomfortable with the whole situation. However, the more time that passes, the more she seems to come to terms with the process and the role she must play.

As they round a corner, they are suddenly bombarded by a slew of reporters.

"Patriot Prime, are you fully recovered?" one reporter asks.

"Are you relieved he is alright, Sentry?" someone else chimes.

A microphone is shoved into Cale's face.

"What brings you out tonight?"

"Is there a threat?" Channel Seven asks.

"Are you on a date?"

Cameras are flashing… flashing… flashing. Cale grits his teeth, annoyed with the onslaught. His head starts to pound, the lights causing a migraine. He's just opening his mouth to snap on the reporters, when Parker interrupts.

"Patriot Prime has indeed, recovered. You can't keep this man down. I am so glad to have such a resilient partner. No need to worry, we're not here due to any threat. Just out for a patrol, which we really must get back to."

Before anyone can ask another question, Parker grabs Cale's arm and pulls him away from the group. He takes slow, deep breaths as she leads him back to where they'd left the car. Once they climb in, Parker starts questioning him.

"Are you alright? It looked like you were ready to tear that group a new one."

"Sorry, the flashes were giving me a headache."

"Well, you have definitely shown you are alive. Let's get you back to headquarters to rest."

"No," he rushes. "I'm fine really. Can we go do a *real* patrol now? I'm not ready to head back, but I don't want to deal with that circus again either."

Parker bites her lip, looking unsure.

"Are you certain you can handle it? You know you aren't fully recovered."

"I'll be fine. My shoulder feels great," he lies.

She sighs heavily.

"If you say so. Where do you want to go?" she asks, starting the car.

Cale gives her directions, ignoring the painful throbbing of his shoulder.

~

Parker follows Cale's instructions and finds herself in the old industrial district of New Edison.

"This area tends to have a lot of crime," Cale tells her. "Most of these buildings are abandoned, making it the perfect places for drug labs, chop shops, and brothels."

"I never realized our city was so… broken."

"It's even worse than that. A lot of the, uh, customers that come through here work for the city."

Parker is only slightly surprised by this. She knows power tends to lead to corruption and debauchery.

"What do you do when you catch them?" she asks.

"Turn most of them into the police."

"What do you mean, *most*?"

"When you catch someone with a city identification card, you are supposed to call the Tribunal. You give them the name, and they'll let you know if you turn them in or if you let them go," Cale explains.

"What? How do they make that decision?"

"Well… sometimes the person may be working with a sting operation."

"And other times?" she pushes.

"And other times the Tribunal likes to collect favors from people who hold certain offices."

"That doesn't seem very *heroic*," Parker mutters after a moment.

"Maybe not, but that's the way it is. We swore to obey the Tribunal's orders."

He's right, she thinks, *and the Tribunal is only doing what is best for the city. I guess…*

"So what are we doing?" she asks.

"Just turn the headlights off and cruise slowly up and down all these side streets. Keep your eyes open."

Parker flicks the lights off and stops the car for a moment to let her eyes adjust to the darkness. Most of the streetlights in the area are burnt out or busted.

When she can see well enough, Parker starts rolling slowly down the first side street, loving how silent the engine is.

"Are you sure it was just the camera flashes that had you going back there?" she asks suddenly.

"What do you mean?"

"I thought you might have been angry about them asking if we were on a date."

"It didn't even faze me," he answers. "I was wondering if it bothered you."

"No, it doesn't bother me. I was kind of expecting it, really. I mean come on, these days, it is impossible for a man and woman to work together without the public assuming they're sleeping together."

"Well," Cale sighs, stretching his arm out and around her shoulder, "I'll, uh, understand if you don't want to disappoint the public."

"Oh, shut up," Parker smirks, knocking his arm away.

Shortly after she and Cale first became friends, they had experimented a bit. One time, after a long training day, Cale had helped her sneak out of the contestant's quarters. They carefully made their way to one of the outdoor training fields. It was dark and no one had spotted them. When they got there, Parker found that Cale had planned a picnic for the two of them. He had a blanket spread out, with a bottle of champagne on ice, and even a wicker picnic basket filled with hors d'oeuvres.

They sat close together, talking and drinking. Eventually, Parker sat with her head resting against his strong shoulder, thinking about what could come next.

They were both fairly attractive, Cale was sweet, loyal, smart, and he really listened to her. The next step seemed quite obvious when she truly thought about it… so she kissed him.

Parker turned her face towards him and leaned up slowly, giving him a chance to back away if he wasn't interested. He didn't move; she took that as a go-ahead and leaned up to kiss him. His lips were warm, soft, and… *wrong.*

She pulled away quickly.

"I'm sorry," she told him. "That was—"

"Awful?" Cale supplied, a slight smirk on his face.

"It's not like it was a bad kiss, but it was just really awkward."

"Way to break my heart," he said, his tone full of mock hurt.

They sat in silence for several minutes.

"We're still friends, right?" Parker finally asked.

Cale laughed.

"I'm pretty sure that's what that kiss just told us. But

if you mean, are we okay? Then, yes. We are definitely okay. I didn't feel any fireworks either. It was kind of like kissing my sister."

"You don't have a sister."

"Well, yeah. But I assume that's what it would be like."

That night they decided they would definitely only ever be friends, but it didn't stop them from making semi-dirty jokes occasionally.

Parker turns onto the next street, sweeping her eyes left and right searching for any sign of movement. When she is satisfied there isn't any, she asks Cale a question that has been nagging her since the ceremony.

"What's the deal with the masks? Not only does everybody already know who we are, but even if they didn't, a scrap of fabric framing my eyes isn't really going to fool anyone."

"I wondered about that at first too, but if you really think about it, they kind of make sense."

"How so?" she asks.

"The whole point of the Patriot Guard is symbolism. They could have shot up a bunch of cops with the injection they gave you, and achieved a much lower crime rate. But that isn't really what this is about," he explains.

"It isn't?"

"No. The PG is about restoring hope in the city, and in the government. A government who can give you real, live, superheroes, can give you anything. The masks are just another symbol, and add to the overall picture."

Parker thinks about this and realizes that Cale is right. He really has a good sense of things, and always seems to pick up on explanations left unsaid. When she first met him, Parker had been expecting a mindless, muscled, pretty boy.

I mean who else would go by Patriot Prime?

She had been pleasantly surprised to find such an intelligent, and understanding man instead.

"Parker, over there," Cale points.

Off to the right side of the road, somebody is spray-painting graffiti onto the side of an abandoned building.

Not exactly a bank robbery, but okay, She thinks throwing the car into park.

Cale is already out of the car, running up to the suspect.

"Hey, you," he calls.

The spray-painter turns, sees Cale, and takes off running.

"Damn it."

Parker jumps out and launches after him. Cale has a head start, but she quickly catches, and surpasses him.

This guy doesn't stand a chance.

In a matter of seconds, Parker closes the distance and grabs onto the suspect's shoulder. She flips him around and sees that he is just a kid, maybe in his early teens. He shakes his curly dark hair out of his face and looks up at her with huge eyes, the moonlight making them appear silver.

Cale finally catches up to them. He's holding his left hand over his right shoulder, and Parker can see he's in pain. Before she can say anything, Cale grits his teeth, grabs the kid away from her and slams him against the wall behind them.

"What the hell do you think you were doing?" Cale asks, looking angrier than Parker has ever seen him.

"I— I'm sorry! It was just a stupid dare," the kid sputters.

"You're out here defacing my city because of a dare?" Cale demands.

The kid's eyes widen in fear, and Parker doesn't blame him. Cale is getting a little carried away. His hand is gripping the kid's upper arm so tightly that Cale's knuckles are turning white. The boy grits his teeth and lets out a hiss, obviously in pain.

She reaches out and puts a hand on Cale's chest,

drawing his attention to her.

"Why don't you let me take it from here, Prime?" she offers. "You go grab the car."

He looks like he is getting ready to snap on her, too, but suddenly the anger in his eyes diminishes and he nods.

"Uh, yeah. I'll get the car," he says quietly, letting go of the kid.

Cale looks like he wants to say something, but changes his mind at the last second. Parker watches as he walks away, and then turns her attention back to the kid.

"What's your name?"

"Thomas," he answers, staring at his feet.

"Well, Thomas, am I right to trust that you won't be doing any more vandalizing?"

He looks up and nods his head quickly.

"Okay then. I am going to let you off with a warning, but if I see you out here again… I'm going to let my angry friend handle you. You understand?"

"Yes, I understand."

"Get on home then," she says, shooing him away.

Thomas takes off running as fast as he can, eager to be away from them. Cale pulls up behind her just as the kid rounds the next block. She goes to the car and takes over driving, not wanting Cale behind the wheel.

"What the hell was *that?*" she asks angrily.

Cale stays quiet.

"Well?"

"I don't know what happened. My shoulder was hurting from running, and the when I saw him… I just felt so angry. That's never happened before, I swear."

"See that it doesn't happen again. You almost pulled his arm out of its socket."

Cale nods sadly and bows his head.

"I think I need to head back for some rest," he says softly.

"Good idea."

Parker pulls a U-turn and heads back the way they

came. As she passes the area the kid was tagging, she slows down to look. He must have just been putting the finishing touches on when they spotted him. It is a giant "SP" with lightning encircling it.

Slavers of the People.

"Didn't he seem a little young to be a gang member?" she asks Cale, pointing at the symbol.

"They tend to bring them in young, so they can brain wash them. Also, I wouldn't really classify Slavers of the People as a gang. You should read their file."

Parker just nods and continues on driving back to PG headquarters. It doesn't take long to get there.

"Do you want me to walk you in?"

She can see he is still in pretty serious pain.

"Not if you aren't staying here tonight."

"I was thinking of going back to my apartment, actually."

"Then don't worry about it. I'll be fine," he assures her. "Just keep your beeper near you in case they call us in."

"Will do."

Cale leaves her and heads inside. As she drives home, she can't stop thinking about how young that kid was… and how strongly Cale reacted. When she climbs in bed for the night, her thoughts are still caught up on the whole situation.

FOUR

A loud, shrill chirping wakes Parker up around six the next morning. The offensive sound turns out to be coming from her PG pager.

Report to War Room, ASAP, it reads.

Groaning loudly, she pulls herself out of bed and stumbles into the bathroom. Going through the motions, she quickly readies herself: pulls her hair up, washes her face, and brushes her teeth; by the time she's done, she feels a bit more alert. Not knowing what she's being called for, Parker decides to dress in practical, casual clothing.

Jeans, tee, and tennis shoes— her wardrobe staples.

The drive from her apartment to PG headquarters takes all of ten minutes, and then she hurries inside, up to the second floor.

Parker is disappointed to find that the War Room isn't as impressive as the name makes it sound. It's really just a large conference room like any you would find in an average office building. There is a big, round table in the center of the room that can seat ten people, though she doubts it has ever seen that many; the Tribunal keeps the area pretty locked down. On one wall, there are three large flat-screen TVs, each turned to one of the main three news channels in New Edison. All are muted with the subtitles on.

The opposite wall has a small cart carrying coffee and other refreshments. Parker grabs herself a glass of orange juice and a muffin before taking a seat at the table. She is, surprisingly, the first one there.

She barely has time peel the wrapper from her muffin when two-thirds of the Tribunal, Senator Scott and General Linwood, walks in.

"Oh, good. You're here already, Miss Linwood," Senator Scott says. "Dr. Bellamy and Mr. Pearson will be along shortly."

Parker wonders what's keeping them, but just nods. You don't question the Tribunal without invitation.

"Do you mind if we get started?" he asks, taking a seat across from her.

"Of course not."

The Senator looks at General Linwood, who nods and takes a seat at the table.

"Excellent. We've had a breakthrough on the robbery case."

"What? I thought that was closed. They tried to rob a bank, and they were caught. End of story."

"Not quite," the General says. "Just listen."

Parker feels her cheeks flush, but nods.

"Sorry."

"Anyway," Senator Scott continues, "it turns out that the robbers were acting on behalf of the Slavers of the People. What do you know of them?"

Convenient timing, she thinks remembering last night's encounter.

"Not much, just what I've seen on the news. They're a group of Variants responsible for a bunch of vandalism around the city, cutting power lines and such."

"Yes, but they are much worse than that. They are a very dangerous group geared towards destabilizing the government."

"By cutting power lines?" she asks, unable to keep the skepticism from her voice.

"We believe they have much more in store. Especially since we have discovered who is leading the group," Senator Scott says, picking up a small remote from the table.

He pushes a button and a panel on the blank wall behind him lifts to reveal a large computer screen.

That's more like it, she thinks.

"We've been tracking the group for quite a while now," General Linwood tells her, "but still don't have as much information as we would like."

"What do you know?"

Senator Scott presses another button on the remote and the computer screen flares to life. An image of a man pops up.

"This is the leader of the group. His name is Konstantine Tesla."

"Tesla? As in—"

"Yes," the Senator nods. "He is the great-great-grandson of the famous Nikola Tesla."

Parker studies the picture carefully. In it, Konstantine is looking over his shoulder as he walks away from the camera. He is tall, thin, and looks to be in his late twenties or early thirties. His hair is black, hanging in layers down to his shoulders, and covering half of his face. She can just make out what she takes to be a mischievous smirk. What she finds most striking about the photo are his eyes; the one not covered by hair is bright blue, and seems to be almost glowing.

"Is he a Variant?" she asks.

"Oh, yes. We think his variation may have been passed down from his great-great-grandfather. Konstantine has an affinity for electricity. Other than that, we don't have much information on him; he has kept a low profile."

Just then, the door opens and Cale enters with Dr.

Bellamy. He has a worried look on his face that he tries to hide when he notices Parker watching him.

"Thanks for finally joining us, Mr. Pearson," General Linwood says angrily. "Take a seat so we can continue."

Cale clenches his jaw and sits down next to Parker.

"It isn't his fault, General," Dr. Bellamy snaps. "As you may recall, I informed you I was going to run some diagnostic tests on his injury. As someone so *invested* in the Patriot Guard, I had assumed you would want your primary superhero in good health."

The General gives Dr. Bellamy a glare that practically shouts his anger, a look that Parker happens to be quite familiar with.

"Continue," he says coolly to Senator Scott, as the Doctor begins to pour herself a cup of coffee.

The Senator clears his throat.

"Well, uh, where was I? Ah, yes. The other members of the group."

He clicks the remote again, but this time the screen fills with a mug shot of a much older man.

"Leon Myles, age sixty-three, Variant, and Tesla's right hand man. This guy is dangerous," Senator Scott assures them.

Parker has to bite back a laugh.

Dangerous? He looks like my pappy.

Leon, with his all gray hair, grandfatherly features, and milky blue eyes peeking out from behind his reading glasses, looks like the furthest thing from criminal.

"What makes him so dangerous?" she asks the Senator.

"His Variation. He has the ability to read and manipulate people's emotions. He has been caught a few times, but often convinces the guards that they want to let him go. The media calls him the Criminal Calmer because, when committing a crime, he usually makes all bystanders feel so content they don't care what is happening around them. It's rumored that when he found his wife cheating on him, he convinced her to kill herself."

"That's terrible," Parker whispers. "How do you fight something like that?"

"If you know it is coming, and you have a strong enough will, you can supposedly resist his powers."

Glancing over at Cale to gauge his reaction, Parker notices that he is zoning out.

"Well, these guys sure sound like a lot of fun," she says sarcastically, turning her attention back to the Senator.

"Oh, we're just getting to the fun part. Show her the next one," General Linwood orders.

The Senator presses another button and this time, a woman comes onscreen. It's another mug shot. Her mouth is open in a snarl, and her dark eyes are glaring so intensely at the camera, Parker almost feels the woman can see her through the photo. She has olive skin, messy long black hair, and an almost feral beauty about her.

"This is Krista Brandt a.k.a. Mother Mayhem, leader of the Children of Freedom," the General explains. "The Children of Freedom," he sneers, "is a militia hell-bent on overthrowing the government. They are based here, out of New Edison, and are believed to have somewhere around a thousand armed members."

Parker doesn't know what to say. She can't believe that there are that many citizens in the city ready to take up arms and wage war against the government.

When the hell did my life turn into a Hollywood blockbuster?

"What is their agenda, their motive?" She asks.

There it is… the look I'm so familiar with.

General Linwood is glaring fiercely at her, a vein popping out of his forehead.

"Since when do a bunch of insane, hippie, terrorists need a reason to act crazy? Really, Parker, at least pretend you deserve this position."

Despite the severe urge to snap, she manages to stay *mostly* calm.

"I mean, what do they say to recruit members? I

highly doubt they go door to door asking 'Do you have a gun and hear voices? You do? Excellent! If you also happen to hate the Man, boy, do we have a job for you!'"

Dr. Bellamy, who at some point had sat down a few chairs away, starts laughing. General Linwood looks about ready to explode when Senator Scott interrupts him.

"Hmm," he clears his throat, while trying to hide a smirk. "They try to convince people that our government is corrupted, the main issue being how high the energy tax currently is."

Parker frowns heavily. She can understand being angry about how high energy prices have gotten. After receiving her last electric bill, in place of her payment, she had wanted to send back a photocopy of her middle finger.

There is only one power company available to the people of New Edison— TEnergy. The TEnergy power plant runs on coal, which it gets from its own personal mines. Recently, the company has started laying off miners, due to the fact that its coalmines are almost completely picked clean.

TEnergy has had to start shipping coal in, which has increased its production costs. These cost increases have been passed down to the consumers, who have no choice but to pay, unless they want to be left in the dark.

"To have so many members, it seems like the Children of Freedom have been around a while. Have you always known about them?" she asks.

"Just about. We were brought up to speed when they reached two hundred members," Senator Scott explains.

"Why the sudden worry then? Because they have joined forces with the Slavers of the People?"

"That is exactly why," the General says, standing up. "They have sought out the help and companionship of those *Variants*! If they are willing to stoop that low, it is only a matter of time before they make their move."

Both Dr. Bellamy and Senator Scott look a bit

uncomfortable. Many people hold prejudices against Variants, but it is one of those things you're not supposed to talk about in civilized conversation.

Not all Variants are criminals, but a large number of them do turn to crime, which only amplifies the distrust that others already feel. Add that to how rare they used to be, and you get the perfect combination for intolerance.

"Well, you are up to speed. Any questions?" General Linwood asks, suddenly.

Parker blinks back the burning sensation in her eyes and clears her throat.

"What do you want us to do with this information?"

"If you see any of these people, bring them in. With the utmost care, of course. We don't want to see you injured." Senator Scott clarifies. "Find any information you can on them."

"Don't forget the boy," Dr. Bellamy pipes up.

"Ah, yes. I had forgotten."

The Senator clicks the remote one last time, and a familiar face pops up, peering out from under a mass of black curls.

"This is—"

"Thomas," Parker interrupts.

"You know him?" the General asks.

"Well, not really. We found him last night on patrol, tagging an abandoned building in the old industrial neighborhood."

"Then where is he now?"

"I… sent him on his way. It was just a bit of spray paint on an empty warehouse."

"Damn it, Parker! This is why you must always, *always*, consult the Tribunal first!" the General slams his fist on the table for emphasis.

"I don't understand; who is he?"

"That is Thomas Brandt… son of Krista Brandt! She had him when she was seventeen and raised him all alone, her family having cast her out as a whore. She would do *anything* for that boy. Don't you see he would be the perfect bargaining chip?"

How can he suggest using someone's child as leverage?

"Sorry, next time I'll be sure to call the Tribunal to assess a person's worth," she snaps.

General Linwood just shakes his head angrily and stalks from the room. Dr. Bellamy wheels her chair closer to Parker's and pats her on the shoulder.

"Don't worry, dear. It was your first patrol. He won't stay angry forever," the Doctor consoles her.

"Have you ever seen him *not* angry?" Parker questions.

Dr. Bellamy furrows her brow, clearly thinking the question over. She opens her mouth, then closes it again. Without saying anything, she then gives Parker another pat on the shoulder and a sympathetic look before getting up and leaving the room.

Senator Scott looks extremely uncomfortable being the last member of the Tribunal in the room.

"Well, here is the folder from the bank robbery. You can look through it if you want. There are some crime scene photos in there," he says, sliding a folder across the table to her. "Have a good day, you two, and keep your pagers close."

He quickly stands up and exits the room, leaving just Parker and Cale.

"Are you alright?" she asks, turning to face him.

"Huh? Oh, yeah. I'm fine."

"You were completely zoned out that whole meeting."

"Sorry, I didn't sleep well last night. Shoulder pain," he explains. "I'm just tired."

"Maybe you should go take a nap," she suggests.

"You know, that is an excellent idea. I think I will. See you later."

Before she can say anything else, Cale is gone.

Poor guy, I hope he feels better soon.

Despite how good a nap sounds, Parker decides to flip through the folder from the Senator. There are a lot of photos from the bank.

Broken pillars... bullet holes in the wall... the vault...

The picture of the vault door catches her eye in particular. It has the Slavers of the People logo painted on it, but instead of "SP" surrounded by lightning, like the tag she saw last night, the letters are encased in a circle.

Creative license, she thinks flipping to the next picture.

~

After Parker dropped him off the night before, Cale had gone straight to see Dr. Bellamy. His outburst had frightened him, and he felt appalled at the way he had acted towards that boy. The kid was just painting on a dilapidated building; it wasn't like he was hurting anybody, and yet Cale threw him against a brick wall. With his strength, he could have really hurt the kid.

He told the Doctor what happened, and expressed his worry that his levels might be off. She listened intently, and then, to put his mind at ease, took a blood sample to have tested. While they waited for the results, they started talking; she wanted to know if anything else was causing him stress or bothering him.

During his final weeks of the Patriot Project, Cale had gotten to know Dr. Bellamy quite well. She had often come to visit him so that his days locked up weren't *so* unbearable.

"It won't be much longer," she told him one evening. "Just think, in a couple weeks you'll be a real life superhero. Think of how proud your family will be."

"I don't have any family to make proud."

"What do you mean?"

"You didn't see my file? I grew up in foster care, bouncing home to home. When I was eighteen I was put out on the street alone," Cale explained.

"What did you do?"

"I jumped from odd job to odd job for a few years, angry at everyone for the position I was in. Then one day, I woke up in my crappy apartment and realized that the only person I had to be angry at was myself. The system, this country, gave me the best chance they could under the circumstances. Who was I to expect any better than everyone else? So I went down to my local recruiter's office and joined the Army in an attempt to offer up thanks, and pay back my dues. You guys scooped me up a couple months after that."

Dr. Bellamy sat quietly for a moment, and then gave him a sad smile.

"Well, you make *me* proud, Cale."

Since then, she had become a motherly figure to Cale, and he always found himself going to her when something was bothering him.

So, as he'd sat with her for several hours waiting for the results on his serotonin and testosterone levels, they'd ended up discussing the robbery.

"How are you feeling about what happened that day?" she asked.

"What, you mean being shot?"

"No, I mean about your 'sidekick' saving the day."

Cale shrugged.

"It was her day anyway, and she saved my life, so I can't hold too much resentment."

"I assumed that would be your answer," Dr. Bellamy smiled. "You're far too good a man to be upset by something so trivial."

"If I feel resentful about anything, it is my own performance. I should never have been in the position where saving my life would be necessary."

"Even superheroes make mistakes. Besides, that robber must have missed Villains 101. He was supposed to go into an overlong monologue about how he beat you, thus giving you the chance to beat him," she said, barely managing to keep a straight face.

"Ah, but you see," Cale explained, "that mistake is made only by the Super Villains, and the bank robbers were but petty thugs."

At that point, a research assistant walked in to give them the test results.

"All normal," Dr. Bellamy told him, looking through the paperwork. "It must have just been leftover weariness from your injury, which, may I remind you, is not yet fully healed. Go get some rest and meet me in the morning so I can check it."

When he met her the next morning, just before they were to report to the War Room, his shoulder was still feeling sore. Once she inspected it, she was both surprised, and worried, that it didn't seem to have gotten much better.

After the initial rate of healing, Dr. Bellamy had assumed the rest of the wound would be better by then. They had no data to consult, because Cale was the only one still alive to have received the injection and its healing benefits.

They spent a short amount of time testing his healing rate by giving Cale paper cuts and then by making small cuts with a scalpel, as they had during the early days of the program. All of the tests were normal, meaning he was healing at the same rate as before.

"This is a more extensive injury," the Doctor said, "so we really don't know what to expect. Although, at this rate, even if your regeneration capabilities are back to the average human speed, this is a wound that *will* heal."

From there, they'd headed up to the meeting in the War Room. Cale noticed Parker kept glancing at him, wondering why he wasn't paying attention, but he couldn't bring himself to concentrate. Then afterwards, when she asked if he was okay, he couldn't even answer her truthfully. He wasn't allowed to.

Oh, yeah, I'm just a bit stressed out. I'm afraid that I may be losing control of myself and becoming dangerous, like the other PG Project members did right before they died. Oops, wasn't supposed to mention that

As he leaves the War Room, Cale decides that he really could use a nap, and heads towards the second floor guest room that he practically lives in. He does have an apartment, but he spends, at most, two nights a week there. He only keeps it as a reminder to himself, that there is more to him than just being Patriot Prime.

The guest room is fairly spacious, and Cale has to admit, furnished a lot nicer than his own sparsely decorated apartment. The room is colored in a theme of cream and earth tones, the whole area radiating warmth. He walks over to the cherry finished platform bed and collapses onto it.

Even with the curtains drawn, the room is still far too bright for Cale to fall asleep. He reaches over and pulls open the bedside table drawer, hoping to find a sleep mask.

I could have sworn there was one in here, he thinks digging through the drawer.

His hand grazes something that is obviously a book and he decides that maybe he can read himself to sleep. When he pulls the object out, though, he finds that it isn't just a book, but a journal. It is bound simply with brown leather backing and he instantly recognizes it. It is the journal Dr. Bellamy had given him during his stay in solitary while they were testing him to be sure that he lacked the negative effects of the serum. She figured recording his days and feelings would help him to pass the time.

Cale flips the journal open and sees that the last entry is dated the day he rescued the students from the collapsing building, the day everything turned around for him as Patriot Prime. He skims over the passage, only pausing to fully read the last paragraph.

The citizens of New Edison have finally accepted me! They, at last, understand that I am only here to help them, and that I am more than capable of doing so. Dr. Bellamy was right that it would only be a matter of time, though I hate that it took such a catastrophe to wake them up. Thank goodness nobody was killed, just a few scrapes and bruises. I look forward to a bright future of providing the citizens of my city with peace of mind, and protecting them… at all costs.

Feeling a sudden urge to write about what had happened the night before with that Thomas kid, Cale grabs a pen from the nightstand.

He knows that some people wouldn't understand why he is so worried— the General for instance; if, god willing, Cale were to actually take his story to General Linwood, Linwood would probably say the vandal deserved it and to act like a hero, not a pansy.

The reason he finds himself dwelling on the situation is because he knows that he would never consciously treat a child so cruelly. Yes, the boy is thirteen, but that's young enough to be considered a child in Cale's eyes.

He flips to a new page and begins writing furiously, and not just about his worries, but also about everything that has been happening with the Patriot Guard since his last entry. He is unsure why, but it seems extremely important that he get everything on paper.

Cale writes until his hand is cramping and his eyes are itching from weariness. His lids grow heavier and heavier, and, deciding he can't fight it anymore, he closes the journal and quickly falls asleep.

FIVE

Knock. Knock. Knock.

"Cale?" he hears Parker ask. "Sorry to wake you, but it's time for patrol."

Cale groans and rolls over in bed and sees Parker standing just inside the room, already dressed in her costume.

"What time is it?"

"It's just before seven. You've been asleep the whole day. Are you feeling any better? I could do patrol on my own."

Cale nods his head and sits up.

"Yes, you're feeling better, or yes, you want me to patrol on my own?" she asks confused.

"Both. We can cover more ground if we split up," he says, stretching. "You take downtown, but stick to the outskirts; that's where most of the crime happens. If you see anyone suspicious, feel free to ask them some questions regarding the suspects we learned about today. Maybe we can get an address."

"Alright. Where will you be?"

"Red Light district, hitting up some 'old friends' for information. Be sure to take an ear piece with you, and be ready to go if I call you."

"Sounds like a plan," Parker grins and turns to leave.

When she's gone, Cale hurries to dress himself, pulling one of the many replicas of his costume from the closet.

It is impossible to keep this damn cape white, he thinks.

Before long, Cale is in his car heading towards New Edison's Red Light district. His vehicle is the same make and model as Parker's, but instead of black, it is a very patriotic blue with a white eagle on the hood. Despite driving basically the same car, Cale prefers being behind the wheel of his Camero. Like a shoe, it just feels more comfortable because he's broken it in.

Cale reaches his destination and pulls into his normal spot, an alley between a strip club and a questionable Chinese restaurant.

He sticks to the shadows and waits about twenty feet away from the side door to the club.

Come on, Benny… I know you haven't changed your routine.

After a few more minutes of waiting, the door opens. A leggy blonde in a short skirt and shimmery tank top comes backing out, pulling a nervous looking older man along with her.

"Are you sure about this? I thought the club was pretty strict on the, uh, 'no mingling' policy," the man asks nervously.

"It'll be fine, baby," she purrs, pulling him by a dumpster. "Nobody's gonna find us out here."

She wraps her arms around his neck and leans in to kiss him.

3, 2, 1…

A man jumps from behind the dumpster and starts yelling.

"Freeze, right there!"

The man yelling has a dark sweatshirt on with the hood pulled up, and Cale can see that he has his hand shoved in the pocket, mimicking a gun.

"No, Benny. You freeze," Cale says as he dramatically steps from the shadows. "You know it's useless to run from me."

"Damn it, Prime! What the hell is that? You scared the shit out of me."

The man, still halfway wrapped in the blonde's embrace, looks back and forth between his would-be mugger, and Cale.

"Go on," Cale tells him, "you should probably get out of here."

"T-thank you," he stammers.

He grabs the girl's hand as if to pull her after him.

"No, she stays," Cale says, "and next time, don't trust a stripper. If it seems too good to be true, it probably is."

The man shoots the woman a shocked look but quickly takes off down the alley, towards the relative safety of the main street.

"Roxie, I thought I told you to stop helping him?" Cale asks the blonde.

She shrugs.

"Yeah, yeah, I know. I just can't resist my Benny. Plus he helps me pay rent," she pouts.

"If I catch you out here helping him again, you won't have to worry about rent. It'll be free in jail. Now, why don't you head back inside? I need a word with Benny."

Roxie totters back to the club's side door, her heels clacking loudly. She looks over her shoulder, giving them both an exaggerated pouty lip and a half-wave before disappearing back into the building.

"Benny, Benny, Benny. How many times have I let you slide under the radar? I think this is it, pal, I'm going to have to take you in," Cale says slowly.

Benny pulls his hood down, worry all over his face. He is almost a foot shorter than Cale and has to look up to meet his eyes. Benny's are all bloodshot and watery; his brown hair is a mess.

"No, no, you can't. P-please, Prime. I'll stop, I mean

it," Benny begs. "For real this time."

Cale sighs heavily.

"I don't think so. I don't have time to deal with your pick pocketing and muggings anymore. I need to devote my time to finding bigger fish."

"Bigger fish?" Benny asks. "Who you need? You know I got this. I can help you."

Cale has to fight the urge to smile.

Too easy, Benny.

Cale first came across Benny about a year ago. He caught him snatching some woman's purse. Benny was only about seventeen at the time and in a really bad place, having grown up in an unstable home. He reminded Cale of himself a bit during his final days in the system. Cale had never robbed anyone, but he knew what it was like to feel desperate, so he had made Benny return the purse and apologize, and then sent him on his way. It was actually his first time not calling the Tribunal for a decision.

Shortly after that, he caught Benny and Roxie working a con together. It was the same scheme every time: Roxie would lead unsuspecting married clients away from the strip club for some fun, only the *fun* ended up being getting robbed in a back alley. Most of the John's wouldn't file a report because they didn't want it getting back to their wives they were mugged while trying to hook up with a stripper.

Cale was getting ready to drag Benny to the police when Benny started offering up information. One piece actually turned out to be quite helpful. Benny had been able to direct Cale to a man responsible for a lengthy string of attacks on women that Cale had been working on. After that, Benny turned into Cale's easy supply of much needed information.

He always has something on somebody.

"What do you know about Konstantine Tesla?" Cale asks.

"I know things that would really *shock* you about

Tesla."

"Ha. Ha. Ha. I know about his Variation. Why don't you tell me where he's at?"

Benny seems disappointed to realize Cale already knows about his prime piece of information.

"I wish I knew. I swear I'd tell you."

"Come on, Benny. I know you have something for me."

"I don't know where his main headquarters are. He likes to keep a low profile. I've heard his group has been laying a false trail of safe houses."

"Safe houses?"

"They have a few actual safe houses spread throughout the slums, for rogue Variants, but they have been setting diversions. Drawing the police to fake hideouts to keep them off of their heels," Benny explains.

That's a pretty good plan.

"What else you got?" Cale asks.

"I swear I don't have anything you don't already know."

"What's that supposed to mean?"

"Well, I'm sure you know Tesla's working with Mother Mayhem, even though that's been kept on the down low, and everyone knows you had a run in with her son. Shook him up pretty badly when you lost your cool. Not very hero like in my opinion," Benny mock chastises him.

Cale feels his anger flare and before he knows it, he has Benny backed against the dumpster, his hand fisted into the conman's collar.

"I don't give a damn about your opinion," he growls. "Who told you about that?"

"Whoa, I was just kidding!" Benny puts his hands up in mock surrender. "I'm on your side, Prime."

"What did you mean when you said 'everyone knows'?"

"What, did you expect to rough up the son of an anti-government militia leader and it would stay quiet? I meant word has been getting around to people in my circuit."

"You mean low-life thugs?" Cale asks, letting go of Benny's shirt and backing away.

"Ouch. That hurts coming from you. But, if that's the way you see us, yes. That's who's talking."

"Wonderful."

"Hey, you should be glad. Everybody's a little spooked by the whole thing, cuz you're usually such a gentleman. I know a few guys who have actually backed off a long planned job out of fear you might be coming to our level. I mean, hell, if you'll rough up a kid for petty vandalism, what would you do to a guy for car theft?"

"I don't see why everyone is suddenly concerned. I *just* shot and killed a bank robber; I *have* resorted to violence before," Cale offers.

"True, but only in defense."

Cale ignores this and tries to get back on topic.

"Look, I need something a little more substantial. Do you know anything about what they are planning?"

Benny shakes his head.

"No, but I know someone who might. There is this guy down on Fourth Street always mumbling about Tesla."

Cale perks up.

"What does he look like?"

"He's a little taller than me, older, black, has long dreads, and he's, uh, always wearing a sandwich board," Benny tells him.

"You mean, like an advertisement?"

Benny nods.

"Okay. Thanks, Benny. Don't let me catch you out here again, I *will* take you in next time."

"You won't. I'm outta the game. Thanks, Prime. Stay cool," Benny calls, before quickly rushing further down the dark alley.

Cale rolls his eyes, turns, and heads back to his car. He is eager to find the man Benny mentioned, to see if the guy actually knows anything.

Fourth Street is only about a five-minute drive from the strip club, but Cale makes it in three. He isn't supposed to speed unless he's in pursuit of a criminal, due to being a public role model and what not, but he feels a little bit of haste is warranted.

He spots the guy right away as he pulls up on the corner of Fourth and Sidney.

Benny, I am going to kill you.

The man Benny directed him to is wearing a sandwich board that reads "THE END IS COMING" and shouting at passing pedestrians while trying to hand out pamphlets.

Reluctantly, Cale exits the car and slowly approaches the man.

"It's coming folks, it is time to wake up and see. Something big is coming. You must cleanse yourself of the dusty film that has coated your lives and prepare to bask in the clean air of the end."

"Excuse me, Sir?" Cale asks. "Can I speak with you?"

"Hero, it's the hero. Patriot Prime, hero of the people," the man mutters.

Oh, yes. I am definitely going to kill you, Benny.

"Sir," Cale begins.

"Jonah," the man interrupts.

"Jonah, I was told you might have some information about Konstantine Tesla. Is there anything you can tell me about him? Maybe where he lives?"

"He is everywhere. He is the storm sent to cleanse this city."

"What do you mean, he is everywhere? Are you saying he moves around a lot?"

"He must protect himself for the end. He is the storm," Jonah tells him very seriously.

"Whom must he protect himself from? Is he in trouble?"

"The hero… the hero searches for the storm in hopes

to quell it, to postpone the end." Jonah starts laughing, "but there is no stopping it. Do not worry though, the hero will not witness the end."

"What does that m—" Cale is cut off by his pager's loud beeping.

The pager has an address on its screen, a request for his presence by the Tribunal.

"We'll have to continue this discussion later," Cale tells Jonah.

As he is walking away, Cale hears the man muttering.

"The hero will not return."

Once in the car, he presses his earpiece to call Parker.

"Did you get that?" he asks.

"Yup, I'm about fifteen minutes away from the address."

"Okay, I'll be there in ten. See you soon."

"Rodger," Parker answers before breaking the connection.

On his drive, Cale contemplates what he just heard from Jonah. The older man was obviously crazy, *and yet...*

Jonah was saying that the "hero" seeks the "storm" to postpone the end. Cale is clearly the hero searching for Tesla...

Does that mean Konstantine Tesla is going to be responsible for some... well, something huge?

Cale shakes his head as if to clear it; the man is just another end of the world nutter, and overanalyzing what he said won't help anyone.

The address he is being sent to is on the edge of the slum area of New Edison, right on the border of town. As he gets closer, Cale notices that the area seems dark. There is a power outage.

The Slavers of the People must have cut another line.

When he finally reaches his destination, Cale is surprised at what he finds. It isn't a downed power line, but a large, smoking transformer—or what used to be a transformer. It is now just a useless hunk of metal.

It looks as if someone overcharged it and then, after it blew, they smashed it and attempted to set it on fire. As if the fact that it is vandalism isn't clear enough, the Slavers of the People's logo has been spray painted on one twisted chunk of charred metal in bright red, a large "SP" surrounded by lightning bolts.

Cale moves to get a closer look of the tag and notices something stuck underneath it. It is a piece of paper, taped up so it won't fall.

He leans in to inspect it and finds that it is a note… addressed to him.

Cale rips the paper down and fumbles to open it.

Patriot Prime,

We have been watching you… waiting for signs. We know. We know you are slipping. We know you are slowly losing yourself. We know it is only a matter of time before you end up like your fellow Patriot Guard Project members, Ike, John, and Walter. We can help you to stop that from happening.

We will be in touch, SP

Cale feels numb all over. No one is supposed to know about the other project members.

How could they know? All those records are sealed.

Even worse than realizing the Slavers must have a mole in PG, Cale feels nauseated at being confronted about his worst fear, that he may be losing control and heading down the same path as the others.

Maybe I'm not immune to the effects the serum caused in them… Maybe it has just taken longer for my system to reach that point.

"Oh, wow. What happened?" Parker asks appearing behind Cale.

He quickly crumples the note and jumps to face her.

"Didn't hear you pull in," he explains when she gives him a funny look. "Looks like the Slavers of the People are escalating things."

"I'll say. I can't believe how many people are without power. What is their endgame here? Are they just trying to cost TEnergy more money?" she asks.

"I have no idea. I guess we'll just have to wait and see."

~

They didn't stay too long at the scene after Parker arrived. Cale assured her there was nothing there to find. They already knew who committed the crime, but there was no sign at the scene as to where the perpetrators were hiding.

Parker felt that Cale was being distant with her. He had practically jumped out of his skin when she came up behind him, and she swears she saw him hide something from her. Being the good friend that she is, though, she hadn't brought it up.

They went straight back to PG headquarters, and after being told they would have a meeting with the Tribunal first thing in the morning, Parker decided to crash there, in one of the extra rooms on the top floor.

When her pager goes off at six the next morning, Parker reluctantly pulls herself out of bed. She can't believe how comfortable the mattress is, and that the one here at headquarters is actually better than her own at home.

Despite the excellent sleeping accommodations, Parker is feeling very groggy.

Late nights and early mornings does not a hero make, she thinks.

She readies herself quickly and heads to the War Room, where she pours herself an enormously sized mug of black coffee, and lazily plops down in the same place she had the day before. She is once again the first one to show up.

This has been one hell of a first week. I think I'm ready for my own *sidekick*.

A couple minutes pass before all the members of the Tribunal and Cale join Parker around the table.

"This will be brief," Senator Scott tells them. "We just wanted to inform you that we will be releasing some of the information we have about the Slavers of the People to the local media."

"You mean a press release about the transformer?" Parker asks.

"More than the transformer. We are going to distribute the names and photos we have of known members and call on the public for help. We will be offering a hefty reward for any information that leads to the capture of a high-ranking member. We must catch them now," the Senator explains.

"I don't understand. Yes, they did break the law, and they created a large power outage in the slums, but last night someone attacked and murdered a mother of two and I don't see all the cards coming out to catch *that* criminal. We don't even know what this group is trying to achieve," Parker says, noticing Cale nodding along with her.

She is happy that he is actually paying attention today.

"Is there something you aren't telling us?" Cale asks.

"Even if there was, it would be our right. You are not to question the Tribunal," General Linwood snaps. "The only reason we even gave you the heads up about this is because we will most likely be receiving a large surge of calls about this since there is a reward. Now that you know what is happening, I think we are done here."

Senator Scott fluidly rises and crosses the room to leave, an unreadable Dr. Bellamy right behind him. When they leave, the General starts speaking again.

"Parker, did you mean your oath at all? Mind your place, and stop questioning the Tribunal," he tells her.

He marches over to the exit, but before leaving turns to address them one final time.

"Rest up if you need it. I expect fast results after the news airs. Anyone with *any* sense will be helping, wanting to get those… *revolting* Variants off the streets of our city."

With that, the General abruptly leaves. Parker immediately bursts into tears.

"Parker? What is it? What's wrong?" Cale begs, twisting to pull her into a hug.

"H-how can he be so cruel?" she asks, unable to stop her falling tears.

"What do you mean?"

"He speaks of Variants as if they are all worthless trash… *My mother was a Variant!*" she sobs, clinging to Cale. "He pretends as if she never existed."

Cale, who had been rubbing her back, abruptly stops.

"Your mother was a Variant?" he asks, barely concealing his shock.

Parker nods as she pulls away from his embrace, not sure how much else she should say. Her father has done an expert job of keeping his dead wife's dirty secret hidden.

"You know you can talk to me, Parker," Cale says softly. "You don't have to if you don't want to, but I'm here, and willing to listen."

Parker takes a deep breath and exhales slowly, attempting to calm her tears. She's never discussed this with anyone, and feels an overwhelming urge to share with Cale, to split the burden so she is no longer the only one shouldering its weight.

Part of her wants to share out of spite, knowing the General would be unhappy having his skeletons released from the closet, but more than anything, the other part just doesn't want to hide her past anymore.

"My parents were high school sweethearts," she begins. "They knew even before they graduated that they would marry. My father spent his first summer after high school working for a construction company and saved all of his money to be able to buy an engagement ring. They eloped, which infuriated my mother's parents. To this day,

I have never met them. My parents didn't want anything to do with them because of their disapproval. Only my grandmother is still alive, or the last I knew, she was, at least. I saw her once, at my mother's funeral, but my father wouldn't let me speak to her."

Parker pauses, taking another deep breath.

"After they eloped, my father joined the Army to support them. Everything was perfect in those early days. She was the doting housewife; he was the determined soldier, climbing his way through the ranks. My mother used to say that things became more than perfect when I was born. They had problems conceiving, and had almost given up when my mother discovered she was pregnant. I had a great childhood for the most part. You may find this hard to believe, but my father used to smile all the time. He even used to laugh," she remembers fondly.

"I *do* find that hard to believe," Cale comments, giving her a small smirk.

"When I turned ten, my mother started developing her Variation. I don't know if you knew this, but not all Variations show from birth. Some can lay dormant for years before becoming apparent."

"What was her Variation?" Cale asks softly.

"She could hear people's thoughts."

Parker pauses a moment, preparing for the difficult part of her story.

"At first it was only people right in front of her, like my father and I. But her power started to grow to the point where she could hear the thoughts of everyone in our neighborhood. It was deafening… she couldn't control it. She was losing her mind. Until she discovered that there was one way for her to silence the thoughts."

"How?"

"Alcohol. If she was drunk, her Variation didn't work. So, she was drunk all the time. My parent's marriage began to struggle; my father didn't know what to do. He stopped laughing, and his smiles became less easy. My mother would cope by drinking even more. Then one day, when I was twelve, I needed something from the store for a school project. Dad was working late, so I asked my mom."

Parker feels fresh tears start streaming down her face.

"She was so drunk, I don't even know how she made it out of the driveway, let alone to the highway. We were swerving all over the place, and she... she ran our car into an oncoming semi. She was killed instantly, but somehow I managed to make it out with a few scratches and a dislocated shoulder."

"You were in the car with her?"

Cale reaches out to take Parker's hand.

"It's my fault Cale! I was old enough to know better than to let her get behind the wheel!"

Parker tries to look away, but Cale reaches up and takes her chin between his thumb and forefinger, forcing her to look at him.

"No. Parker, it was *not* your fault. She made the decision, not you. You cannot blame yourself for something your mother did when you were twelve."

"*He* blames me," she whispers.

"The General?"

"Yes. He may hate her for being a Variant, but he hates me for killing the love of his life. That's why he always makes digs at me about not doing what I'm told. He thinks I'm an incompetent fool."

This time Cale lets out a deep breath.

"Your father doesn't hate you, he just wants you to be the best."

"No, he hates me. Haven't you noticed how he can barely look at me? And when he does it's with disappointment."

"If that's true, then he is a worthless human being who doesn't deserve your tears. You were twelve; you can't keep blaming yourself for something that was beyond your control. Understand?"

Parker just nods, unsure whether or not to trust his words.

"I mean it. You have to let this guilt go. If you don't it will eat away at you. Maybe..." Cale hesitates.

"Maybe what?"

"Have you considered speaking to the General about this?"

Parker almost laughs.

"Are you kidding?" she asks. "He doesn't acknowledge that she ever existed. Can you imagine how upset he would be if I brought her up?"

She can tell Cale doesn't know what to say, and she really doesn't want to keep talking about this.

"Thank you for listening, Cale. I do feel better after sharing with someone. I can expect your silence on this, right?"

"Of course, I'm always here if you need to talk, and don't worry. I would never share this with anyone else."

"Thank you. Now, I don't know about you, but I feel like blowing off some steam. I'm going to head down to the training floor. Want to come with me?" she offers.

"Actually, that sounds perfect. You head on down and I'll meet you there. I have to get the okay from Dr. Bellamy."

Parker agrees, and heads to the room she stayed the night in. The PG staff keeps the room amazingly well stocked and she finds that there are workout clothes, in her size, in the closet.

Parker can't believe she finally told someone about her mother. When she'd started to tell her story, she felt she would probably regret it, but as of now, she only feels relief. Having someone else in on it helps her feel less alone. With her father refusing to acknowledge the past, there were some days Parker was sure she was insane and had imagined the whole thing.

But now Cale knows, she sighs inwardly. *I'm not alone anymore.*

SIX

Cale joined Parker shortly after she began her workout, telling her he was cleared to train, granted he took it easy. They did a couple of laps around the track, Parker leaving Cale in the dust, and then switched to one-on-one combat.

He seemed a little reluctant at first, until Parker goaded him into action.

"Come on," she urged. "Are you afraid I might hurt you?"

"Ha ha, no. I just don't like making girls cry, and with how bad I'm going to whoop you, trust me, you'll be crying."

"Bring it."

Cale flashed her a perfect, if a bit mischievous, smile and followed Parker to an exercise mat. They only spent an hour on the training floor, each winning two rounds, but with Parker feeling like the trash talk victor. Both are worn out as they head to their separate locker rooms.

"I'm starving," Cale tells her. "Meet in the lobby after you're done and let's go get some breakfast. I know a place with killer pancakes."

"Mmm, pancakes. What a great sugary, fattening, and

calorie-conscious way to end a workout."

"Oh, stop. You know your injection makes your metabolism act differently. You need all those calories."

"I know," she laughs, "I was just joking. I am definitely in if pancakes are involved. Oh! And there has *got* to be bacon."

"Obviously."

Parker makes her shower a quick one and leaves her hair hanging freely to dry naturally.

It'll be a mess, but I am too hungry to care.

Cale is already waiting for her when she gets back to the lobby and they head to the car without hesitation. The drive doesn't take long and he points out the restaurant when they get near. It looks like a little mom and pop place, and Parker asks how he'd found it.

"My apartment is actually right across the street," Cale tells her as he parks in front of the restaurant.

"Do you spend much time there?" she asks.

"Not really, but I can't make myself let the place go."

When they walk into the little diner, the owner rushes over to greet them and urges them to take the best and most private booth the place has to offer.

"I don't think I'll ever get used to that," Parker tells Cale as they sit down.

"I never thought I would either, but eventually the novelty fades."

Parker glances at a TV mounted near the counter of the diner.

"Look," she points. "They're talking about last night!"

Cale turns around to watch the report.

"It has now been confirmed that the group who organized the robbery of New Edison National Bank, Slavers of the People, has struck again. As you may already be aware, this group has been responsible for many acts of vandalism this summer. Last night, they attacked again, blowing a transformer in West New Edison and leaving hundreds without power," the female news anchor reports. "The Patriot Guard is currently seeking information on those involved. If you have information on the Criminal Calmer, Mother Mayhem, or the leader of the group, Konstantine Tesla, aka 'the Thundertaker,' you are urged to come forward. Any tips that lead to the capture of one of these three will be repaid with a ten thousand dollar reward. If spotted, do not engage these criminals. They are extremely dangerous, and two are Variants. Instead, immediately call the police."

"Ten thousand dollars?" Cale asks.

"The Thundertaker?" Parker says at the same time.

Both glance at the TV as the message is repeated once again.

"Wow," is all Cale has to say.

"Yeah... I mean I thought 'Stolid Sentry' was bad, but hell."

A short, elderly waitress comes to take their order before hurrying back towards the kitchen.

"I notice they officially tied the robbery to them," Parker says casually.

"I take it you don't approve?"

"It's just... I don't know. Doesn't it seem odd to you? This whole summer, they have been active. Spray-painting old buildings and cutting a couple power lines. There is even a rumor they put a potato in the tailpipe of the owner of TEnergy's car. Then, out of the blue, they escalate things and try to rob a bank... attempt to kill a hero. It just doesn't fit."

"I understand your reasoning," Cale tells her. "But their tag was at the scene."

"But it wasn't!" she insists.

"I saw the photos—"

"Yes, the vault said SP, but it was circled. Every other version of their tag is surrounded by lightning bolts, not a circle. "

Cale sighs.

"They were in a hurry. Maybe they didn't have time to spray paint a bunch of mini lightning bolts. Why are you so concerned with this?"

"I just feel like we are missing something, like the Tribunal is hiding things from us. They should tell us why they are so worried, we have a right to know what we're facing."

"A couple things… First, we gave up our rights when we gave our oaths. Second, I really don't think they are hiding anything. The Tribunal is just nervous that the Children of Freedom are gaining another ally, a powerful ally, with Variant followers."

Parker thinks this over, conceding that he makes a good point.

"I suppose you're right. I'm just overly paranoid because it has been such a crazy week."

"What were you expecting being a hero to be like?" Cale asks.

"Hmmm… more random crimes. It seems weird that we haven't had to chase any purse snatchers, or rescue any kittens from a tree."

"A kitten in a tree is a random crime?"

"You know what I mean."

Their waitress returns in record time, laden down with food. She quickly spreads the plates out before them, tells them to enjoy their meal, and walks off. Parker immediately dives into the pile of bacon, thankful for the amazing new metabolism her injection has provided.

"Parker, why did you try out for PG second gen.?" Cale asks. "You really don't seem like the kind of person to take orders from anyone."

She thinks her answer over carefully before speaking, not wanting her words to come out wrong.

"When you and the Patriot Guard were unveiled, my father became even more unavailable than he had before. He took longer to return my calls, he started missing our longstanding weekly family dinner night, and he was just all around more difficult to get along with than ever before. When they released that they would be doing tryouts for a chance to join the Patriot Guard, I couldn't stop myself. I figured that if I won, he would have to spend time with me, and he would admit that I finally did something he felt was worth while."

"Let me get this straight… you did all this, just to earn your father's time and approval?"

Parker nods.

"He's the only family I have. Pretty sad trying so hard, considering it didn't work, huh?" she asks.

"Well, let's just say we disagree on that. I've seen the General watch you train, and the only way to describe the expression on his face is 'pride.'"

She doesn't know what to say to that, so instead of responding, Parker changes the direction of the conversation.

"What about you? How did you get involved in all of this?"

"I'm an orphan, grew up in the system, you know, the normal hero background story. I joined the army to pay back my dues, and right after basic, I was recruited for PG. Now, here I am," he shrugs.

Cale has briefly mentioned his past on other occasions, but he has never gone into detail before. Parker decides to push a little further.

"What happened to your parents?" she asks.

"I have no idea. I just know that I was in the system for as far back as I can remember. I'm sure if I really wanted to know, I could get someone at headquarters to help me, but I don't see the point."

"You're not interested in them at all?"

"I tend not to waste time on people who don't care about me. Besides, if I met them now, I would be paranoid that they were only interested in Patriot Prime, not Cale Pearson."

Cale's hand is resting on the tabletop, so Parker

reaches across to hold it.

"I understand."

"I just hate that people no longer see Cale; they see Patriot Prime."

"I see Cale," she says, giving his hand a quick squeeze.

"Thank you."

"I mean, after working with you, I definitely don't see a hero."

"Oh really?"

"You got *shot* on the first trip out with your new sidekick, come on."

Cale opens his mouth but nothing comes out. Parker bursts out laughing.

"I'm screwing with you," she says. "You are an excellent hero."

"I'm done talking to you," Cale says dramatically, crossing his arms over his chest and turning his head to the side.

"You better stop pouting, they'll think we're having a lover's spat," she jokes.

Cale sighs.

"That is the last thing we need," he says, turning back to his breakfast.

They eat the rest of their meal in a comfortable silence. Parker keeps glancing up at the TV, which is repeating the story on the Slavers of the People.

They are really playing this up, she thinks. *There has got to be something else going on here.*

It's not that she thinks the Tribunal is hiding things from them just for the hell of it; she understands they probably have a legitimate reason, but she hates that, after everything she and Cale have been through, the Tribunal still treats them as children.

Go save the city from an unknown threat, but be back by dark. Wouldn't want to miss your bed time, would you?

"I'm stuffed," Cale says, pulling Parker from her

thoughts.

He pulls out some cash and throws it on the table.

"Aren't you going to take that to the register?" she asks.

"No. If I do, they won't accept it. I usually just leave it here."

Parker follows Cale through the diner, nodding hello at all the staring customers. Cale holds the front door open for her and makes a sweeping arm gesture to let her through. As she steps outside the door, Parker almost bumps into a short man who seems to be snapping pictures of them. Cale doesn't acknowledge the photographer, so she decides to follow his lead.

"Do you mind coming back to my apartment with me?" Cale asks. "I need to grab something."

"Sure, I'm in no rush."

Cale offers Parker his arm and they cross the street to his building. The apartment complex isn't as upscale as she would have imagined, but it isn't exactly low-class either. Cale's apartment is on the third floor.

"Whoa."

Parker can't hold back when he leads her in.

"Yeah, yeah. I know."

"When you said you couldn't let the place go, I assumed it would be a little more… homey," she says.

The living room is only furnished with a single plain sofa positioned in front of an enormous TV and video game collection. The walls are bare, and their bright white color makes the room seem all the more barren.

"I take it you're a gamer?" Parker asks, indicating the piles of game cases. "I'm surprised you have time for that."

"Are you kidding? I made time. Do you know how many scores I had to settle online after my injection enhanced my reflexes?"

"How many?"

"Let's just say… if I knew who my birthmother was, I might have been seriously offended at some of the comments."

Parker starts laughing.

"Awesome."

"I just want to grab a couple things from my room. It sounds like we're going to be getting busy and I'll probably just crash at PG headquarters."

~

When Cale finishes loading up at his apartment, he drives Parker by hers. She decides that his plan to stay at PG is probably for the best, and has to pick up some things of her own. Her place is the exact opposite of Cale's.

Where his walls are bare, Parker's are covered in family photos and knick-knacks. Her life is spread out in a timeline before him. When Parker steps into her bedroom to pack a bag, Cale walks slowly around the living room, studying the pictures. He stops at one and does a double take. There is a woman he at first mistakes for Parker, sitting in a hospital bed and holding a baby. Looking closer, he notices her eyes are green, not brown.

Parker's mother, he thinks, moving onto the next photo.

This one is of all three of the Linwoods, and to Cale's astonishment, he sees that the General does, in fact, know how to smile.

Or at least he used to.

Cale continues his exploration of the room, pausing here and there to look more closely, or smile at a picture of a young Parker. His favorite is one of her around the age of ten, atop a large black racehorse and smiling ear-to-ear, with her two front teeth missing. She looks so genuinely happy, it almost radiates from the frame.

He's just paused at a framed diploma when Parker walks back into the room.

"Associate of the Arts?" he asks, pointing to the

frame.

"Yeah, with a concentration in communication. I wanted to go into Public Relations," she explains.

"Well…you kind of did," Cale shrugs.

When they finally make it back to headquarters, one of the staff members is there to greet them. She has a list of leads about the Slavers of the People, its allies, and some possible whereabouts of its members that the PG has received from the new tip line.

"This is quite a list," Parker comments. "Should we split up?"

"Even though I doubt any of these are legit, I think we should stick together. If by some miracle one of these is actually the address, we shouldn't go in alone."

"Good point."

They quickly change into their costumes before meeting up to head out.

"Where are we going first?" Parker asks as she climbs into the passenger seat of Cale's car.

"Looks like some address in the slums. It's near the transformer that blew."

"That seems convenient."

"Oh, I forgot. How did your patrol go the other night? Did you run into any crimes or find out anything useful?" Cale asks.

"I questioned a couple iffy looking people. Didn't get much, although, one guy told me to head over to Fourth and Sidney; he said there was some guy named Jonah who would be worth talking to. I guess he's a Variant."

"Really? I actually talked to him. He seemed like he might know something, but overall just came across as crazy. He was wearing a sandwich board that said 'THE END IS COMING.' I wouldn't trust much of what he says. What's his Variation?"

"I think they said he was a 'psychic,' but I've never heard of that one before. I don't even think that's a real Variation."

"Huh, I haven't heard of that one before either."

"Was he seriously wearing a sign for the end of the world?" Parker asks, amused skepticism clear in her tone.

"Well, an end of something sign. It didn't specify the world, but he did seem to have limited advertising space, so…"

Cale sees her shaking her head from the corner of his eye, a smile on her face.

"Here it is," he tells her as he stops in front of a rundown, old Victorian-style home.

"It looks abandoned."

"Let's check it out."

As they are walking up the path to the house, Cale notices an elderly lady ambling down the sidewalk, staring at them. Even after eighteen months in the uniform, Cale still feels ridiculous walking around in broad daylight wearing a cape. He's half tempted to say "trick or treat" when they knock on the door.

Parker makes it up the front steps before him and raps on the door. They wait, and after no response, she knocks again.

Cale walks across the porch to peer into one of the front windows. The blinds are half busted, and he can see most of the front room.

"I don't think anyone actually lives here," he says. "The front room is empty."

Parker tries the doorknob and Cale is surprised to see that it twists with ease.

"Let's check it out," she offers, pulling the door open.

The inside of the house is a mess. Glass from broken windows and crumpled newspapers litter the floor, which is missing several floorboards. Everything is covered with a fine layer of dust that looks as if it hasn't been disturbed in years.

"Let's split up and check the rest of the house," Cale suggests. "I'll take the upstairs, and you take this floor."

"Got it," she says, making her way towards a hallway

on the opposite side of the room.

Cale takes the stairs in the corner and climbs to the second story of the house. He does a slow walk through, finding two empty bedrooms and a mildew-infested bathroom.

This is such a waste of time.

As he is checking a hallway closet, he hears Parker calling from below.

"I found something!"

He hurries down the stairs two at a time.

"Where are you?"

"I'm in the master bedroom!"

Cale follows the sound of her voice down the hallway and into a room on the right side of the house.

"What did you—" he stops mid-sentence, immediately seeing what she'd found.

On one of the walls in the bedroom, the SP logo is painted, surrounded by lightning. It is right next to a window and, as he moves to better inspect the emblem, he notices the window's view.

"You can see the blown transformer from here," he notes.

"Did you find anything upstairs?"

"Just a bunch of dust and dead bugs."

Cale walks a circle in the room, looking over every inch. He thinks he sees something flash out of the corner of his eye, but when he turns to look he can't find a source.

There it is again.

He fixes his gaze on an air vent that is on the opposite wall of the Slavers tag, just above their heads.

"Parker, look! There is something in there."

She looks up to where he is pointing.

"Is something red flashing in there?

Cale stretches up and pries the vent cover off with, then reaches into the dark hole. As he feels around, his fingers graze something. He grabs hold and when he pulls it out, he finds himself holding a tiny video camera. He looks the camera over, trying to determine if there are any signs of where it may have come from.

"This is a wireless camera… and it's transmitting right now."

"You mean someone is watching us?" Parker asks, sounding a little freaked out.

"Well, they were. The light just stopped flashing. They probably didn't want us tracking the transmission. In any case, I think we should get out of here. I don't like the thought of a group of criminal Variants knowing where we are"

"I'm with you there. I'll call headquarters and get them to send a team to sweep this place for any more electronics."

As Parker makes the call, Cale twists the camera around, searching it one more time, as if staring at it would make everything clear to him.

What was this doing in an abandoned house, aimed at the Slavers of the People logo?

"They're sending people now, and in the General's exact words, we should quit our 'damned lollygagging and check on the next tip.'"

Cale resists the urge to roll his eyes and just signals Parker to follow him back to the car.

"Who do you think made the tip to send us there?" she asks, after they get on the road to the next address.

"I don't know. It might have been an actual tip, or it could have been a set-up on Tesla's end."

"First, what is the point on spying on us? And second, the name 'Thundertaker' is too horribly awesome to be ignored."

This time, Cale can't prevent himself from rolling his eyes.

"Sometimes I swear that the Tribunal is trying to convince this city we are living in a comic book."

"Well, I say in an effort to show the Tribunal our

loyalty and support, the next time we get into a fight with a criminal, we start shouting 'WAM,' 'BAM,' and 'KA-POW!' every time we punch them."

"You'd better watch it," Cale warns. "You'll go straight from Stolid Sentry to Loony Lookout in no time."

The next address on the list leads them to a house in the suburbs. When they knock on the door, a man in a business suit answers it and seems beyond shocked to see them standing on his welcome mat.

"Patriot Prime?"

"Good afternoon, I was wondering if you could tell me what you know about the Slavers of the People—"

"Or the Thundertaker," Parker adds

Cale shoots her a hard look and can tell she is biting back laughter.

To say that the man seems confused is a large understatement. He looks back and forth between them with complete bewilderment.

"Are you two going door to door?" he asks.

"What? No. We received a tip that you had information regarding this case," Parker explains.

After a moment, the man's face clears as if he has just figured something out. He lets out a heavy sigh and turns to yell back into the house.

"Carl! Get your butt out here, now."

A small boy, no older than seven, comes bolting down the hall towards the open door. When he spots Parker and Cale, his jaw drops comically.

"Did you have something to do with this?" his father asks him.

Carl snaps his mouth shut and looks down at the ground.

"Carl?" the man insists.

The little boy nods his head twice, very slowly, still refusing to take his eyes off the ground.

"What exactly did you do?"

He waits so long, Cale doesn't think the boy is going

to answer, but finally he begins to speak.

"I called the tip line and said you knew where the Thundertaker is so that the heroes would come here and I could meet them, and maybe become a sidekick too."

Cale looks over at Parker and can tell she is on the verge of saying "aw."

"Son, you know that was wrong don't you? You've wasted the heroes' time."

Carl looks up at them, his eyes full of unshed tears.

"I'm so sorry! Please don't throw me in jail. Then, I'll never be a hero like you!"

Parker starts talking and Cale finds himself surprised at her words.

"I don't know… lying, especially to heroes, is a big no-no. Maybe if we took you in you would learn your lesson."

The boy's father nods along in agreement.

"No, please! I've learned my lesson, plus I'm gonna be grounded anyway. I promise never to do it again!"

"Hmmm," Parker ponders.

"I suppose we could let you off with a warning, but just this one time," Cale tells the boy. "Don't let us catch you doing anything naughty, understand?"

Carl nods, eyes huge.

"And remember," Parker adds, "Santa watches you all year round. Don't think he won't rat on you."

Somehow, the little boy's eyes get even wider.

"Thank you for being so understanding," the father says as they prepare to leave.

"Of course. Just keep the phone out of his reach for a while," Cale instructs.

After the door closes and they turn away, Parker groans loudly.

"I really don't want to do the rest of list," she whines, getting back into the car.

"Oh come on," Cale tells her, "they can't all be fake."

The rest of the day is spent proving his earlier

statement wrong. Not one single tip they look into, aside from the Victorian house, leads to gathering any real information.

This really needs to end.

SEVEN

After two days of following pointless leads, Cale can
tell Parker is getting restless with the tip line's wild goose
chases. She seems distant and uninterested in their
inquiries, but the most obvious sign of her displeasure
comes from the fact that she won't stop complaining.

"I mean *come on*," she starts, for what is probably the
tenth time in the last hour. "How likely is it that other
crime has actually slowed down or stopped?"

"Well, you never know. One of my sources, Benny,
said that he knew some guys backing off a job they'd been
planning," Cale tells her, conveniently leaving out that he
was the reason they were stepping down.

"Yeah, but I doubt that the day the Tribunal opened
the tip line, all the city's criminals woke up and decided,
'hmm, I think I'll be a productive member of society
today.' Isn't it more likely that the Tribunal is only
assigning us tasks related to the Slavers of the People and
pushing the others aside?"

"Maybe… but do you really want to ask them? They
are trying to do what is best for the city."

Parker sighs heavily and gives him an undeniably
pouty look.

"No, I don't want to ask them. My father is already giving us looks like it's our fault the tips suck. I don't want to annoy him more."

"So, onto the next tip?" Cale asks plastering a cheery smile on his face, knowing it'll annoy her.

"Ugh... I guess so," she groans.

"You know, you are adorable when you pout."

"Oh, shut up."

"Just adorable," he repeats, barely dodging the punch she aims at his shoulder. "Be careful. Bellamy will skin you alive if she sees you trying to further the injury to my shoulder."

"Shouldn't you be healed by now?" Parker asks in all seriousness as they exit PG headquarters and walk to his Camero.

"Dr. Bellamy isn't sure why the accelerated healing stopped working on the gunshot wound," he explains. "My healing still works on all other minor injuries, but for whatever reason, my shoulder is healing at a normal human rate."

"Does it hurt?" she asks.

"Oh, only when I run, or stretch, or train."

"It's still that bad?"

"No, it's really not," he lies.

In truth, his shoulder has been aching nonstop and doesn't appear to be getting any better. Even though Dr. Bellamy said that it is currently healing at the average human rate, Cale doesn't feel like any progress is being made, after seeing how quickly the injury had started out healing. He tries not to let the pain bother him, but when he does something that makes his shoulder twinge, like turning in the wrong direction, he gets annoyed with how long the process is taking.

As the week progresses, they do start to see a little more action, though not the kind Parker would prefer. Over a period of six days, three more transformers are blown. They never make it to the scene until after the vandals have gone, but at least on these trips, they know they are on the right trail. Every other tip they've followed up on has been for nothing.

They have found no evidence of the Slavers of the People since the first day, when they had discovered the video camera in an old abandoned house. The Tribunal later sent a tech team to sweep the place, but they hadn't found any other cameras or indications as to why that one was there.

"We are never going to find these guys," Parker grumbles as they walk around the scene of the latest transformer blow out.

"We might get lucky one of these times and make it to the scene before they bail," Cale offers.

"What we need to do is catch them before they blow it. Maybe if there was a..." she drops off

"A what?"

"I need a map! Is there one in the car?" she asks, excited.

"Um, yeah. Should be in the glove box. Why?"

Parker doesn't answer him, and instead runs to the car to pull out the map. She spreads it out on the hood of the Camero and starts tracing it with her finger.

"Look! Here is where we are, the fourth transformer they've blown."

"Ok..."

"Here are the other two they've done this week. It's a pattern! The last three they have blown have been done at two day intervals, and if you look at the map," she points to the other transformers' locations, "they are moving this way down a line of transformers. If they keep it up—"

"Then in two days, they are going to blow this transformer, right over here," he taps the spot on the map. "Brilliant! We need to tell the Tribunal."

After making sure there is nothing of use at the scene, which, as usual, there isn't, they make their way back to

PG headquarters and call a meeting with the Tribunal.

General Linwood, Senator Scott, and Dr. Bellamy are all in the War Room waiting for them when they arrive.

"What's happened? Have you found something?" the General asks, before they are through the door.

"Not at the scene," Cale explains, "but Parker has figured something out."

Parker hurries over to the table and spreads the map out in front of everyone.

"I found a pattern," she starts, and then points out her evidence while explaining everything.

"We think we should plan an ambush," Cale says, once she has finished.

"Oh, this is excellent!" the Senator exclaims. "I'll make sure the press is prepared for a big story!"

"This is more like it, you two," the General nods at them, the closest he has ever come to openly showing approval of Cale.

"No."

Everyone turns to face Dr. Bellamy, who is the only person in the room who doesn't appear to be excited.

"What do you mean, 'no'?" General Linwood snarls.

The Doctor ignores him and turns her full attention on Cale.

"Cale, you are not well enough to take on something like this."

"I'm fine, really. I've been doing great this week."

"Yes, while running fools' errands on bogus tips," she pauses to throw a glare at the two men of the Tribunal, "but you aren't ready for a confrontation like the one you could end up facing if you do this. Do you really think you can handle these Variants in your condition?"

"He'll be fine, Maura. Stop coddling him," the General forces out through his gritted teeth. "Now, if you are done, you may leave. We have an ambush to map, and that isn't really your area, now is it?"

"It doesn't really matter what my damned area is,

does it? You wouldn't listen to me anyway!" she yells, stepping towards General Linwood as if to challenge him. "You've already got what you wanted from me and now you two expect me to sit back and watch as you exploit my hard work for your own selfish endeavors! This is not what I signed on for, Sampson!"

Cale and Parker stand perfectly still, frozen in shock. Dr. Bellamy may have, in the past, made a few snide remarks, but she has never yelled at anyone outright, let alone disrespected the other members of the Tribunal. Anger is etched in every line of her face, and she has her pointer finger buried in the General's chest.

"I think this is a discussion best left for later, Maura," the General tells her; his voice is low and dangerous.

Before she can answer him, he reaches out and grabs her by her upper arm, then proceeds to lead her from the War Room.

Cale glances over at Parker and he can tell she has no idea what to make of the situation.

What did she mean about her work being exploited for 'selfish endeavors?'

"I'm, uh, going to go check on those two," the Senator tells them. "Just wait in here, and General Linwood will be back to help you plan momentarily."

He gives them his politician's smile and hurries from the room.

"What the *hell* was *that?*" Parker asks immediately.

"I have absolutely no clue."

"What did she mean about her work being exploited?"

"Well, technically we are her work. Maybe she shares your view that putting all of our time into finding the Slavers of the People is wasteful."

"Maybe... I feel like there is an awful lot going on here that we aren't being told." Parker lets out a sad sigh. "At least I know you'll be honest with me."

Cale nods at her and gives her a small smile, feeling a

knot form in his stomach.

In the beginning of the *Patriot Guard: Second Generation*, when he had been told he wasn't allowed to share the facts about the original Patriot Project with his new sidekick, Cale hadn't questioned the decision. He hadn't anticipated he would become such close friends with the competition's winner, or that he would want to tell them. Now he feels extremely guilty about keeping this information from Parker, but is tied by his loyalty to the job and the fact that the Tribunal swore him to silence.

Cale takes his oath very seriously; he won't break his promise, however much he may want to. He grew up on broken promises from social workers and foster parents, and he refuses to be like them… to make his word meaningless.

After about ten minutes, General Linwood returns alone.

"Sorry about that," he apologizes gruffly. "Dr. Bellamy has been overtired. She has been spending a lot of late nights working on new research. She didn't know what she was saying."

Cale has to refrain from pointing out that she was completely right about them never listening to her.

"We should start planning your strategy," General Linwood tells them. Then, though it clearly pains him, he asks Cale, "you are well enough for this, aren't you?"

"I'll be fine," Cale assures him.

"Excellent. Now you'll want to stake out here… and here."

They spend several hours going over the logistics of the ambush, and by the time they finish, Cale has a pretty good feeling about the plan.

"I think this is going to work," Parker smiles.

"Of course it's going to work," the General says. "Now, why don't you get some rest? Also, you should take tomorrow off."

Wow, Cale thinks.

Then, even more shockingly, General Linwood reaches out and pats Parker on the back, giving her a smile.

"Nice work, kid. I'm proud of you."

"T—Thank you..." she manages to stammer out through her shock.

After that, the General bids them goodnight and leaves them alone.

"Can I walk you to your room?" Cale asks, pretending not to notice the obvious wetness forming in the corners of her eyes.

Parker nods at him and clears her throat before following Cale through the door and into the private room section of the second floor.

~

It's not often Parker finds herself with free time these days. Almost every minute of her life since she auditioned for the Patriot Guard has been planned out for her. So, when Parker wakes the next morning and remembers she has the day off, she is a little unsure what to do.

She spends the morning lazing around, flipping through daytime TV, but is bored with that before eleven.

She texts Cale but doesn't get a response.

Probably settling some more video game scores, she thinks with a smirk.

Parker is just getting ready to toss her phone on the bed when she rethinks it and begins scrolling through her contacts; she doesn't want to spend all day cooped up and alone. Before she can second-guess herself, she sends two texts and waits anxiously for the responses.

In less than two minutes, her phone chimes and she has her answer. Parker is going to lunch with some old friends, and she is pretty excited.

She met Lucy Gales and Cynthia Watford in college. Lucy used to be Parker's roommate, and Cynthia had lived in the dorm across the hall. Parker hasn't seen them for months, the last time being when she got them both tickets for one of the *Patriot Guard: Second Generation* obstacle course tapings.

Parker throws open her wardrobe, suddenly wishing she'd grabbed more street clothes from home. She manages to find something safely between training clothes and hero garb, and sets out to meet Lucy and Cynthia.

They are already waiting for her with a table when Parker gets to the small Italian Bistro. Both jump up when they see Parker walk through the door.

"Parker!"

"Over here!"

Parker smiles brightly as she approaches them. Lucy tackles her in a hug that, had it been the days before Parker's injection, would have knocked her over.

"Oh," Lucy groans, "you're a lot sturdier than you used to be."

Parker just laughs and turns to give Cynthia a hug.

"Luce, what happened to your hair?" Parker asks.

The last time she'd seen her, Lucy's blonde hair had hung to her waist, and now it's cropped into an extremely short pixie cut.

"It was way too much maintenance," Lucy answers, taking a seat at the table. "I was going to just do braids like Cyn's, but she said I couldn't pull it off."

"You are far too white," Cynthia says, her and Parker taking seats as well.

"Well, I like it," Parker insists.

Their waiter, seeing everyone now present, swoops in to take their drink orders and drop off a basket of bread.

"*So,*" Lucy starts, smacking Parker's arm after the waiter leaves. "Spill. Tell us everything!"

"Um…what do you want to know?"

"How have things been going, *hero?*" Cynthia asks. "What's it like being famous?"

"I'm not *that* famous."

As if waiting for that cue, a little girl from a neighboring table comes bolting over, placemat and crayon in hand.

"Sentry! Can I have your autograph?" the little girl asks.

Parker feels herself start to blush as she takes the crayon and signs the placemat.

"Sure."

Lucy has her hand over mouth, trying to stifle her laughter, while Cynthia is just giving a very clear '*I told you so*' look to the table.

"Thank you!" the little girl exclaims, throwing her arms around Parker for a quick hug before running back to her own table.

"You were saying?" Cynthia questions.

"Okay, it can be a bit disconcerting at times," Parker admits.

"But there has got to be a lot of perks!" Lucy says. "You know, like getting to stare at Patriot Prime all day."

"That man is too gorgeous to be real," Cynthia sighs. "Have you two—?"

"What? No!" Parker snorts, laughing. "Cale and I don't see each other that way."

Lucy shakes her head disbelievingly.

"He is so good looking," Cynthia insists, "that if you have a pulse, you see him *that* way."

The waiter interrupts then, dropping off the drinks and taking their lunch orders.

"What about you guys?" Parker asks. "Are either of you seeing anyone?"

"No time," Cynthia says. "I've been so focused on my internship at the hospital. Luce is still seeing Jason though...they've moved in together."

"Yeah, we've taken the next step. Oh! That reminds me, Cyn, Jason's friend Chad saw you when we were at the mall last Thursday and asked Jason to ask me if I could set you two up. He's really interested."

"I'm not dating someone named *Chad*. Let me guess, he works with Jason?"

"Uh-huh."

"I'm not dating a telemarketer."

"What's wrong with telemarketers?"

Parker sips her drink and zones out of the conversation. She tries to follow along, but it quickly jumps from who's dating who, to who got a new job, to who is going to win some singing talent show, and Parker has no clue what they are talking about. She nods and smiles when they look to her, but mostly remains quiet.

It's not that Parker didn't miss her friends, but the top forty chart seems a lot less important when she is verging on taking down an affiliate organization of an anti-government militia.

When the check comes, Parker insists on paying, and tells them how much fun it was to see them both. In all honesty, though, when she leaves the restaurant, Parker just feels relieved…which leaves her feeling lonelier than ever.

I'm not lonely, she insists to herself, *I'll always have Cale.*

Cheered up a bit at that thought, Parker heads back to headquarters to review the plan for the ambush.

Parker feels confident as she and Cale set up their stake out at the transformer they suspect is next. They position themselves behind a cluster of bushes, where the lack of streetlights ensures they are out of sight.

The dirt lot the transformer is in is large and rather open. Cale and Parker know that, if the Slavers do show up, they'll see them. Other than the bushes they are hiding in, there isn't much coverage available. The only other obstacle on the lot, aside from the transformer itself, is a four-by-four TEnergy maintenance truck, sitting straight across from Cale and Parker's hiding spot.

Parker is feeling pumped.

Nothing can go wrong.

Logically, she knows that *everything* could go wrong, but the high she's had since the meeting when they planned the ambush has made her sure of its success.

I'm proud of you, she repeats in her head for the three hundredth time. *He actually said he was proud of me, and he smiled!*

Parker knows this is monumental for their relationship. If she catches the Thundertaker, or Mother Mayhem, she truly believes everything will be perfect between her and her father.

She is so wrapped up in her thoughts that Cale has to nudge her to point out two figures arriving at the transformer. At first, their identities are too hard to make out, but as they step beneath a streetlight, Parker can see them clearly.

It's Mother Mayhem *and* the Thundertaker. They are whispering to each other, but are too far away to be overheard.

Mayhem is pointing behind her, towards one of the side streets. The Thundertaker nods emphatically, and she takes off on her own down the shadowed street.

Cale taps Parker, points after Mother Mayhem, and then points to himself. Parker nods in agreement and watches as Cale follows the woman with stealth.

They had previously agreed that, if it came to a fight, which it undoubtedly would, Parker would face Tesla. His Variation made him extremely dangerous, so their best chance against him is speed, and Parker *is* speed. In addition to her normal costume, Parker is wearing shock-resistant rubber gloves. If she has to grab him, he won't be able to electrocute her.

She holds her position, not wanting to move too soon, waiting to see what he is going to do. She watches as Tesla paces back and forth, inspecting his target, trying to find the perfect spot.

He stands in front of the transformer, facing away

from her, and places his feet shoulder width apart. He then slowly spreads his arms, and Parker stares on in amazement as glowing balls of pure energy appear in the palms of his hands. They start out small, as merely sparks, but then start to get brighter, growing in intensity and size.

He gets ready to strike out at the transformer, and Parker comes to her senses.

"Hold it right there, Thundertaker!" Parker calls, stepping out from her hiding spot. She has her gun drawn and trained on Tesla.

The spots of energy disappear from his hands, and his arms fall limply to his sides. He tilts his head and then turns to face Parker, a look of complete exasperation on his face.

"Are such… vulgarities completely necessary?" he asks, his crisp voice coming off as extremely bored.

What?

"I wasn't aware I was being, uh, vulgar."

"Don't stand there, *Stolid Sentry*, and pretend that our media-concocted names are not completely ridiculous."

He crosses his arms and watches her expectantly, his eyebrow arched, waiting for her response.

Parker has no idea what to say; she hadn't exactly planned on a lot of conversation when they mapped how this would go down.

"I like to think that my name is nowhere near as ridiculous as yours, but, I'll tell you what, if you cooperate with me, you can put whatever name you wish on your arrest report."

Tesla starts laughing, general delight on his face.

"I'm really not planning on being arrested, but I like your style," he says, pointing at her. "In your line of work, a healthy dose of sarcasm is a must… sadly, your partner doesn't understand that."

"What would you know about Prime? You've never faced him."

"No, but your Tribunal makes sure every fight he gets

in goes around, and I have to say, I'd much rather listen to snarky comebacks than gag-inducing promises of 'justice.' He takes this hero thing *far* too seriously."

Parker has to resist the urge to smile. She knows super villains are supposed to be smart-asses and all, but she wasn't expecting this.

"That's only because he wants to keep our city safe from criminals like you," she says, keeping her tone level to hide her amusement.

Tesla looks around dramatically, and then points at himself.

"Criminals like me? All I've done is a little vandalism. Shouldn't you be out there looking for that serial killer? The one who has murdered three single mothers?"

"What are you talking about?"

"Ah… you don't know. Well, they have been keeping it out of the news, but I assumed your Tribunal would be keeping you up to date. I guess you've been too busy chasing *me*. How about I just give you my number, then next time you want to chat just give me a call and we'll have a little dinner or something?"

Tesla gives her a wink, and she notices that his blue eyes are glowing.

"I don't go on dates with criminals."

"What about revolutionaries? Because if you just wait, you'll see me usher in the dawn of a new era in energy."

Parker is getting frustrated.

This guy is making no sense.

"What are you talking about?" she asks. "What is the point of all this?"

"The point, Sentry, is to free the citizens of New Edison from their reliance on TEnergy's corrupt system."

"That's a new one. People called 'slavers' aren't usually into freedom."

"Always with the vulgar names. We never said we were the *Slavers* of the People—"

"I've seen your logo," she interrupts.

97

"Are your manners always so appalling?" he asks. "Calling complete strangers names, and interrupting… I expected better from the General's daughter."

Tesla sighs heavily and begins pacing back and forth. Parker is careful to keep him in her sights.

"Not to mention aiming a weapon at an unarmed man."

"*You* are a weapon."

"Again with the name calling. Now, as I was saying, we never claimed to be the Slavers of the People. Your media did that, and I am guessing it was on the orders of the Tribunal. Yes, our logo is SP, but it stands for *Servants* of the People."

"I'm done with this conversation. The only thing you've served to the people is a hike on their already outrageous energy bill. Ever since TEnergy has had to start importing coal, their prices to operate have increased, which in turn *must* be passed to the customers. You know what happens when you blow up extremely expensive pieces of their equipment? Guess what? They need to be repaired, and the costs of said repairs get passed on to the citizens you are claiming to be helping!" As her anger rises, so does her voice. "Now, put your damned hands on your head, because your little protests stop tonight."

"I'm sorry you feel that way," he says quietly, lifting his hands into the air.

Somehow Parker anticipates his next move and throws herself to the ground, rolling to the left seconds before Tesla throws a ball of energy where she had just been standing. The ground explodes, sending sizzling pieces of dirt flying.

Son of a bitch!

She quickly jumps up and dodges his next blast, all the while trying to get a clear aim at him. Tesla stays on the move and out of her cross hairs. She sees him clench his hands tightly and, when they open, he has two more orbs of energy ready to fly at her.

She just barely escapes them by ducking behind the TEnergy maintenance truck. Her heart is racing, pounding loudly in her ears, and she can feel adrenaline coursing through her veins.

"You're quick," Tesla calls. "I can see why you stayed behind and Prime followed Krista. I *am* assuming Prime followed Krista. I doubt you came alone."

Parker bites her lip to keep from answering, knowing that's what he wants her to do, to give away her position.

"I hope he doesn't get too angry about what he finds. I wouldn't want anything to happen to him," he continues, his voice getting closer.

Parker presses her back against the truck, crouching to keep her head below the windows. Slowly, she starts edging around to the front of the vehicle, attempting to keep her footfalls light and quiet.

"Oh, Sentry. Do we really have to do this? I don't want to hurt you," Tesla tries to assure her. "I'm really not a bad guy, here."

She can tell his voice is coming from around the back of the truck. Parker rounds the front of the vehicle and twists to peer at the side she's just come from, one hand clutching her gun, with the other placed on the hood of the vehicle.

Suddenly, an arm wraps around her neck, putting her into a headlock. Parker begins to fight back, but the cold barrel of a gun pressed into her temple makes her pause.

"Drop it," a female voice whispers coldly.

Parker grits her teeth, but does as she's told and lets her gun fall to the ground. She is seething with anger, hating herself for not realizing there was another assailant.

Tesla walks around from behind the truck, seeming cautious until he sees the position she is in. A playful smile spreads across his face. If he weren't a lousy criminal who had just tried to incinerate her, Parker might think the genial expression made him look quite handsome.

"Krista, play nice," he admonishes. "No need to hurt

her."

Just. Freaking. Wonderful. Mother Mayhem has me in a sleeper hold.

Parker reaches up to grab Krista's arm, trying to loosen the hold around her throat, and just barely resists the urge to dig her sharp nails into the other woman's exposed flesh.

"You know this would be a lot easier without her in the way," Krista says coldly, cocking the gun.

"I disagree. Think of her friend," Tesla offers. "He would not be very understanding."

What the hell is he talking about?

Krista lets out a deep breath, but doesn't remove the gun from Parker's head. In fact, she pushes it even harder into her skull.

"Well then, would you rather I knock her out, or have Leon handle her?" Krista asks.

"Why don't we let Leon do the honors? Wouldn't want to bruise that pretty face."

Krista just snorts, as Tesla places a hand to his ear.

"Leon. I have a job for you," he says into what Parker realizes must be an earpiece.

Parker knows she needs to act, and holds out hope that Krista will listen to Tesla and not shoot her. After bracing herself and taking a deep, silent breath, Parker tightens her grip on her assailant's arm and sweeps her leg out to wrap her ankle around the back of Krista's leg. Parker twists away from the gun and uses all of her force to knock Krista's legs out from under her. The woman falls to the ground, landing hard on her back with a loud grunt.

Parker quickly grabs her own weapon from the ground and aims it at Tesla, all the while backing towards Krista to kick the gun out of her hand.

"You don't want to do that, dear," a new voice tells her.

An older gentleman, easily in his sixties, comes

around the vehicle to join Tesla. He has a soft, gentle expression on his face, though he seems to be chastising her.

Parker barely has a chance to recognize the man before she realizes he is absolutely right. She doesn't want to do this.

Why would I want to hurt these people? They're my friends.

Parker drops her gun once more, and smiles at the men before her.

"I'm sorry," she says. "I guess I *do* have appalling manners. I hope you can forgive me."

Tesla starts laughing, and turns to the older man.

"Laying it on a little thick there, aren't we, Leon?"

"She's quite strong, it needs to be thick," Leon tells him.

Next to her, Parker can hear Krista groan as she tries to sit up, her joints popping loudly.

"Oh, my. Here, let me help."

Parker reaches down to offer a hand to the fallen woman, but Krista only growls and slaps the proffered hand away, choosing to help herself up.

"Let's get out of here," Krista says, shooting a glare at Parker.

"Where are we going?" Parker asks, taking a step towards Tesla.

"I'm sorry, Sentry," he chuckles, "but you can't come with us. Maybe one day, but not today."

Parker gives him a reproachful look, but can't seem to muster up any real annoyance.

"Will I be seeing you again?" she asks.

"My best guess says you will."

Krista starts walking towards the street and signals that the other two should follow. As they turn away, Parker remembers something Tesla said earlier.

"Wait! You never gave me your number like you said!" she calls.

She hears Tesla laughing again, and he pauses to

respond, turning to shoot her another wink.

"I'll call *you*," he assures her. "I have your number."

As the three depart, Parker can hear Krista complaining.

"Really, Konstantine? Did you really have time to make a date?"

Once the trio are out of sight, Parker's emotions return to normal and she feels as if she has been punched in the face. All of her anger and adrenaline come coursing back and she curses under breath, feeling ashamed.

The Criminal Calmer strikes again.

Looking around, Parker notices something that makes her breath catch and gut turn to lead.

Cale is nowhere to be seen.

"Damn it," she mutters, and then quickly takes off towards the street she saw him follow Mother Mayhem down.

EIGHT

Parker rushes down the shadow-strewn street, desperate to find Cale. She knows that the Tribunal, or most of it, would prefer that she chase down the Thundertaker, Mother Mayhem, and the Criminal Calmer, but there is no way she can just abandon her partner.

"Cale!" she calls.

She continues running down the alley until she reaches a dead end; a ten-foot tall fence blocks her path.

"Cale!" she tries again.

Parker scans her surroundings and notices an oddly shaped pile of newspapers on the ground beside a dumpster. Approaching the pile cautiously, she bends down to move some of the papers away, and lets out a loud gasp when she finds Cale beneath them. She pushes the rest of the trash away and leans in to rest her head on his chest.

He's still breathing.

He seems only to be sleeping. Parker reaches out and lightly smacks the man's face.

"Cale, wake up!" she urges.

"Ugh," he groans.

"Oh, thank goodness."

Cale's eyelids flutter open, but it takes a moment for the glazed expression to leave him.

"Where am… *damn it*!" he exclaims, remembering where they are.

"What happened?" Parker asks.

She grabs Cale's arm and wraps it around her shoulder, then helps pull him to his feet.

"I followed Mother Mayhem," he groans. "But she knew I was coming. This whole thing was a set-up."

"What?"

"I got here and there was an ambush waiting for me. They knocked me unconscious."

"Why? I don't understand," Parker says. "What was the point of this?"

"I don't know, but we should get back to PG headquarters."

"Can you walk, or should I bring the car to you?"

"I'm fine. It's not that far."

Cale has a slight limp, but the further they go, the better it seems to get.

"Looks like your accelerated healing is working," she notes.

"Huh? Oh, yeah. I guess it is."

It takes them ten minutes to get to the car. They parked a few blocks away, not wanting to give anyone a heads up that they were there.

Yeah, because that worked out, she thinks bitterly.

It's not until they are back in the Camero that Parker really thinks about their failed mission, about all of the soon-to-be disappointed people back at PG headquarters.

They drive back in complete silence, neither wanting to acknowledge what they are about to face. Parker cruises below the speed limit, trying to put off the inevitable.

"I really don't want to go in there," she tells Cale as she pulls into the PG parking area.

"Yeah… me either. How about we make a break for Mexico?" Cale jokes. "I could be okay with you and me

104

living the rest of our lives out on a beach."

"Let me guess, is it a—"

"Nude beach? Well, obviously."

Parker gives him a small smile before climbing out of the car.

The walk to the building is one of the longest she can remember. She doesn't want to go through the front doors to confront all of the anxiously waiting people, to face her father and say that she failed.

To make matters worse, she was walking in still in perfect health. The only damage she seems to have sustained is a little dirt on her costume from rolling. She looks as if she hadn't put up a fight, which was, unfortunately, true. She stood there watching her targets walk away, wondering if Konstantine Tesla meant what he said about calling her.

Granted, it truly *wasn't* her fault. Dozens of others have been had by the Criminal Calmer. Sadly, that doesn't offer any comfort.

He's going to return to hating me, Parker thinks dejectedly as her thoughts drift to her father. *They were right there within my grasp, and I let them escape.*

She looks to Cale as they push open the front door, hoping for a reassuring glance, but is disappointed to see him tied up in his own puzzled thoughts.

The lobby is mostly empty, for which Parker is grateful, but there are a handful of people waiting for them. All three members of the Tribunal are there, plus two of Dr. Bellamy's assistants, and a security guard. The Doctor and her assistants are sitting on a couch talking quietly, while General Linwood and the Senator stand in the corner of the room speaking with the security guard.

"The heroes return!" Senator Scott booms as they enter.

Everyone in the room looks up expectantly.

"How did it go?" he asks. "Should I call the news? I told them to expect a big story."

Parker feels like she is going to be sick, and turns her gaze downwards, inspecting her shoes. She knows it's cowardly to expect to Cale to explain by himself, but she can't muster the strength to speak first.

"Well?" the General asks.

"It didn't go as planned," Cale says.

"What is that supposed to mean? They didn't follow the pattern?"

"Yes… well, no. It's— the pattern was a setup."

"What do you mean it was a setup?" Senator Scott asks.

"They knew we were coming," Parker rushes, looking back up. "Mother Mayhem took off down a side street, so Cale followed, leaving me with Tesla. I tried to fight Tesla, but he called in the Criminal Calmer… and there was nothing I could do."

She hates that it sounds like she's pleading, but she can't seem to help it. She looks at her father, begging him to understand, but his face is unreadable. His eyes are dark and empty, leaving Parker feeling empty as well.

I'll even accept anger. Please, just give me something.

"What happened to you?" the General asks Cale.

"Mother Mayhem led me straight into an ambush. They knocked me unconscious, and I woke up next to a dumpster with Parker kneeling over me."

"You were unconscious?" Dr. Bellamy asks, speaking for the first time since they arrived.

Cale nods at her.

"We need to get him to the lab now," the Doctor tells her two assistants. "We need to be sure they didn't give you anything. Any needle marks would have healed before you woke, so we'll have to run some extensive blood tests."

At her signal, the two assistants converge on Cale, and despite his protests, lead him to the elevators, presumably to take him to the lab. Dr. Bellamy follows closely behind them, muttering.

"I knew this was a horrible idea."

The Senator just stands still, clearly not sure what he should be doing. His skin has taken on a slight sickly pallor.

He's probably wondering how to appease the reporters he led on. This won't help him with his upcoming reelection.

General Linwood sneers, turns away from Parker, and starts to walk away.

"I'm sorry," she says, following him.

He ignores her.

"Please," she begs. "Dad—"

"Stevens!" the General commands, signaling the security guard. "Please escort the Sentry to her private room upstairs. I'm sure she needs to rest."

Then, without so much as giving Parker a second glance, the General continues off down the hall, towards his private offices.

Cold shock runs through her.

She had expected anger, disdain, and even disappointment, but being completely dismissed as if she were no one of importance strikes Parker to her very core.

He wouldn't even look at me.

Stevens comes up and takes her arm to lead her to her room, but she knocks his hand away forcefully, and gives him a furious scowl.

"I know where it is," she growls before stalking off to the elevators.

When she gets to her room, Parker throws herself onto the bed, not even bothering to remove her costume. She had expected tears, but none come. She is too numb, and still in shock.

What the hell happened tonight? Cale said it had been an ambush, and that they knew we were coming.

If that was the case, what had been the point of it? Why hadn't they killed them? The Slavers of the People had led the heroes there just to knock one of them unconscious? It makes no sense.

And there's another thing…

What Had Tesla been talking about when he said they weren't the "Slavers," but the "Servants"? Everything he said was in an attempt to make his group seem like nothing more than a bunch of extremist protestors who were against the rising energy costs.

But his logic made no sense.

How would making citizens pay for major repairs help ease their financial burden?

Honestly, the guy came off as kind of crazy. I doubt anything he said was true.

Parker has the overwhelming urge to pile blankets on top of herself, curl up in a ball, and sleep for a week. She almost succumbs, too, but then remembers something else Tesla had said.

"Shouldn't you be out there looking for that serial killer who has murdered three single mothers?"

She knows he must have been making it up, trying to throw her off guard. Parker remembers, though, that there recently *was* a murder involving a single mother of two. She had even voiced her concerns as to why the Tribunal wasn't concerned with looking for the murderer.

Surely, there haven't been two more murders since then…

Unable to banish the troubling thought from her head, Parker decides that she needs to look into it.

Tesla told her it wasn't in the news, but she knows if it is anywhere, it will be in the Patriot Guard file room. They monitor and compile files on every crime in the city, so there is bound to be *something* there if the crimes really did occur.

Parker forces herself to climb out of bed. She decides to change into something a bit more comfortable, and then is on her way downstairs to do some digging in the file room.

~

After Dr. Bellamy draws a fifth vial of blood, she tells Cale to lay back, get some rest, and she'll be back in a bit for some more.

He feels awful, not just because of the lack of blood, but from lying to Parker.

This is becoming a far too often occurrence.

He does know what the point of tonight had been. The Slavers of the People wanted to talk to him directly.

He took off after Mother Mayhem when she ran down that side street, determined to bring her in. Looking back, he wishes he had been a bit more vigilant tonight.

If only we can catch them, then everything will return to normal, Cale thought. *We can go back to dealing with "random crime," as Parker put it.*

He hadn't lied when he told Parker the whole thing was a set-up. He chased Mayhem all the way to the dead end, and when they got there, he realized something was up. He barely had time to wonder what she would be doing over here before he was surrounded by almost a dozen armed Children of Freedom members, popping out from behind dumpsters.

"You are quite hard to get alone, Patriot Prime," Mother Mayhem said, as she paced back and forth in front of him.

Her expression screamed satisfaction. He could tell that she was proud of catching him off guard.

"You've seemed to manage it, though," Cale answered. "If you count this as *alone.*"

His eyes darted side-to-side, sizing up his opponents, trying to find the best plan of action.

"Don't bother," she said," or I'll just have Leon handle you."

She points to an older man with glasses on her left, one of the people to come out of the shadows. Cale hadn't noticed him before, because he wasn't holding a gun, but now that he was looking straight at him, he realized who it was, and just how dangerous he was, even unarmed.

The Criminal Calmer.

"What do you want? Why am I here?" Cale asked.

"You're here because you were too rude to answer our note, and because you didn't check out that tip in the slums by yourself."

"The house with the camera?"

"Yes. We planted it in hopes you would go alone, then when you showed up on screen, we would have met you there to talk. Sadly, you had your *partner* with you. We had to resort to blowing up more transformers in a 'pattern' to get you here. As if we would be so careless."

"I still don't understand. Your note made no sense. Nothing you said meant anything to me," Cale lied.

Mother Mayhem let out a harsh bark of laughter, giving him a knowing look.

"Come now, don't lie to me. You're awful at it. We know all about the Patriot Project, and its unfortunate victims."

Cale decided to drop all of the pretenses.

"Nobody was a victim. Everyone gave their informed consent."

"Oh, really?" she laughed again. "I don't doubt you all signed medical waivers, but did anyone really understand the possible effects? Did you, Cale? Did you read and understand that you were signing your life away?"

"What do you *want*?" he asked, not willing to admit she was right.

"Despite what the propaganda against us may say, we want what is best for this city, and it would be best if there weren't a mindless, rage-infused, super soldier running about, tearing citizens limb from limb."

"I haven't torn anyone limb from—"

"No, not yet. But you did react rather strongly to a child painting on an old building. Not to mention, you roughed up that petty thug, Benny to get answers. Not very heroic, I must say."

"I'm in control. There is nothing to worry about."

"Are you really in control? *My son* still has the bruises from your hand digging into his arm. His shoulder was almost dislocated. That doesn't sound like *control* to me," she growls, her eyes flashing dangerously.

Cale didn't know how to respond. He felt guilt burning through him, and averted his gaze from the angry mother.

"Look," she sighed, "I'm not here to make you feel guilty. As we mentioned in our note, we want to help you."

"*If* there were anything wrong, how could you help me?"

"We may have a cure for the serum Dr. Bellamy injected you with."

Cale's head shot up.

"A cure?"

"Yes," she nodded, "something along those lines."

"What makes you think I'd accept anything from you? You are a group of wanted criminals. You expect me to just trust you?"

"Of course not. I know you'll be stubborn. I know that right now you are claiming to yourself that everyone is overreacting, and that the boy *was* breaking the law. *But*," she continued, "I also know that you will slip up again, and you will hurt someone else a lot worse. At that point, despite your lack of trust, I expect you to come begging for the help that no one else can provide you."

"You're wrong," Cale whispered.

"And you, hero… you are a time bomb. I just hope that when your timer hits zero, you're not with someone you love."

Mother Mayhem nodded at the Criminal Calmer, who took a few steps closer to Cale.

"When you decide you want our cure, just tell your pal Benny that you're in. He'll know what to do. And before you get any ideas, he isn't one of us. He's just a kid who knows how to get the word around," she added.

"You seem sleepy," the Criminal Calmer told him, his voice sounding gentle and concerned.

That was the last thing Cale could remember before he woke up with Parker kneeling over him.

He wishes he had asked how they knew about the other project candidates. They must have a mole at PG, or someone who worked on the project had broken their confidentiality agreement. Cale knows he should tell someone about this— probably the General—but he is afraid of what will happen if he does.

The General would demand that Cale be locked up for further testing, and then demand that Parker find and take down the Slavers' organization. It's not just that Cale is afraid of being locked up again; he doesn't want Parker out there alone, with no one to cover her back.

Cale also wishes he would have asked more about this so-called "cure." What exactly is it, and what does it do? A shot, a gas, a pill? Would it completely counteract the serum, taking away all of his enhanced abilities, or would it just control his adrenaline, testosterone, and serotonin levels?

Could it really take away everything that makes me Patriot Prime?

He sighs loudly and reaches up to rub his temples, feeling a headache coming on. It's an odd sensation because it isn't a real, physical, headache; his healing capabilities prevent that. He is just mentally weary.

Thinking it over carefully, Cale decides that the best thing to do for the time being is to keep the Slavers of the People's knowledge to himself. He will bring up his worries one more time to Dr. Bellamy, but if the tests come back normal again, Cale is going to forget about it. There is no reason to live his life in fear.

NINE

When Dr. Bellamy returns to draw more blood, Cale decides to share his fears with her; he is just unsure how to begin.

"Arm please?" she asks.

He holds his arm out for her and watches as she ties a tourniquet around his bicep. She asks him to clench his fist, and then carefully inserts a needle into his arm, easily finding the vein.

He is still a bit surprised at how casually he can sit there and watch her draw his blood. Cale used to hate needles, but now, though he still doesn't like them, he is so used to them that he is barely fazed.

"Almost done," Dr. Bellamy assures him, moving to attach another empty vial to the tube coming from his arm. "Just one more."

He sighs as he watches the red liquid swirl into the clean glass, filling it up slowly.

"There," she says. "All done."

She caps the last container of blood and then eases the needle from his arm. She pushes down on the needle site gently with a cotton swab, and when she pulls away after a few seconds, the area has already healed and cannot be spotted.

"I would prefer if you stay down here tonight, Cale. The results may take a while, and we can't be sure they didn't give you anything."

"Doctor?"

"How many times have I told you to call me Maura? We are surely on first name basis by now," the woman smiles at him.

"Sorry, Maura. I was wondering if you might be able to check my levels one more time?" he asks, avoiding looking at her.

She lets out a gentle sigh, and moves to sit next to him on the hospital bed.

"Is this still about that boy? Thomas?" she asks.

Cale nods.

"You have to stop beating yourself up about this. Do you know how likely it would be for you to *just now* be having the negative effects of the serum, like the others?"

"No," he answers looking back over to her.

"Not very likely at all." Her expression is earnest, begging him to listen. "I think it is much more likely you were just reacting because of being tired and sore. Everyone has bad days, Cale, and you are bound to have more. If you worry about every little outburst you have, you are going to drive yourself mad. Do you understand?"

"Yes, but—"

"Cale, you have to stop. I will check your levels one more time when I run this next blood sample, but, after that, I am not wasting any more resources on this. I'm sorry."

"I understand. Thank you."

Cale feels a wave of relief wash over him.

"Now," Dr. Bellamy says, standing up. "Let's have a look at that shoulder."

Cale strips his shirt off, being careful with his right arm. It still hurts to lift higher than his torso.

Her fingers feel cool on his shoulder as she examines

the wound.

"Oh, dear," she whispers. "I think it may be infected."

Cale twists his head to look at the wound and is surprised to see the skin around the bullet hole looking red and swollen. The wound itself seems to be oozing and Cale feels his stomach clench at the sight.

"I'm going to go get you some antibiotics for this. Just stay still and try not to irritate the wound any more than it already is."

She circles around the lab, gathering equipment, concentration etched on her face. Once she is laden down with medical supplies, she hurries back over to him, dumping everything onto the stainless steel tray next to the bed.

Dr. Bellamy starts by cleaning the wound with alcohol, and Cale lets out a soft hiss at the sting.

"Don't be such a baby," she tells him, giving him a small smirk.

She then fills a syringe with what she says is an antibiotic, and injects it right into the wound.

"I don't know how effective that will be," she comments. "Your metabolism is so fast that you might burn through it before the antibiotic has a chance to do its job. We'll have to keep a close eye on it and see what happens."

She slathers the injury with a thick cream, which is letting off a distinctly medicinal smell, and then wraps his shoulder in gauze.

"You need to be careful; all of this running around is not letting you heal. I'm going to go get these blood tests started. You get some sleep."

She clears the table of medical supplies and signals him to lie down.

"If I come back and you're not sleeping, I *will* give you a sedative," the Doctor warns him, just before exiting the lab.

Cale leans back onto the bed, knowing he won't be able to get any sleep, and thinks about what Dr. Bellamy has told him.

Is it possible that everyone, including myself, is just reading far too much into this? She does have a point... what are the odds that the negative effects wouldn't kick in until now? Maybe the Slavers are just trying to mess with my head, he thinks, *and this whole thing is a way to put me off my game.*

This thought makes him feel slightly better, though his mind won't be totally cleared until the Doctor runs her final test.

A soft rapping draws Cale's attention to the lab's door, and he looks up just in time to see Parker duck inside, crouching.

"I take it you're not supposed to be here?" Cale asks, smiling.

"Shh! Keep your voice down," she whispers, coming closer to him. "Bellamy, is crazy protective over you. She told me to leave you alone or she'd call the General, who, by the way, pretty much banished me to my rooms. I think I might be grounded or something," she jokes.

Cale can see the hurt she is hiding behind her words.

"Are you okay? How did things go with him?" he asks, scooting over so she can climb up next to him.

Parker settles in beside him and rests her head on his shoulder.

"It was awful," she starts. "After you left, he wouldn't look at me, or even speak to me. He ordered that security guard to take me to my room."

"I can see that lasted."

"Honestly, I was contemplating going into hibernation, but then I remembered something Tesla said tonight."

"Don't you mean the Thundertaker?" Cale asks, nudging her with his elbow.

Parker laughs.

"That name really pisses him off. He called it 'vulgar'

and said I have 'appalling manners.'"

"All the more reason to use it, and, well, you *do* have appalling manners."

This time Parker elbows him.

"Better watch it," he says. "I'll stick Dr. Bellamy on you. Now, what did Tesla say that made you sneak out after curfew?"

"He mentioned something about a serial killer running loose, targeting single mothers, and said three had been killed already. He also said that the Tribunal has been keeping it out of the news," she tells him.

"You know he was just trying to get you going, right?"

"Well, the thing is, I remembered hearing about a mother of two being killed last week. So, I snuck into the PG file room, and, Cale... he wasn't lying. There *has* been someone going after single mothers, but now the body count is up to four."

"What? Why haven't we been told about this? This is usually the kind of thing the Tribunal has me doing along with regular patrols."

"I don't know. There is something going on here, and I have no idea what. What I do know is that the Tribunal is hiding things from us."

As if things aren't confusing enough.

"What else did Tesla say?" he asks. "Sounds like you had a long conversation with him."

"Well, he did ask me on a date."

"What? No he didn't."

"Yeah, he kind of did. You jealous?"

"Devastatingly so," he says, dramatically clutching his heart. "What else did he say?"

"Let's see... he said that he was a revolutionary, that they were the 'Servants,' not the 'Slavers,' and he wouldn't let Krista kill me because it wouldn't make my 'friend' happy, whatever that is supposed to mean. Also, as I stood there in a trance watching him walk away, he promised he would call me."

Cale feels his stomach lurch. He has a pretty good idea who the friend they want to keep happy is.

"What did he mean about being Servants?" he asks.

"He wasn't making a whole lot of sense, but he seemed to think that they were helping 'free the citizens from TEnergy's corrupt system.'"

"Corrupt how?"

"I don't know, and he was probably just making stuff up."

"While I *am* inclined to believe that; he wasn't lying about the serial killer," Cale offers. "I think it's worth looking into TEnergy."

"I suppose so, but after we catch this serial killer."

"Of course. You do know the Tribunal isn't going to approve of us looking into this, right? They didn't give us that case for a reason, and whatever the reason, they probably aren't going to change their minds."

"I know, and I don't care. We'll take care of this ourselves, and they'll get over it. Especially if Senator Scott can put a good spin on it for the media."

"That's true," Cale nods.

They both lay quietly, thinking about all of this new information. Before long Cale feels his eyes drifting close and he falls fast asleep, with Parker's head still resting on his shoulder.

Which is exactly how General Linwood finds them the next morning.

~

"What the hell is going on down here?" General Linwood yells, causing Parker to jerk awake.

She jumps up looking wildly around, trying to find the cause of this noisy outburst. What she finds is her father glaring daggers at her. Parker realizes that she must have fallen asleep in Cale's hospital bed the night before, and feels herself blush at what her father must think he walked in on.

Next to her, Cale stirs awake and looks around. If the situation weren't so tense, his reactions would be hilarious. He looks from the General, to Parker lying next to him, and then his eyebrows shoot up in shock as he looks back to the General, a denial on his lips.

"Sir," Cale starts, "It's not—"

"I don't want, or need, to hear anything from you. Either of you," General Linwood spits. "I have all the answers I need right here!"

The General holds up a copy the *New Edison Daily*, the local newspaper, and tosses it on the bed before them. The bold headline shouts up at them, 'CRIME RUNS RAMPANT AS HEROES SHACK UP!'

Parker scoops up the paper in shock, looking at the pictures that accompany the story. They look like they were taken the day she and Cale went out to breakfast. There is one of them holding hands while leaning across the table towards one another, one of her and Cale arm-in-arm crossing the street, and a final one of him holding the door of his apartment building open for her.

Oh, god.

She quickly scans over the article.

Our heroes were spotted up and early having a cozy breakfast together at a diner across from Patriot Prime's apartment. This raises questions as to where the heroes had been before breakfast, and why the Stolid Sentry still has bed head? After leaving the diner, Patriot Prime was overheard asking the Stolid Sentry if she would return to his apartment with him, to which she quickly agreed. They were witnessed holding each other on the way to the apartment building, where they disappeared inside for quite some time. Perhaps if the heroes weren't so busy investigating one another, there would be less crime occurring throughout the city.

"This article is a lie," Parker says, passing the paper to

Cale.

"Really?" the General asks angrily. "Those pictures don't look like a lie. What were you two thinking?"

"The pictures are misleading! We only stopped at his apartment so he could grab things to stay here at headquarters," she pleads.

"General," Cale says, "I assure you she is telling you the truth. There is nothing going on between us."

General Linwood sneers at Cale.

"Yes, I'm sure that's why I walked in on you two in bed together."

Before Parker can offer any more protests, the General advances on her. He grabs her upper arm and drags her off the bed, and across the room.

"Hey! Be careful!" Cale shouts, getting up to follow them.

"Cale, I'll be fine. You just stay here and rest," Parker instructs him.

The General's fingers are biting into her arm roughly, and she knows she could twist free; she is, after all, stronger than he is, but she doesn't resist and allows him to pull her from the room. He leads her to the nearest secluded area, the stairwell.

The door latches shut behind them, the metal click seeming ten times louder than it should be. For a moment, neither of them speaks, but instead size each other up. He looks Parker up and down, anger clearly boiling in his dark eyes.

"What were you thinking, Parker? I thought you were going to take this seriously?" he asks, his voice low and hard.

"I do take this seriously, and I didn't do anything! Cale and I are just friends, I promise you. Is that not allowed?"

"What isn't allowed is you making the Patriot Guard look like a bunch of randy, incompetent fools! You and Prime need some space," he tells her.

"What does that mean?"

"It means you'll be running patrols alone. You two shouldn't be seen in public together for a while. I want you to take the rest of the day off, let most of the media fire burn out, and tomorrow night you'll start patrolling an area the Tribunal designates for you."

Parker stares at him, mouth hanging open, not sure what to respond to first. How could they give in to the media like that? They should be dispelling the rumors, and not hiding. Separating the two will only make it seem like the paper was right and that they are ashamed of themselves.

I don't have anything to be ashamed of.

"This is ridiculous! We did nothing wrong! If anything, this is Senator Scott's fault for leading all those reporters on yesterday about a big story!" Parker insists.

"Do not try to push your mistakes off on someone else. I raised you better than that."

"You stopped raising me when my mother died. Don't play parent of the year with me. I happen to remember the truth and won't be fooled like the idiots you surround yourself with."

Shock, followed quickly by anger and… *Was that sadness?* flash across the General's face.

"This conversation is over. You may not obey me as a father, but you will obey me as your commanding officer. You are just lucky I don't have you replaced, Miss Linwood."

"What does that mean?" she asks. "Who would you get to replace me?"

He lets out a harsh laugh.

"What? Do you think we sent the other twenty-four contestants of the PG Second Generation on their merry way with their enhanced capabilities?" he asks. "We've continued training them, as an elite military force. Watch yourself, or you could find yourself swapping places with one of them."

Before Parker can respond, the General climbs to the main floor and leaves her alone in the stairwell. Parker blinks back the tears threatening to spill and hurries back towards the lab, wanting to speak with Cale. When she gets to the door, she notices two armed guards standing outside of it. They block her from entering.

"I'm sorry, Sentry," one of them tells her. "We are not allowed to let you through."

"What?" she asks in disbelief.

"At the moment, by order of the Tribunal, you are not allowed to see Patriot Prime."

Parker glares back and forth between the men, but neither budges beneath her gaze.

"This is ridiculous," she spits, turning away from the lab.

Parker storms (there is really no other word for it) up a flight of stairs and into the training arena. She quickly launches herself into a ferocious workout session. Every target she shoots and every dummy she punches is wearing her father's face in her mind's eye.

When her knuckles are red and swollen from boxing, she switches to running laps, urging herself faster and faster around the track until she is almost certain she has beat her personal best.

"You look like you could use a break," someone calls, from the side of the track.

Parker turns to see Dr. Bellamy standing there holding a bottle of water and a plate of food. She almost ignores the woman and keeps running, but her stomach gurgles loudly at the sight of the plate.

She sighs and follows Dr. Bellamy to a wrestling mat in the corner of the arena, knowing that the meal won't be free. She is positive the Doctor will want to talk.

"Thanks," Parker says as she sits down, taking the water from the Doctor.

"You're welcome. The guards said you came up here a couple hours ago, and I know you haven't eaten yet," Dr.

Bellamy says, pushing a plate of food across the mat towards Parker.

Have I really been in here for hours?

Parker takes the offered plate and grabs the turkey sandwich on it, taking care not to shove the whole thing immediately into her mouth.

"I know you probably aren't looking too kindly on the Tribunal right now," the Doctor says, causing Parker to snort on her mouthful of sandwich.

Dr. Bellamy gives her a wry smile, but continues.

"I just want you to know, that I had nothing to do with keeping you and Cale apart. I know that nothing is going on between you."

"You do?" Parker asks after swallowing. "How?"

"Cale and I are quite close, and no, not like that," she adds, seeing Parker's questioning look. "I think he views me more as a maternal figure. As I was saying, we are close, and I know he would have told me if there was something going on between you."

"I'm glad someone believes us."

I know you came to say more than this.

"Now, that being said, I think it would be best if you and Cale *remained* just friends."

Parker hates being told what to do, but she agrees with the doctor.

"Of course," she says. "A relationship could interfere with our abilities to perform our job."

"Yes, but that's not my reasoning," the Doctor continues. "Cale is having a rather difficult time with some personal issues at the moment, and the last thing he needs is an unstable, new, relationship.

"Are you saying that I'm unstable?"

"No! Of course not! I meant that *all* new relationships are unstable."

"What did you mean when you said Cale is having a difficult time?" Parker asks, concern outweighing her annoyance.

"That is not my place to share, though, I do beg you do not approach him about it. If he wishes to share, he will come to you."

Dr. Bellamy stands up and brushes the wrinkles from her dress pants.

"I'm glad we had this talk, Parker. I just hope you'll heed my advice."

The Doctor exits the arena, leaving Parker alone with her thoughts, which are growing more and more confusing by the minute. She finishes her meal, and decides to head upstairs for a nap.

Her legs are rubbery from her work out, so she decides to take the elevator, not even wanting to think about stairs. She's so exhausted she doesn't even waste the effort to roll her eyes over the fact that the Star Spangled Banner is playing in the elevator. Once in her room, Parker climbs into bed and quickly falls asleep.

Her father's angry face swims before her.

"You may not obey me as a father, but you will obey me as your commanding officer. You are just lucky I don't have you replaced, Miss Linwood," he spits at her.

"You would replace me?" she asks, her voice quiet and weak.

"I would have replaced you years ago if I could have, you incompetent fool. You knew better than to let her get behind that wheel, didn't you?"

"I'm sorry, daddy. I knew better, I should have stopped her." semi yourself."

Parker feels tears pouring down her face.

"Please, I'm sorry. Forgive me," she begs.

"How could I ever forgive you? I thought you were going to take this seriously, Parker?"

Parker sucks in a loud gasp of air and her eyes bolt open.

It was a dream, she tells herself, panting.

Her father has never said those things to her about her mother's accident; they are a creation of her own mind, and she knows this, but she suspects that they are his true feelings.

A sudden burst of anger hits her as she thinks about everything that had happened today. The paper, her father's accusations, not being allowed to see Cale, and Dr. Bellamy telling her that a relationship with Cale would be bad for him.

She has no intention of a relationship with Cale, but, for some reason, the Doctor telling her not to have one makes her blood boil.

Needing to let off steam, Parker decides to go out. Maybe she can put some of this angry energy to use and find out information on the serial killer.

She decides not to wear her hero costume and dons a simple pair of jeans, boots, t-shirt, and a red leather jacket to conceal her holster and pistols.

I'm coming for you, you son of a bitch.

TEN

Parker receives a lot of questioning glances on her way out of the building, but nobody approaches or stops her. The staff members who don't know Cale and Parker very well (along with some of those who do) openly study her with distaste, obviously believing the lies of the newspaper.

The sun has just set, and there is a chill in the air as Parker makes her way to her Camero. She is a bit surprised that the General didn't confiscate her car keys, but attributes it to him assuming she would actually listen to his orders.

As if.

Once in the car, she takes the folder containing all of the info on the serial killer and opens it, spreading its contents on the passenger seat. After rifling through a few papers, she finds what she is looking for and starts the car.

The killer tends to stay in the same area with each attack, and Parker decides to head to the scene of the last crime.

Maybe I can find some people in the area who witnessed something and didn't come forward.

She soon finds herself, once again, in the slums. She

parks her car near the latest crime scene, a dank back alley.

Parker gets out and walks around, examining the scene. All of the real evidence has probably been bagged by the police, but she feels the need to look around and get a feel for the place. She is overwhelmed by sadness and disgust when she sees that the chalk outline is still clearly sketched on the pavement.

"I'm sorry I couldn't help you," she whispers, staring at it.

Parker lets out a miserable sigh, and starts towards one of the main streets. Despite it still being fairly early in the evening, there are not a lot of people out. After darkness falls, citizens tend to avoid the streets in this part of town.

The first stop she makes is at a nearby gas station, to question the clerk. He has himself locked behind a barred counter and insists that he has no knowledge of any murder, and would she please just leave him alone. She questions a few patrons in the store as well, but no one knows anything.

Parker hits the street again, feeling a little frustrated at the lack of information she is getting. She almost wishes she had worn her costume; people may have taken her a bit more seriously.

She continues a few more blocks until she comes across a poorly cared for basketball court. There is a group of about eight guys standing around, talking and joking loudly. They seem to be in their late teens or early twenties, and immediately zone in on Parker as she approaches.

"I was wondering if I could ask you a few questions?" she calls, as she gets closer.

"You can do whatever you like," one of the guys says, stepping forward and winking at her.

She has a hard time making out his features in the darkness, only clearly able to see that he has cropped dark hair. All of the others stand in angles directed at him, and

Parker has a feeling he is the leader of the group.

"Two nights ago a woman was murdered about six blocks from here. Do you know anything about it?" she asks, cutting to the chase.

"You just assume we would know something about a murder?" he asks, crossing his arms and glaring at her.

"No, don't think that I'm singling you out. I'm asking everyone I see out on the street tonight."

"How many others have you seen?" he asks.

"Well, none so far."

"You know why that is?"

"I suppose because this isn't the safest neighborhood in the city," she offers.

"There isn't anyone on the streets because, when night falls, these are our streets."

Parker studies the man carefully, wondering if she might have found her guy already. He seems more like a street thug though—someone who would act in the heat of the moment, not someone who'd stalk and plan an attack. All of the murdered women had been followed, their lives and movements tracked.

How else would the killer have known they were all single mothers?

"These streets belong to everyone," she tells him.

"Who the hell are you to say what anything belongs to?" he asks angrily, advancing towards her a few more steps.

"You don't recognize me? I'm the Stolid Sentry, and, if anything, this city is much more mine than yours."

Murmurs break out among the group, and Parker senses that she may have made a mistake in revealing her identity.

"*You* are the Stolid Sentry?" the leader asks, pacing a circle around her. "I guess I didn't recognize you without your murdering partner by your side."

The other men let out a cry of agreement.

"Your pal, Patriot Prime, killed one of our friends last

year during a drug bust. Maybe we should show him how it feels when someone he works with gets hurt."

Parker begins to back away from the man and bumps into someone behind her. Turning around, she notices that, while she had been focused on the leader, the other members of the group had surrounded her.

Parker quickly flips back to look at the leader and notices that he has drawn a switchblade.

"You really don't want to start with me," she tells him levelly.

"Oh, I think I do."

He lunges at Parker, trying to slash at her with his blade, but she dodges him by feinting right and going left. She ends up in the line of another attacker who attempts to strike out and punch her. Parker catches his fist in her hand, twists his arm, and when he cries out in pain, she punches him in the nose and pushes him away.

Another attacker attempts to grab her from behind, but she uses his weight against him and flips him over and onto his back. She can hear his head make a sickening crack against the pavement.

Too easy…

After flashing a triumphant smile, Parker turns around to find two more assailants rushing at her. Too late, she realizes it is a diversion as she feels the cold metal of a blade against her throat.

"Far too cocky," the leader whispers, pushing the blade harder against her neck and wrapping his other arm around her waist. "Just like your partner."

Parker feels panic set in as the remaining five members of the group move in closer. Her mind is running through so many different escape options that she can't seem to settle on one.

"I *really* wouldn't do that if I were you," she hears someone call out from behind her attackers.

At first, she is so relieved because she thinks it *must* be Cale, somehow come to rescue her, but as her ears catch up with her, Parker realizes that it isn't his voice.

The group parts before her, allowing the leader, and thereby Parker, to see the newcomer. She is shocked, and a little less relieved than she had been a moment before, as she realizes that the voice belongs to Konstantine Tesla.

The leader starts laughing loudly.

"What? This so-called hero couldn't beat us. What makes you think that some ordinary man can do it?" he asks.

"Ah, but you see, I am *far* from ordinary," Tesla smiles.

Before anyone has time to respond, Tesla raises his clenched fists and opens them, revealing two glowing orbs of power.

"Dude's a Variant!" one of the group members yells, turning to make a break for it.

Tesla launches the first orb at him, and quickly follows up with a second at another group member, leaving both men unconscious on the ground, twitching as if they'd just been tasered.

Parker feels the blade loosen on her throat as her captor looks on in horror at his men being taken down one by one. She uses his distraction to her advantage, and stomps down hard on his foot. He cries out in pain and Parker leans away from him, into the blade, and then slams her head into his face. She hears his nose give a satisfying crunch. He releases her and falls to the ground, cupping his broken nose.

Being pretty pissed off, Parker hits him on the head for good measure, knocking him out. She jumps around wildly, positioned in her fighting stance, just to find the only person left standing, aside from herself, is Tesla.

She eyes him suspiciously, but when he holds his hands up in mock surrender, she relaxes her stance.

"Thank you," she says, and then begrudgingly adds, "I guess I owe you one."

"Well, I would appreciate it if you didn't try to arrest

me tonight," he tells her, smirking.

She momentarily debates tricking him into letting her close enough to knock him unconscious. Things would be so much easier if she showed up at headquarters with him in custody. Her father would be so happy.

That's all she needs to think about to make her change her mind.

Screw him and his happiness.

"Arresting you *would* make a lot of my problems disappear, but I guess I can pretend you are not a wanted criminal for one hour."

Parker looks around at the group of unconscious men and lets out a groan, then pulls out her phone to dial the police.

"This is the Stolid Sentry," she says, "I have a ten-fifteen on the basketball court of South Christopher. Eight suspects tried to attack me, all are now unconscious. You may need a bus. Thank you."

"That's my cue to leave," Tesla tells her.

"Mine too. I don't feel like dealing with them today."

"Well, in that case, let me walk you back to your car. I still have fifty-five minutes until you remember I'm a wanted criminal."

Parker gets ready to protest, but decides she doesn't have the energy for it, so instead just signals him to follow her.

Maybe I can get some info out of him about where the Slavers are based. He may have my word not to arrest him right now, but I will have to go back to hunting him tomorrow.

They walk the first block and a half in silence, and she is surprised that it isn't as uncomfortable as she'd imagined. Parker studies Tesla out of her peripheral vision, trying to size him up. His dark hair is hanging loose, he has a definite five o'clock shadow going on, and his clothes look a little worse for wear. If she had to take a guess, Parker would say that the criminal life isn't treating him that well.

"I saw you made the front page today," Tesla says, a bit too casually.

She shoots him a sideways glare, and he starts chuckling.

"Don't start. I'm not going to defend myself to *you*."

"Manners, manners," he says. "Do you really want to offend one of the few people in the city who knows that story was a complete lie?"

"You know it was a lie?" she asks.

"Obviously," he snorts. "Prime couldn't handle you."

Parker doesn't know how to answer this, so instead says nothing.

"I also know," Tesla continues, "that you are currently being slammed by the media because of me. They were promised a big story... If you had caught me last night, this wouldn't be happening. I want to apologize, but I'm not entirely sorry that I'm not behind bars."

She feels herself smile a bit.

"Yeah, I wouldn't expect you to be. I guess I accept your half-assed apology. I should have been better prepared last night. Just understand that next time I'll be ready, and won't hold back."

"I wouldn't expect anything less," he assures her. "Now, what were you doing out here tonight? I would guess business, but you're not in uniform."

"Well I received a tip from someone about a string of murders, and thought somebody should look into it, and I am...uh, off duty today."

They round the corner to the alley that Parker left the car in, both walking a bit more slowly as they approach it.

"Does this informant happen to be tall, dark, and extremely handsome?" he asks, waggling his eyebrows at her.

Parker snorts.

"I believe *he* thinks so."

"Tut, tut. So rude."

Parker leans back against the driver's door when they

reach the car, looking around the alley.

"Did you find anything?" Tesla asks, becoming serious.

"No, unfortunately. Apparently nobody saw anything, or so they say."

"Naturally."

Parker groans and leans her head back, feeling overwhelmingly frustrated. When she looks back up, she sees Tesla staring at her, eyes squinted. He suddenly reaches his hand out to touch her neck.

"You're bleeding," he tells her.

"It must have been from the knife."

His fingers graze her skin and she feels a slight shock.

"Sorry," he murmurs pulling his hand back, and clearing his throat

"It's, uh, all right," she whispers.

They stand there in silence another moment, giving each other an appraising look. Tesla glances down at his watch and lets out a sigh.

"I should probably be on my way; my hour is almost up."

"Yeah, I guess you should."

"Tell you what," he says, giving her a wide smile. "Next date, we'll actually go for something to eat."

"This wasn't a—"

He waves off her words before she can finish and turns away, towards the entrance of the alley.

Before he rounds the corner, he pauses, turns back towards her, and sees that she is still watching him.

"Parker? Another thing about those murders…" he starts.

"Yes?"

"The only reason the killer hasn't been named a priority by now is either to protect someone, or to expose someone, but at the *opportune* moment. Be careful."

Before she can think of a reply, Konstantine Tesla disappears around the corner, leaving her feeling extremely confused.

~

Cale marches down the sidewalk, away from the house that his latest tip has led him to. It is, of course, another false trail. He seriously believes he is on the verge of losing his mind.

I'm a soldier for goodness sake, not a freaking census employee.

In the week he and Parker have been split up, Cale has chased down over two-dozen dead-end tips on the Slavers of the People. If he weren't so desperate to get his partner back, he would raise hell over the worthless jobs the Tribunal has him doing, but, as things are, he knows he must listen obediently or he'll never get to work with Parker again.

They may not have been partners for long, but Cale feels like they work really well together, aside from him getting shot, that is. He also just misses the companionship of someone who understands him and the life he must live. Someone who knows how difficult it is to balance two identities; the one you display for the public, and the one that is really you.

Things wouldn't be so bad if he could at least *see* Parker, but the Tribunal is doing a pretty good job at keeping them separate, especially since Parker decided to go all commando and take out eight gang members last week.

She said she didn't know that the group was wanted when she confronted them, but the Tribunal ignored this and sold the story to the papers as a daring bust by the young hero. Cale is proud of her, but worried.

What if she would have gotten into trouble and no one was there to help her?

With the local news now singing nothing but praise for the Patriot Guard, Cale hopes he and Parker will be reunited soon. He has only talked to her once in the last week, and it was just in passing.

Cale grunts as he climbs into the car, having accidentally bumped his shoulder.

The infection hasn't gotten any worse, but it doesn't seem to be going away either. Dr. Bellamy has been pumping him full of antibiotics at every opportunity, but his metabolism burns away the dose before the medicine can do its job. The main issue is that his shoulder seems to have stopped healing, and is causing him more pain as every day passes. The only good news is that the infection doesn't seem to be spreading.

Cale looks over the list of tips he is supposed to check into, and after making sure he is done for the day, he decides to take a short cruise around town to check on things.

Maybe I can do something useful today, like prevent a mugging.

It is late afternoon, and still pretty light out, so Cale doesn't expect to see much crime. He rolls his window down and enjoys the fresh, cool breeze that comes rushing in.

He drives around for ten…twenty…thirty minutes and doesn't see anything. He has just given up when he rounds a corner and notices a suspicious-looking guy on the sidewalk near a school.

The man has dirty, unkempt hair, overlarge clothing, and keeps darting his head around, surveying the area. Cale watches as he approaches a group of young kids, and immediately steps into action.

He quickly parks in the school lot and heads towards the group. The man is so caught up talking that he doesn't hear Cale approaching.

"I'm telling you," the man says, "this stuff will blow your mind! Take two drops of this before class and you won't ever be bored through another lesson."

He holds out a bottle of clear liquid with a shaking hand.

"It's usually one-twenty for a bottle, but I'll throw

you guys a sample for ten each, since you're first-timers."

"Selling drugs is bad enough, but peddling to children? You make me sick," Cale says loudly.

The man goes rigid and the kids look at him with large, round eyes.

"We weren't gonna buy any, Prime. Promise!" one kid exclaims.

The drug dealer turns around slowly. When he sees that it is, indeed, Patriot Prime, he throws the jar of drugs at Cale's head and starts running.

Cale easily dodges the container and takes off after the man, chasing him around the back of the school, onto the playground. The drug dealer tries to cut through the recess equipment, but Cale catches him by the swings.

Somewhere between the front of the school and the swing set, the man had picked up a medium rock; it looks like he's hoping to use it as a weapon. It is easy to see the dealer is high on whatever product he was trying to sell the kids.

He positions himself so a swing is between him and Cale.

"Look, put your rock down," Cale tells him, distaste emanating from his voice. "This will be a lot easier on you if you just come with me calmly."

Completely disregarding Cale's words, the man lets out a high-pitched war cry and throws the rock at Cale, striking him in his injured shoulder. He then tries to push the swing at Cale, as if the chains would unbalance him while he is clutching his aching shoulder.

Cale growls and grabs the chains faster than the drug dealer can process. He then twirls the swing, twisting it around the man's still extended arm and puts all his effort in pulling the dealer closer to him.

There is sickening crunch, and when the lowlife cries out, Cale realizes the chain must have snapped his wrist. He doesn't let this faze him as he unwraps the man's arm and drags him by his shoulder to one of the swing posts.

136

Cale then takes out a pair of handcuffs, and fastens the man's uninjured arm to the frame of the swing set.

"You won't be sullying any more lives," Cale snarls.

The man huddles up and whimpers in pain, cradling his broken wrist to his chest as Cale phones the police for a pick-up.

As Cale heads back to his car, he notices that a couple of the kids stuck around to see what happened. They are all looking at him with what he could swear is fear.

"Drugs are bad," he says before walking past them. "They ruin lives."

The kids just stare at him and nod in agreement, no one saying anything.

It isn't until he is back at PG headquarters in his private room that he starts questioning whether he could have handled the situation better.

Did you have to break his wrist? he asks himself.

I gave him the option to surrender peacefully, he counters.

His levels had come back as normal on the final test Dr. Bellamy ran, and he had promised himself not to overthink things like this. Even if there were at least four different ways for Cale to apprehend the subject, the guy deserved what he got.

Right?

Cale urges himself to just move past it, and not to dwell. Dr. Bellamy is right—everyone has bad days—and he'll drive himself mad for sure if he sits around waiting for his control to waiver.

Someone knocks lightly outside his room, and Cale shoots a suspicious glare at the door.

Probably more crap work from the Tribunal...

He crosses the room, opens the door, and is immediately thrown back by a blur of color launching at him.

"Whoa," he says.

He looks down and sees that Parker has him wrapped in a tight hug.

"What are you doing here?" he asks.

"Well that's a fine hello," she huffs, pulling away from him and crossing her arms.

"No! I'm very glad to see you, but I don't want to get in trouble and risk not getting to work together for even longer."

"Worry not, my dear Patriot Prime. I come with good news," she beams. "Thanks to my 'outstanding' take down of that gang, PG has been scandal-free for a week. So... the Tribunal says we can be partners again!"

"Really? That *is* great news!" Cale smiles.

"The only condition being, in the General's words, that we 'do not disgrace our city, or our country, by publically displaying any more sexual misconduct.'"

Parker moves to sit on the couch in his room, lounging back comfortably.

"So," she asks, "What do you want to do to celebrate?"

"I feel the *obvious* choice is going to a *severely* public place and making out," he says with a sigh, moving to sit in a chair near the couch.

"Of course, but after that?"

"Solve some crime, I guess," he shrugs.

"Sounds like a plan. Hopefully, we'll be able to do that... eventually. The Tribunal already assigned us a bunch of tips to follow up on tomorrow."

Cale huffs loudly, unable to control being pouty.

"I'm *so* sick of trying to find the Slavers of the People. They haven't acted at all this week; seems like we could cool it a little."

"I know," Parker sighs, "I still feel like we're missing something, but my mind is so dull from the tedious assignments we've been on that I can't seem to muster any real concern anymore."

"Maybe this whole thing is a medical experiment," Cale offers. "A surgery-free lobotomy."

She starts laughing loudly and smiles at him.

"I missed you."

"I missed you, too."

"It's been a boring week," she confides.

"Busting up a wanted gang is boring? I'm just glad you are okay. When I heard about that, I was so mad I wasn't there with you."

"Trying to steal my glory?"

"No," he says seriously. "What if you had needed back up? I don't like thinking about what could have happened."

Parker swallows loudly and whispers,

"Neither do I."

ELEVEN

"Is there something you want to say?" Cale asks Parker, glancing over at her in the passenger seat.

She has been practically bouncing with nervous energy ever since they got in the car and started chasing tips.

"What do you mean?" she asks.

"What do I mean? You are about to spontaneously combust over there. You can't sit still. I think that, by now, I can tell if you have something on your mind."

He watches as she starts chewing her lip nervously.

"Parker, what is going on?" he asks, practically begging her to tell him.

"I lied!" she exclaims. "Well…not entirely, but I didn't tell you the whole truth, and I feel really, really bad about it."

Her words come tumbling out so quickly that it takes him a moment to catch up with her.

"What are you talking about? What did you not tell the 'whole truth' about?"

Parker takes a deep breath and looks over at him nervously.

"You know the night I took down the gang?"

"Yeah?"

"I *didn't* do it alone. I had help."

"What?" he asks, more curious than anything. "From who? What happened?"

"I got cocky," she starts. "I let myself become overconfident and ended up pinned from behind with a knife to my throat. I'm not entirely sure what they would have done, but…Konstantine Tesla showed up and took out five of them using his Variation. That caused enough of a distraction that I was able to free myself from the one with the knife. I think that Tesla may have saved my life."

Cale has a difficult time thinking of what to say.

"Then I am very grateful to him for being there to help when I couldn't be," he finally tells her.

"You're not mad that I didn't arrest him?"

"Did you have the opportunity?"

"Well…kind of. I guess. He walked me to my car."

Cale gives her a questioning look, but chooses not to push.

"He just saved your life, as you said, so I think you not arresting him is justified. Just don't mention this to the Tribunal."

"No, of course not," she agrees.

"Is there anything else you would like to share, or talk about?" he asks.

She pauses so long he doesn't think she'll say any more.

"Why do you think he saved my life? I've been wondering…his life and plans would be a lot easier with one less person chasing him."

"That is a good question, Parker. I wish I had an answer for you."

"I feel so much better," she confides. "I hate keeping secrets from you."

Cale tries his best not to look as completely guilty as he feels, hoping Parker doesn't see through his guise.

"Anything else exciting happen this week?" he asks.

"Hmmm," she thinks. "Oh! Dr. Bellamy basically called me unstable and told me to stay away from you."

He practically gives himself whiplash cranking his neck to look at her.

"What?"

"Well, she didn't say to stay entirely away from you, just that we shouldn't pursue a relationship. So, basically, she warned me not to put any moves on you. Sorry. Guess you're out of luck."

Cale snorts.

"First, that is really strange, and second, I'm never out of luck. No one can resist Patriot Prime."

"Tesla says you can't handle me," she laughs.

"When you said he walked you to your car, I didn't realize you two became best friends forever."

"Now, now. Don't get jealous. Green isn't your color," she chastises playfully.

"Is he better than me? At fighting, that is."

Despite his effort, Cale is unable to keep a straight face. Parker leans over to punch him, but stops just short of hitting his shoulder.

"Grr... you're lucky you are still broken."

"Hey, where are we headed again?" Cale asks.

He knows the general direction, but doesn't recall the street or house number.

Parker grabs the tip list from the glove compartment and quickly scans it.

"Um, 394 Borage Avenue. Sweet! A tip not in the slums! I know the people there can't help it, but, jeez, is that place dreary and depressing."

Cale finds himself in complete agreement. All of the "leads" they've been following have been nothing more than chasing shadows, most of the time in the slums.

Spending so much time in such a desperate area of town can really wear you down, Cale thinks. *Especially when you aren't doing anything to help matters.*

"It hasn't been *as* bad since those gang members were arrested. We've seen a lot more people out and about, and children outside playing instead of inside cowering," Cale says.

"Yeah, that's true."

"You really served the community with that bust."

"All with the help of a fellow *servant*," she mutters.

"What?"

"Just something Tesla said when we first encountered him and Mayhem, about how they were Servants not Slavers."

Parker seems to be stuck halfway between their conversation and some deep nagging thought.

"It is really bugging the hell out of you that you can't figure him out, isn't it?"

She draws her lips into a tight line and gives a small nod.

"Well," Cale sighs, "let's just arrest his ass, and then you can ask him all you want."

"Good idea, let's follow this tip," she says, holding up the tip list and tapping it. "The resident is supposedly a Variant."

It doesn't take Cale long to find the address they are looking for. The house is in a very nice neighborhood; the surroundings couldn't be more different from the slums. Instead of litter and weeds, yards are perfectly mown and surrounded in ideal white picket fences, children play out in front of houses, laughing loudly instead of cautiously looking over their shoulders, and the houses themselves look like model homes from a magazine.

Cale pulls into the empty driveway of a powder blue, two-story house. The walkway to the front door is lined with rose bushes in full bloom, and the yard is perfectly manicured.

"I can't help but imagine a little old lady living here," Parker says as she gets out of the car.

"I guess we'll see."

They walk to the door together, and Cale presses the doorbell. They both wait patiently, hearing someone shuffling around inside. When the door creaks open, they *are* actually faced with a tiny, older woman.

The woman is only just over five feet tall, and wears

her silver hair in a short bob cut. She peers out at them, surveying first Cale, and then Parker. When her pale green eyes fall on his partner, Cale sees them widen in surprise.

"Parker," the older woman says, voice thick with shock. "What a wonderful surprise!"

"You two know each other?" Cale asks, looking to Parker.

After the smallest of pauses, she answers.

"Not really, but I recognize her. This is my grandmother."

~

"Come in, come in!" the old woman urges.

Parker can tell Cale is still looking back and forth between her and the elderly lady, attempting to process that she is indeed Parker's grandmother.

"Thank you," Parker answers stiffly, following her inside.

Close behind, Cale closes the front door silently, and then follows her into a cozy sitting room.

"Please, have a seat," the woman instructs, gesturing to a floral patterned loveseat.

"Thank you, Mrs.—?" Cale starts.

"Mayes, but you can call me Aida."

"Thank you, Aida."

"Please, make yourselves at home, and I'll just go fetch some tea!" Aida tells them.

Before either Parker or Cale can object, Aida bustles from the room.

"Is that really your grandmother?" Cale asks.

"Yes. I recognize her from my mother's funeral."

"Are you okay?"

"I guess. I am a little surprised, though. I'm not sure how to feel about this… I always wanted to meet her, but my father forbade it."

"If you want to go, I can handle this," Cale offers,

placing a reassuring hand on her knee.

"No, no. I'm fine for now. I'm pretty curious about why she is on the tip list. I wonder if she has any real information."

Cale nods in understanding and turns his attention from her, choosing to survey the room.

Parker can't believe how stereotypically *grandmotherly* the place is. It smells like fresh baked goods, little knick-knacks line the walls, and there is even a crystal dish filled with questionable candy on an end table.

After a few minutes, Aida returns with a tray, laden down with tea and a plate of what looks like homemade chocolate chip cookies.

"Please, help yourself," she tells them, sitting in a chair across from the loveseat.

"Well," Parker starts, clearing her throat, "let's cut to the chase, shall we?"

Despite being immensely curious about her grandmother, Parker tries to keep herself on task.

Hopefully there will be time for questions later, she thinks. *For now, though, I must stay professional.*

"I've been expecting you," Aida smiles. "I suppose you have some questions for me?"

Parker and Cale exchange a surprised look.

"Um, yes we do," Parker says. "Do you know anything about the Variant, Konstantine Tesla, leader of the group called Slavers of the People?"

Confusion clouds the older woman's face.

"You are here about Konstantine?"

"Yes. You know him?" Cale asks.

Aida nods.

"He is a very nice young man."

"Do you know where he is?" Parker asks quickly.

"I'm not sure, no."

"How do you know him? Are you a…member of his group?"

"I was a friend of his mother, Clara. She was a good

woman," Aida tells them. "She really raised that boy right."

Parker resists the urge to roll her eyes.

"That *boy* is a wanted criminal. It's been all over the news."

"I'm not sure I believe the news. They don't always tell the truth. Or was that bit about you two true?" Aida asks, looking back and forth between Parker and Cale.

"No," Parker answers, "*that* wasn't true. The photos were taken out of context. But there is evidence of Tesla's crime."

"Perhaps that, too, was taken out of context."

Parker looks to Cale to see if he will intervene with this infuriating old woman, but he just looks away and reaches out for a cookie.

"These are delicious!" he tells Aida, after taking a large bite.

"Thank you, dear," the woman smiles.

"Earlier, I asked if you were a member of Tesla's group, and you didn't answer."

Aida shrugs.

"I am not a member, but a sympathizer. I wouldn't be much use at my age, although I do feel TEnergy needs to be put into their place. They are ripping their customers off and getting away with it because they have a monopoly on energy around here."

This time, Parker does roll her eyes.

"Why would blowing up equipment help matters?" she asks, her voice rising in frustration. "It is only going to end up cost—"

Cale cuts her off, holding up a hand to stop her.

"You said you weren't sure where he is…do you have any idea at all?" Cale asks.

Aida looks unsure if she should answer.

"Please, ma'am. This is important. We don't want any harm to come to Mr. Tesla, but the longer this goes on, the more danger he is in. The police are becoming desperate, and who knows how they will react, or what they will do if they find him in action."

Cale gives her an imploring look, his clear blue eyes begging her to help. Aida lets out a low sigh and nods.

"He is a good boy," she says. "I honestly don't know where he is staying, *but* I know his mother is buried in a local cemetery, and he pays his respect quite often."

"What cemetery?" Parker asks.

"The one on Marvin."

We could place surveillance on the cemetery.

Sounds a little harsh, though…jumping a guy at his mother's gravesite.

"Thank you, Aida," Cale tells the woman. "Do you have anything else you think might help us?"

"I'm sorry, no."

"In that case," Cale starts to rise. "I think we should—"

"Wait," Parker tells him, and she turns back to her grandmother. "You said you have been expecting me, but when I asked about Tesla you seemed surprised. Why have you been expecting me?"

"I assumed you would be experiencing signs and would want to know more," Aida says simply.

"Signs of what?"

"Your Variation, of course. You should be developing it any time now. Your mother was a bit of a late bloomer, but I have a feeling you'll be right on track."

Parker's mouth falls open and she stares at Aida in shock. It takes her a moment to form a reply.

"What? I'm not a—a Variant. I'm a hero."

"Can't you be both?"

"That's not the point! I can't be—" Parker tries, but is interrupted.

"Dear, there is no use protesting. The women in our family are all Variants. *That* is why your grandfather and I objected to your parent's marriage. It wasn't because of your father, although now I feel he is *quite* the jackass, keeping our only grandchild away from us," Aida mutters angrily. "We just wanted your mother home until her Variation developed so I could help teach her to control it."

Parker has no idea what to say; she feels blindsided by this whole conversation. She turns to look at Cale, but he seems to be in as much of a shock as she is.

"Have you started displaying any signs?" Aida asks her. "Perhaps hearing things without people saying them, having a strong feeling someone is lying, advanced reflexes, or maybe seeing things that aren't really happening?"

"I—no. No, I haven't. You must be wrong about this."

"My poor Annie was the same way," Aida smiles sadly. "You look just like her, you know? She was such a beautiful young woman."

Parker tenses upon hearing her mother's name.

"You are wrong," Parker finally says. "You were wrong to try to control my mother's life, and you are wrong about me. I am *not* a Variant. Cale, let's go."

Parker stands up briskly, ready to bolt from the house and the unnerving accusations. She signals Cale to move along, and begins to follow him from the house.

"Parker, please wait," Aida calls after her.

Parker pauses briefly, turning to see what the woman wants. She is holding out a small card.

"Take this. My number is on the back. If you ever need anything, do not hesitate to call me. When you do start experiencing signs, I can help you. That's how I met Clara, Konstantine's mother; I am a counselor for young Variants."

Parker clenches her jaw tightly, but takes the card and nods, before hastily leaving the house and bolting for the car.

TWELVE

I am not a Variant. There is no way that I can be. I mean, I would know, right? I would feel it, and know that I'm different. Aida is wrong. It must not be every generation of women in our family. Maybe my father's DNA was so anti-Variant that it overpowered the gene.

Parker has been trying to convince herself of this since they got back to headquarters. First, she made Cale promise not to say anything about the tip leading to her grandmother's, and then Parker disappeared into her room.

I haven't had any signs at all! She asked if I have been experiencing advanced reflexes, but I only have that because of the serum. Right?

You are a lot faster than anyone else who received the serum, even Cale, who received the stronger, first generation, serum.

She shakes her head.

No. I can't be. The General hates me enough as it is, I can't be a Variant!

Parker stomps back and forth across her room, her nerves making her unable to quit. She wonders what would happen if it were true.

Would the Tribunal kick me off the Patriot Guard? Would they lock me up and study me to see how the serum interacts with a gene mutation?

No. I don't think Father would go so far as locking me up, and Dr. Bellamy isn't that cruel.

Parker stops pacing.

That's it! I should go to Dr. Bellamy. I bet there is some sort of test she can do to find out if I am a…Variant.

But should I trust her?

Parker shrugs the last thought away. Cale trusts Dr. Bellamy; surely she can trust the woman too.

Maybe I should double check with Cale first.

Parker is certain that, conveniently enough, Cale is in the lab, having his shoulder examined. She decides to head down there straight away.

She doesn't pass anyone on her way downstairs, and she wonders what everyone has been up to. The Patriot Guard staff, when they are around, have all been frazzled and rushed.

They are probably under just as much pressure to find information on the Slavers as we are.

Parker finds Cale in the lab alone, sitting on his normal hospital bed.

"Oh, good," she says. "You're here."

"Yes, goody," he answers sarcastically.

"Oh, shut it. Where is Dr. Bellamy?"

"Just went to run some more tests. Do you need her?"

Parker pauses. She is sure Cale knows what she has been thinking about since they left her grandmother's, but she isn't sure she wants to voice her worries, and let him know how badly they are affecting her.

"Um…I don't know. I was thinking about, maybe… asking her to test me, and see if I am a Variant."

Cale looks at her, and she can tell he is unsure what to say.

"Are you certain that's a good idea?"

"Why wouldn't it be?" Parker asks him.

"Well, say it comes back positive. Are you going to be able to handle knowing it will happen someday? Or are you going to sit around and stress every second until it the Variation actually pops up? That could take years, Parker.

Do you really want to do that to yourself?"

Parker bites her lip and begins pacing.

"I don't know! It's just… which is worse? Knowing it is going to happen, but not when, or not knowing if it is going to happen at all? At least if I know I am a—a Variant for sure, I won't spend every waking second wondering *if* it could happen."

Cale nods, understanding what she means.

"I guess that makes sense. I just want you to be sure."

"I am. I am positive this is what I want. Only…"

"Only what?" Cale asks.

"Can I trust Dr. Bellamy to keep quiet about this? I don't know what my father would do if he found out."

"Of course she wouldn't say anything, if you didn't want her to. She is bound by the doctor-patient confidentiality agreement, but, Parker, there is something you should probably consider."

"What?"

"Don't you think it possible that your father already knows the likelihood that you could be a Variant? Surely he knew your grandparent's reasoning for opposing the marriage."

Parker's eyes widen as she considers this.

Of course he would know. That bastard has been hiding this from me…Maybe this is one of the reasons he remains so distant.

"He knows," she whispers. "I'm certain of it. Either way, though, I would prefer to keep him out of the loop on this. You are positive I can trust Dr. Bellamy?"

Cale nods, and Parker hears the door to the lab open behind her.

"Trust me about what?" Dr. Bellamy asks.

Parker swallows and slowly turns to face the Doctor. The woman is standing just inside the door, holding a medical chart and a cup of coffee with a curious expression on her face.

"I just received some information about my family's medical history… I was wondering if you could, perhaps, test me to see if I might be a Variant?"

Parker practically holds her breath, waiting for the doctor's response. There is barely a change of expression on Bellamy's face as she nods her agreement.

"Sure. I'll just need a blood sample. The results could take as long as a month to come back, I warn you."

"Okay, thank you," Parker says. "I was also hoping that this—"

"Would stay between us?" Dr. Bellamy finishes. "Naturally. This is your own, private, business. Quite honestly, after the article on you two, the last thing PG needs is another scandal, like the one there would surely be if it were to get out that the Stolid Sentry *may* have a Variation."

"That's a good point," Cale murmurs, and Parker has to agree.

Dr. Bellamy sets to work straight away, hurrying around the room to collect her blood draw equipment. In a matter of moments, she has Parker seated with a plastic tube tightened around her upper arm, and is drawing a sample.

Parker wonders what her blood will reveal.

Am I really a Variant like my mother? Or will it show that I am truly more like my father?

"There. All done!" Dr. Bellamy tells her cheerfully, as she withdraws the needle. "Now, we just wait and see."

The doctor stands up and gathers her things to leave the lab.

"Oh, and Cale?" she says on her way out. "Your results are staying quite the same as they have been. Don't worry, though, we'll figure this out."

After Dr. Bellamy leaves, Parker rounds on Cale.

"What does that mean? Don't worry, we'll figure this out? Have you been hiding something from me?" Parker demands.

"It's nothing," he tries to assure her. "Just my shoulder injury."

"What about it?"

"It's infected, and all the antibiotics Dr. Bellamy has given me to fight the infection are ineffective."

Parker hurries over to sit next to Cale on the hospital bed.

"What does that mean? Is the infection spreading?"

"No, no," Cale shakes his head. "It seems to be staying confined to my shoulder, but the wound isn't healing, and it is still causing me a lot of pain."

"Why didn't you tell me?" Parker asks, hurt.

"I didn't want to worry you unnecessarily, and we haven't seen a lot of each other lately."

"You're my partner; I'm supposed to be worried about you!"

Cale gives her a small smile and shrugs.

"You better not be keeping anything else from me, you ass," she tells him playfully.

"What else could I be keeping from you?" he asks.

Parker shrugs.

"I dunno. You don't have a secret girlfriend, or anything, do you?"

"Is that jealousy I detect?" Cale asks.

"You wish."

"Nope. No secret lover. I'm afraid that you're the only one of us hiding a relationship."

"What? Who the hell would I be hiding?" Parker laughs.

"Oh, just your BFF and possibly more, Mr. Konstantine Tesla."

Parker shoves Cale and prepares to stand up.

"I'm just kidding," Cale says, taking her hand to keep her in place.

"You better be if you know what's good for you."

Parker and Cale sit in silence for a while, neither sure what to say to comfort the other.

"If it comes back positive," Cale finally asks, "what are you going to do?"

Parker shakes her head.

"I honestly have no idea, but at least if I know, I can prepare myself. I just don't want to end up with my mother's problem."

"That won't happen," Cale assures her. "You are too strong. Plus, it sounds like your mother was in denial and unprepared when her Variation showed up. You are trying to meet it head on."

"Thank you."

Parker leans over to give Cale a hug, which he quickly returns. The door to lab busts open loudly, making them pull apart quickly.

"Didn't I tell you two to lay off?" General Linwood asks angrily. "Here you are in that same damn bed."

"General, it's not—" Cale starts.

"Save it," the General growls. "We have more important matters at hand."

"What is it?" Parker asks.

"There was another transformer blown. The one that was next on that 'fake' pattern you spotted."

"What?" Cale asks, disbelief clear in his voice.

"You heard me," the General says. "Get over there and check it out, and for God's sake, keep your hands to yourselves."

"Yes, sir," they both answer.

Now Tesla is just trying *to screw with me,* Parker thinks angrily as she climbs off the hospital bed and stalks towards the door.

~

Cale and Parker waste no time in heading out. Before they know it, they are in the car and on their way to the transformer.

"Why would Tesla go back and blow that transformer?" Cale asks.

"I dunno. I thought they were clear on the pattern

being a set-up."

"Do you think this may be a set-up?" Cale wonders.

"I doubt it. If anything, I have a feeling they just chose this one to mess with and taunt us."

"So…you mean like how a little boy will use a stick to poke a girl he has a crush on?" Cale asks, giving Parker a cheeky grin.

"I really will hurt you," she warns.

Cale just laughs and keeps driving. He doubts the Slavers of the People will still be there, but he can't justify wasting time on a hunch.

When they get to the scene, they decide to split up. Parker goes to investigate the surrounding area while Cale checks out the actual transformer.

It looks just like the rest, and was obviously destroyed in the same manner. Also helping to confirm this is the Slavers logo spray-painted on the smoking transformer. As he gets closer to it, Cale notices two pieces of paper taped to the charred metal.

More notes.

One is addressed to Patriot Prime, while the second is addressed to the Stolid Sentry. Cale takes a deep breath and pulls the note for him from the transformer.

"Find anything?" Parker asks from behind him.

Cale quickly shoves the note into his pocket, and turns to face her.

"Just this," he says, pointing to the other note. "It's addressed to you."

Parker looks back and forth between Cale and the note, surprise all over her face. She slowly walks over and pulls the note down, then flips it open to read. Shock, and then anger, flashes across her delicate features and she drops the note. Parker quickly draws her gun and starts twisting around, aiming in all different directions.

"Come on out, you jackass!" she yells, looking wildly around.

Cale bends down to pick up the discarded note, and

reads it.

Dearest Sentry,

Have you missed me?
I told you I had your number.

K.T.

"Parker, I don't think he's here," Cale tells her.

"No, he has to be. He's too egotistical; he'd want to see me read it."

"You nailed it. He's egotistical; he already thinks he knows how you'll react. He isn't here. He wouldn't risk it."

Parker looks around the surrounding area again, surveying each shadow before lowering her weapon.

"You're right," she sighs. "Can we not tell the Tribunal about the note?"

Cale pretends to think this over before answering her.

"I suppose not knowing won't hurt."

"Thank you," she says, relieved. "The last thing I need is the General thinking there is something happening here as well."

Cale is eager to read the note addressed to him, but doesn't want to answer any awkward questions from Parker. He, again, feels the burn of guilt in his stomach, but knows it is better for her if he remains quiet.

"Should we look around some more?" he asks.

Parker shakes her head.

"What's the point? You know they didn't leave anything behind they didn't want us to find."

"Yeah, I guess we should go back to headquarters," Cale offers.

Then I can read this note…

"Oh, come on," Parker says. "We're already out, *and* we actually have permission to be out. Let's go do something useful."

"What if the Tribunal asks what took us so long?"

"We'll just tell them we thought we found a lead, but it didn't pan out. Come on," she continues, seeing his uncertainty. "You don't really want to hole up at PG headquarters when you could go out and make a difference, do you? Because that's not the Patriot Prime I know."

"Alright, what do you want to do?"

"Well, I was hoping to do some more follow-up on that serial killer. He's killed another woman," Parker explains.

"Sounds like a plan. We really need to find this guy. Have you learned anything else about him?"

On their way from the transformer site, Parker begins explaining the killer's pattern. He always strikes in the same general area, seeming to prefer the slums. Parker suspects it is because of the lack of witnesses willing to come forward.

After they inspect the latest crime scene, Cale and Parker start walking the neighborhood to see if anyone has seen anything. Everyone is completely oblivious, or at least they claim to be.

One resident, whose window overlooks the crime scene, admits that the window was open the night of the murder, but claims he didn't hear anything.

"Were you home that night?" Parker asks the young man.

"Yeah."

They are standing just outside the front door, and the guy looks almost nervous enough to slam it in their face.

"How did you not hear anything? There was a woman being brutalized and murdered below your *open* window, and you didn't hear a thing?" she presses.

"I—I just..."

Just then an older woman walks into the hallway and sees Parker and Cale. Her features closely resemble the young man's and Cale decides she must be his mother.

"What's going on here?" she asks.

"We are just working our way around, asking questions about the murder that happened the other night," Cale tells her.

"Is this a test? Jake, what did you tell them?"

"Nothing, mom. There…there's nothing to tell, right?" Jake says, looking between the two heroes.

It's almost like he's asking if that is the right answer.

"What do you mean, 'is this a test'?" Parker questions.

"I didn't mean anything by it. Just a slip of the tongue, that's all," the woman insists. "Now, if you don't mind, I need to get ready for work. I would appreciate it if you left."

Without another word, she turns and heads further into the house.

"Your mother works third shift?" Cale asks.

"Yeah, for a while now."

"And is it *just* you and your mother here?"

Jake nods.

"My dad left a long time ago."

"How old are?" Cale questions.

"I'm seventeen."

"Jake, if you know *anything* you need to tell us. This guy, he is targeting women just like your mother. Single mother, out late…she is the perfect target, and until we catch this guy, she will be in danger every time she leaves this house. Now, what do you know?"

Jake looks over his shoulder nervously, checking for his mother.

"I won't get in trouble for talking to you?" he asks.

"No, of course not," Parker assures him.

"O—okay, well, that night…the night it happened, I was home and I could hear it. She was screaming, real bad, and I rushed over to the window to see what was happening. I saw a man attacking her. He was wearing all black and had a black beanie covering his hair. He was too far away to make out any facial features." Jake pauses for a breath, before hurrying on. "I called the police, and they said not to intervene; they were on their way. I stayed in the window, and I watched."

Tears start running down Jake's face, and he turns away, refusing to look at either of them.

"I just watched it happen, and didn't do anything to save her! She died, and I could have helped. Instead, though, I was too much of a coward!"

"No," Parker whispers, placing a gentle hand on his shoulder, "no, Jake, you did the right thing. You did what the police told you to do. You don't know what he might have done if you tried to step in. Don't blame yourself."

Jake wipes his eyes on the back of his hand and glances at Parker. Cale can see that he desperately wants to believe what she is saying to him.

"She's right, Jake. Where would your mother be if something happened to you?" Cale asks.

"In the same place as the children who just had their mother murdered while someone just looked on and watched."

"Jake..."

"No, no," Jake interrupts, "I— I know. It's just going to take some time to accept that. I wish I had something more useful about the guy's description."

"That's okay," Parker says. "It was a lot to take—"

"Wait! I do remember. When he was...done, as he was leaving, he had a limp. He was using a cane. He used it to— to beat her, I thought I was just a weapon, but he was definitely relying on it when he rushed off."

Cale and Parker shoot each other a quick glance.

"Does that help?" Jake asks.

"Yes, it helps a great deal," Cale assures him. "We had literally nothing to go on, so you have been extremely helpful."

"Can you tell us what your mom was talking about when she asked about a test?" Parker asks.

"Um… I'm, uh, not sure."

"Jake!" the mother calls from somewhere in the house. "Are you almost ready?"

"I have to go. I need to walk my mom to work."

Parker looks like she is getting ready to push further, but Cale cuts her off.

"Alright, we'll just be going then. Stay safe, Jake."

"I will, thank you, Patriot Prime."

After the door closes, Cale quickly retreats, waiting for Parker to round on him.

3, 2, 1, he thinks, hearing her rush up behind him.

"What was that? There is something else going on, and that boy may have some of the answers!"

"That may be true, but his mother has to work, and I did not want to risk her leaving without him. It's not safe out… especially for women like her," Cale explains.

Parker lets out a loud huff, but doesn't protest any further, which Cale takes to mean she knows he is right. He feels a small, satisfied, smirk spreading across his face, and Parker playfully punches his side.

"Stop feeling all brilliant," she says. "Everyone has their moments."

"You're just jealous because mine come at closer intervals than yours."

Cale's pager starts buzzing, interrupting whatever smart remark Parker is getting ready to make.

"It's the Tribunal," he tells her, checking the pager. "They want us back now."

"Oh, joy. Why do I get the feeling we're in trouble?" Parker asks him.

"Because you are always *getting* me into trouble."

Back at headquarters, General Linwood is waiting for them in the lobby.

"Oh, boy," Parker mutters.

He does not look happy…scratch that. He looks angrier than usual.

"Where the hell were you two?" the General asks, as soon as they get close enough to hear him. "You were only instructed to check out the transformer."

"We were following up on a, uh, lead," Parker tries.

"Bullshit. I know, for a fact, you were out asking questions about a murder. You don't need to worry about that."

"Someone needs to worry about it," Parker counters.

"*Someone* is. The police, you know, the *real* detectives. You two are just a couple of crime fighting muscles. The only reason you are *investigating* the Slavers case is because you are the only ones that could handle them if you actually found them," the General spits. "As unlikely as that is looking."

Cale sees Parker flinch at the cold way General Linwood refers to them, and he knows it has got to be hurting her.

"Now, I want you two to separate. You are a bad influence on one another. From now on, you are only permitted contact for training, or assignments *I* give you. Understood?" he asks.

Cale and Parker both nod dejectedly.

"*Understood?*" he repeats.

"Yes, General Linwood," Cale says quietly.

"Yes, sir," Parker responds at the same time.

"Good. Now head to your chambers."

"I was actually going to head home...sir." Parker tells him.

"At this time the Tribunal would prefer you both to remain at headquarters," General Linwood tells her.

"What? That's not fair!" she exclaims, and Cale nods in agreement.

"Do not push me, or the Tribunal will have both of your leases severed so you two have no other option but here."

Parker's mouth hangs open, ready to tear into the General further, but Cale shakes his head once, warning her off of it. She snaps her mouth shut, shoots General Linwood a withering glare, and storms off.

"Do you have anything to add, Prime?" the General asks.

Instead of answering, Cale shakes his head in disgust, and, he too, walks away. He heads straight up to his rooms, cursing the General the entire way.

Bastard. What the hell is the Tribunal's problem lately?

Cale is so furious when he reaches his room, he almost forgets that he has been eager to be alone all evening.

The note!

He pulls the partially crumpled paper from his pocket and opens it as quickly as his fumbling fingers can manage.

Patriot Prime,

We know you are getting worse. We have been watching you and can see the decay. You keep slipping. First the boy, then your street source, and now you used unnecessary force and broke the wrist of a practically homeless man. When will you see you need us? We have your cure. We are waiting for your word, but we won't wait much longer. Send us your response…soon.

Always watching you, S.P.

Cale growls angrily and crushes the paper. He can't believe they are pestering him for using force on a man who was trying to sell drugs to children.

They must be insane if they think breaking some druggy's wrist is going to make me trust a group the whole city is after. It would take a lot more than that…

THIRTEEN

When Cale wakes up the next morning, it isn't because his body decides it is time to get up, but instead because of an obnoxious ringing telephone near his bed.

"Hello?" he mumbles groggily, after stumbling his way to the receiver.

"Aren't you up yet?" Parker asks cheerfully.

"Oh, good God. Where is Parker and why have you replaced her with this morning person imposter?"

"Oh, shut it. I guess this schedule is finally getting to me."

"What do you want?" he groans.

"I wanted to see if you were up for training? Seeing as it is the only way we might see each other today."

"Fine…but you better have coffee waiting."

"Of course," she chirps.

"And…a muffin."

"Okay. See you in ten," she laughs, hanging up the phone.

Cale continues to curse Parker under his breath while he gets around. He'd stayed up a bit later than planned, thinking about the note, and how presumptuous the Slavers of the People are.

Like I am just going to blindly trust them, he thinks as he steps in the elevator and pushes the button for the training floor.

When he steps off, he sees Parker across the room,

163

already stretching.

"You have far too much energy today," he tells her as he approaches.

"And you don't have enough! Here's your coffee," she says, passing him a steaming cup.

"No muffin?"

"Sorry. There was only one left, and I ate it."

Parker starts laughing at the disappointed look on Cale's face and pulls something out of a bag by her feet.

"Now, now. Don't cry. Here's your muffin."

"Blueberry? They didn't have banana?" he asks, trying to keep a straight face.

"I'm gonna hurt you."

Cale sticks his tongue out at her and proceeds to quickly down his breakfast.

"You ready?" he asks, leaning into a stretch.

"I've been ready forever, just waiting for your old ass," she jokes.

"Old? I'm not old."

"Maybe not in years, but you are the first generation. Face it, the new model is *much* better," she goads, and then takes off racing for the track.

"Cheater!" Cale calls, chasing after her.

They run a couple miles and not once does Cale come close to catching up with Parker.

"You're just showing off," he says, breathing a bit heavily.

"It's not my fault you're so slow," she says, not a single sign of a workout apparent.

She looks as if she just took a leisurely stroll instead of running four miles. Cale fares better than any average person, but he still feels slightly worn by the exercise.

"Maybe it's your Variant," Cale jokes.

The look Parker gives him says he has crossed a line, and he immediately begins backtracking.

"Sorry. That was uncalled for. I know you're nervous about the test result, and I spoke without thinking."

"It's okay," she sighs. "You're right, though; I am nervous."

"I just want you to know," Cale assures her, "no matter what the results say, you are still the same old Parker to me."

"So now you're calling me old?" she asks, but interrupts when she sees him open his mouth to protest. "I know what you meant. Thank you."

"Anytime."

Parker looks around the arena, eyeing all of the equipment, and sighs.

"So, what next?" she asks him.

"How about some combatives?" Cale suggests.

"Sounds great, but are you sure you should, with your shoulder and everything?"

"Yeah, I'll just be extra careful."

"Alright, just as long as you don't hurt yourself. I really don't want Dr. Bellamy coming after me with a scalpel or something."

"Bellamy wouldn't come after you with a scalpel," Cale says. "She'd use something much subtler... like killer nanobots."

"Oh, that's comforting," Parker snorts.

When they get on the training mats, they start with Parker on the offensive and Cale trying to fend her off. She does pretty well for herself because her speed makes her hard to get ahold of, but when Cale finally does manage to catch her arm, he is able to use his weight against her and flip her onto her back.

"I'll get you back for that one," she tells him, climbing to her feet and going back to attack mode.

Out of the next ten attacks she mounts, he manages to catch and divert her four times.

"That all you got?" she goads.

Cale's shoulder is starting to protest, and sting, but there is no way he is going to give up that easily. He can already imagine the self-satisfied grin on her face and the comments on the second generation being better.

"Why don't we switch?" he asks. "You go on defensive."

"Oh, I suppose."

Parker plants her feet shoulder-width apart and eyes him warily. Cale begins pacing a circle around her, keeping her on the move. Every once in a while, he changes directions to throw her off. A few times he feigns like he is doing it again— he leans right, but continues going left. Parker realizes what he is doing, but just a second too late. She turns right just a fraction far enough and gives Cale the perfect opening for an attack.

He quickly takes the opportunity, and before she can blink, he has her flat on the mat.

"Point to me, I think," Cale says triumphantly.

"You were bound to get lucky at some point," Parker offers. "Again."

Cale can tell she is annoyed that he got the best of her and he has to admit he is enjoying her displeasure.

This time, as she places her feet shoulder-width apart, she crouches down slightly, into a wrestler's position. Cale decides to take her head on, but as he rushes her, she gracefully steps off to the side and turns to stomp down on the back of his upturned ankle as he is running, sending him sprawling onto the mat.

"Someone's feeling feisty," he groans, rolling onto his back.

"Oh, I'm just getting started," Parker smiles, offering a hand to help him up.

When he reaches up to take it, she quickly pulls it away.

"Psych."

"Ha, ha, very mature."

Cale pulls himself up without help and shakes out his arms.

"Limbering up won't help you in this case," Parker taunts, getting into position.

"Ready?" Cale asks.

Parker nods.

Cale doesn't move. Instead, he stays still while sizing her up, trying to read her intentions and find the best attack. She doesn't give him anything to work with, so he tries another feign, faking left, and rushing her from the right. Parker is too quick for him, though. Just as he is about to grab her, she snags his arm and sidesteps him. She twists his arm behind his back and sweeps her leg out to knock him off his feet.

Cale lands hard, on his stomach, with Parker kneeling down next to him. She still has his arm twisted behind his back. The pressure and angle of her hold has Cale seeing stars. The pain in his shoulder is blinding and he feels like he might pass out. Suddenly, white-hot rage rushes through him, and with a surge of strength, he breaks her hold on his arm.

As he breaks free, he knocks Parker off balance and sends her sprawling onto the floor. Before Cale can even process everything that is happening, he is up on his feet and hovering over Parker.

"Not bad, old m—" she starts, but something in his expression must make her pause. "Cale, are you al—?"

Cale doesn't hear her words. He doesn't care what she has to say. The only thing that matters to him is his anger and pain, and *she* caused both.

Cale snarls ferociously and cuts off Parker's question. He reaches down, grabs her by the hair, and drags her onto her feet. She screams out in pain, but he barely hears her. There is a loud buzzing in his ears that's drowning out almost everything.

With his hand still firmly twisted in Parker's hair, he drags her over to the wall and throws her against it. Her shoulder hits the wall and she tries to turn away from him, but Cale grabs her by her upper arms and forces her back against the wall.

He can feel a snarl on his face as he studies her, trying

to decide on his next plan of attack. He sees her lips are moving, but he can't hear her words over the buzzing in his ears. When he looks up at her big brown eyes, he sees she is scared. Terrified, of *him*.

Parker is scared of you, his brain whispers.

It's like a bucket of cold water hits him, and all his other senses come rushing back. He feels Parker trembling beneath his iron grip on her arms, and hears her voice, calling to him.

"Cale! What are you doing? Cale! Let me go!"

His fingers release her like he's been burnt, and he takes a step back, holding his hands up in surrender.

He sees Parker reach up to feel the back of her head and when she pulls her hand away, there is blood on it.

I did that. When I threw her against the wall. I hurt her. I lost control… and I hurt Parker.

His shoulder is still twinging in pain, and he feels like he is going to be sick.

"I—I'm sorry," Cale whispers.

He quickly turns away from her and sprints towards the stairs.

I need air.

He glances over his shoulder, and Parker seems to be in too much of a shock to follow him.

"What the *hell* was that?" Parker yells after him.

He doesn't answer or turn to look again, and keeps running until he makes the stairs, then the lobby, and then the street.

I need air.

~

What the hell just happened?

Parker watches in shock as Cale flees from the training arena. She cannot figure out what just happened. Never before has Cale lashed out at her like that, and she doesn't understand why he reacted the way he did.

The back of her head is stinging painfully and she reaches her hand back to feel where she hit. When she pulls her fingers away, Parker can see she is still bleeding and decides to go visit Dr. Bellamy, just to be on the safe side.

In shock, she barely realizes she sets out, and by the time Parker makes it to the medical floor, she is feeling a bit woozy and almost trips on her way into the lab.

"Parker? Are you alright?" Dr. Bellamy asks.

The Doctor was hunched over a table on the other side of the room when Parker stumbled in, her head shooting up immediately as if sensing something was off.

"I had a, uh, bit of a training accident," Parker explains, covering for Cale, but not quite sure why. "I hit my head, and now I am bleeding."

"Let me have a look at it," Dr. Bellamy says as she crosses the room.

Parker sits down on a stainless steel stool to allow the Doctor easier access to her scalp. Her head stings as the older woman gently probes the area to assess the damage.

"Hmm," Dr. Bellamy murmurs. "If you were anyone else, well, aside from Cale, I would say you need stitches, but, for you, I think a little glue will do the trick and this should be healed by morning."

"Great, thanks."

"How exactly did this happen?" the Doctor asks as she reaches for a tube of medical glue.

"Cale and I were doing combatives and… I fell back and hit my head on the wall," Parker rushes, mumbling.

"I'm surprised Cale didn't escort you down here."

"Oh, well, as I'm sure you know, we aren't allowed to interact outside of training or missions assigned by the Tribunal."

Dr. Bellamy doesn't respond and instead continues working on Parker's injury. Parker briefly wonders if the woman's silence is from guilt, or anger at her fellow tribunal members.

It's not long before the wound is sealed.

"There," the Doctor says. "All set, but I think you should rest for a bit. Why don't you take a nap in here? I have to run an errand, so you won't be bothering me," she adds before Parker can protest.

Not having the energy to argue, Parker just sighs and goes to lie down on the hospital bed.

"I'll just be out for a little while. You should still be here when I get back," Dr. Bellamy tells her with a stern, matronly, look.

Before the older woman can leave, Parker stops her.

"Doctor? I know it is still really early, but has there been any news about my… possible Variation?"

"No, not yet. I put in a rush order, though, so it shouldn't take as long as it usually does to hear back."

Parker nods and leans back on the bed, closing her eyes. She hears the door close behind Dr. Bellamy and lets out a long sigh.

What is wrong with me lately?

More like: what is wrong with my life?

Parker is overwhelmed by her sense of frustration. She feels so suffocated by the crushing weight of it all.

I thought things were going to get better when I joined the Patriot Guard. I was going to make something of myself, win my father back, and oh, I don't know… ride off into the sunset or something? Live happily ever after?

She hates how ridiculous it all sounds, thinking about it now. She must have been crazy to think her life was going to magically turn itself around. If anything, joining the Patriot Guard had made her life, if not worse, then at least way more complicated.

Before I joined, my biggest problem was my shaky relationship with my father and my questionable employability. Now, I have so many problems I can barely count them all… like catching the Slavers of the People for instance, and Konstantine Tesla.

Though, if she were truly honest with herself, she counts Tesla as a completely separate problem. Putting the

Slavers away is a cut-and-dry issue for Parker, if she could ever find them, that is. She knows that if she managed to catch Tesla now, she would turn him in too, but he just doesn't quite seem the evil super villain the Tribunal paints him as.

Parker groans and hangs her arm over her face.

He helped you out one time. No reason to start questioning the Tribunal about him. I mean come on! He is, in fact, a criminal. You don't owe him anything.

Pushing Tesla from her mind, Parker tries to focus on the general problem of *finding* the Slavers. How will she ever catch them? They are always two steps ahead and Parker can't find a pattern. She feels useless.

You are useless, her brain provides. *This city is counting on you to protect them, to be a symbol of hope, and what are you doing? Lying in a hospital bed because you have a boo-boo, thinking of arguments to throw at the General, or worrying about being a freak.*

Parker shakes her head, trying to chase these thoughts away, but they won't budge. Waiting for results of her Variant testing is eating away at her nerves already, and it's barely been twenty-four hours.

He'll hate you. He'll hate you so much if it's positive. That's why he's never brought it up—because he doesn't want to think about it.

Pain hits her; she feels anxiety fill her chest and she forces herself to focus on something else, steering away from the uncomfortable subject. Her mind lands on Cale and Parker finds herself momentarily relieved, at least until she remembers the training incident.

What happened? Why was he so angry? I've never seen him like that before. He looked at me like…like he hated me.

Parker's eyes start to burn.

Could Cale really hate me? What could I have done to cause that?

She tries to recount their training, to see what led up to his outburst, but can't think of anything out of the ordinary.

Was it something I said? I didn't say anything that out of line. It was just our usual banter. Could I have hurt his feelings? Or maybe his pride?

Parker racks her brain but still cannot come up with an explanation for Cale's behavior.

Before long, her eyelids start to grow heavy, and she drifts off to sleep.

Parker immediately falls into a nightmare.

She's sitting in her private room at PG Headquarters, when all of the sudden her father bursts in waving a piece of paper. There is a large, red, "V" stamped across it.

"Variant? You're a Variant? You disgust me!" he shouts, crumpling the paper and throwing it at her. "You aren't fit to be in the Patriot Guard."

He charges her and rips the mask she didn't realize she was wearing from her face.

"But... I—I'm sorry. I didn't know," she tries to reason.

"Get out of my sight!"

Parker stands and runs from the room, her face buried in her hands. She can feel the tears pooling in her cupped fingers. She runs and throws the door open to Cale's room.

He is on the far side, facing away from her and looking out a window.

"Cale," she calls miserably.

When he turns to face her, Parker jumps back in fear. His face is contorted in white-hot rage. Hatred emanates from him so strongly she can feel it burn her skin.

"What is it?" she whispers fearfully. "What did I do to drive you away? Why do you hate me?"

Cale doesn't answer her. He lets out a feral growl and charges across the room. Parker steps back through the door and slams it shut. The whole thing shutters as Cale hits it. The door begins to buckle so Parker turns and runs.

She runs so quickly it takes her moment to realize she is no longer in the hall of PG Headquarters. Wherever she is, it is much darker and has a dank, musty scent to it.

When Parker glances over her shoulder she sees that Cale isn't chasing her, so she slows her pace. There is a light in front of her. She gets closer, and closer, and just when she glimpses a room, her surroundings change.

She is kneeling and unable to move.

Parker looks around, terror coursing through her.

Konstantine Tesla is standing over her, grim expression on his face. He's talking, but his words are muffled.

"Believe me, it's for the best."

A loud clang jolts Parker awake. She sits up gasping, her hand clutching her heart. The dream lingers briefly and she flips around, searching for Tesla.

Instead, she finds a very apologetic looking Dr. Bellamy.

"I'm so sorry," she whispers, as if that will balance out the racket she just made.

The Doctor is stooped over a spilled medical tray, gathering up her instruments.

"I was trying to be quiet, and I suppose I utterly failed."

Parker glances up at the wall clock and is surprised to see how late it is.

"It's practically dinner time. I can't believe I slept so long. Isn't that bad for a concussion?"

"Not for you," Dr. Bellamy smirks. "You needed the rest."

Parker grimaces, not really classifying the nightmare as 'restful.'

"How are you feeling?"

"I'm okay," Parker says. "I have a bit of a headache, but nothing I can't handle."

"No need to be so stoic; the public isn't watching."

Parker tries to protest as Bellamy approaches her, needle in hand, but the older woman is having none of it.

"Don't be such a wimp. Now hold still; it's just a mild pain killer."

Parker grumbles as she rolls up her sleeve. She barely feels prick of the needle.

"I don't want you leaving until that sets in," Dr. Bellamy instructs.

Parker braces her hands on the side of the bed and looks down at her feet, impatiently kicking them. Bits and pieces of her dream start to come back, causing a knot to form in her chest.

Parker jumps off the hospital bed and stalks towards the exit, ignoring Dr. Bellamy's questioning protests from behind her.

FOURTEEN

Parker's thoughts are a muddled mess, making the trip upstairs a blur. Even as she is knocking on the office door, she realizes that she doesn't know what she is going to say. She's not entirely sure why she came in the first place. She thinks, perhaps, that she is so close to a mental breakdown that her body has reverted to 'factory settings,' and sent her to the person who *should* be the one to protect her.

When he opens the door, the General's face is an unreadable mask, but as he looks down at Parker's expression, he lets his normally cool demeanor slip. Concern clouds his features, and she realizes she has been crying since she left the medical floor.

"Parker? What's wrong?" he asks, confused.

Instead of answering in any coherent way, she launches herself at him, sobbing, and he catches her in an awkward hug. After a short pause, he begins to stiffly pat her back.

With his arm around her, General Linwood carefully leads Parker into his office and over to a small couch, closing the door behind them.

"Shh, shh," he whispers, pulling her to sit down next to him.

He doesn't say anything else, doesn't push her, or demand answers. He just sits there, making quiet sounds of consolation.

They stay like that for quite a while; Parker crying onto his shoulder as he shushes her and strokes her hair. Even when her sobs seem to stop, he gives her a few more moments before speaking.

"Please," he whispers, worry clear in his tone, "please tell me. What's wrong?"

"Everything," she responds hoarsely.

He waits.

"I thought things would be better," she starts. "I thought that life as the Stolid Sentry would be much better than the boring life of Parker Linwood. I was wrong. Everything has went straight to hell since I put on the mask."

She pulls back from the General a bit so she can wipe her swollen eyes, and lets out a humorless bark of laughter.

"I thought my life was bad before. What a fool I was. As Parker, I only let one person down, but as Sentry, I have a whole city's disappointment sitting on my shoulders."

"Parker, the city loves you."

"Maybe for now. What about when I can't catch the Slavers? I keep letting them slip through my fingers. My limelight is almost up. They'll be calling for blood soon, and won't care if it's mine, Cale's, or the Slavers."

"Don't be ridiculous—" General Linwood tries, but she interrupts him.

"It's already started," she says. "That fake story about Cale and I being an item. It's the first shadow on our dedication to the job. That article was written because there are already people becoming bored with us being 'heroes.' Don't deny it. You know the truth, and that's why you were so angry."

"Did you consider that maybe my anger stemmed from my daughter being involved with some cocky poster boy?" he asks.

"We weren't—"

"I know that now, but at the time I didn't. What did

you expect?"

Parker shakes her head and ignores the question.

"You really shouldn't talk about Cale like that," she says. "He isn't a 'cocky poster boy.' He is a good person, and a good fr— hero."

She had been about to say he was a good friend, but couldn't get it out.

Does he still consider us friends?

Parker's eyes start to water again.

"Is this all about not catching the Slavers yet?" General Linwood asks.

She doesn't answer.

"I'm...sorry if I've been pushing you too hard," he says, clearing his throat, obviously uncomfortable.

Did he just apologize for something?

"It's not that...well, it's not *just* that," Parker rephrases. "I—"

"What?"

"How could you not tell me I might be a Variant!" she exclaims. "How could you not give me a warning or something? Mention that it runs on mom's side?"

The look of alarm on the General's face tells her that Dr. Bellamy indeed kept Parker's request of a blood test quiet. She can tell he had no idea she discovered the secret he'd been hiding.

"How did you find out?" he asks quietly.

"Aida. Her address was on the tip list. Needless to say, I was a little shocked as to why." Parker stands up and begins pacing. "My own grandmother is a counselor to young Variants. She also has it in her mind that I'll be showing signs any time now."

"There's no guarantee," the General tries.

"Maybe not, but I had the right to know! My whole life, you've acted as if mother's Variation was a huge, shocking, surprise."

"It was!" he snaps, frustration cracking his tone. "She didn't develop on time. She... we thought it wasn't going to happen, that it skipped her. Your grandparents disagreed, but we didn't want to sit around and wait for something that was never going to happen. We wanted to get married, start a family…"

"Why didn't she go to them when her Variation *did* present?"

"Your mother was too proud…too stubborn. I begged her to go to them, Parker. You don't know how hard I tried. Do you think I wanted her to turn down the path she did? That I wanted her to get in the car that day?"

"No…and I'm sorry!" Parker bursts into fresh tears.

"What? What are you sorry about?"

General Linwood stands up and blocks Parker's path, forcing her to stop pacing.

"I'm sorry I asked her to take me to the store. I'm sorry I didn't see how drunk she was. I'm sorry she was on that highway because of me, and I'm sorry I took her from you!"

Her vision is so blurred Parker doesn't see the look of complete shock and outrage on the General's face.

He places a hand on either of her shoulders and turns her to squarely face him.

"Parker Elizabeth Linwood, don't you *dare* stand there and try to foot the blame for what happened to your mother. You were twelve years old, and she was a grown, albeit sick, woman who made her own decisions."

Parker looks up at him, slowly absorbing his words.

"Please don't tell me you've been blaming yourself all these years?" the General asks softly.

"You mean…you don't…you don't blame me?" she asks, trying to quell the tiny spark of hope she feels. "You don't hate me for not stopping her?"

He opens his mouth to speak, but pauses and buries his face in his hand. When he finally looks back up at her, there is a single tear trailing down his face.

"Parker, of course I don't blame you. I have never blamed you, and I could *never* hate you. Don't you know how much I love you?"

A giant, invisible, weight that has plagued her half of her life lifts, and Parker almost doesn't ask her next question, not wanting to ruin the moment.

"Then why did you shut me out? You distanced yourself from me. Why?" she begs.

"Because I hated myself!" he snaps, turning away from her. "I knew how bad your mother was getting, that she was becoming a danger to herself. I left you alone with her, and you almost died. The one thing I am supposed to do as a parent is protect you, and I failed miserably."

"Dad—"

"Don't. Just...don't. I know I failed you when I pushed you away, I see that now. I saw it a while ago, I just haven't known how to fix it, and I'm afraid I've been taking my anger at myself out on you."

"If you were mad at yourself...why did you sell Tempo? That seemed like more of a punishment to me."

"I suddenly felt like a twelve year old girl owning a racehorse was perhaps not the safest pastime she could have had. I just wanted to protect you."

The General turns to face her again, giving her his most sincere look and taking her hand.

"I'm truly sorry for everything I've put you through, Parker. I had no idea how you were feeling, and that you have been blaming yourself all these years."

Parker can't think of anything to say. Her mind is full, thoughts buzzing so loudly, they're keeping her from pinning any single one down. Instead, she just leans in and hugs her father.

"Is there anything else that has been bothering you?" he asks, leading her back to the couch.

"I'm pretty nervous about my blood test," she admits.

"What blood test?"

"After I met Aida, I asked Dr. Bellamy to test me. I want to know if I am a

Variant."

"Bellamy didn't inform me?" he asks, more to himself than Parker.

"I asked her not to."

"Are you sure you want to know? What if you find out you are a Variant and spend years waiting for it to happen?"

"That's what Cale said. I would rather wait a couple years, expecting it, then wonder my whole life if it is or isn't going to happen."

"Even Prime knew before me?" the General asks.

"I didn't want to say anything until I knew for sure. I know you hate Variants—"

"I don't hate Variants."

"But, whenever you talk about them," Parker starts, "you seem so…disgusted."

"That's just a bitter old man dwelling on memories. If you are a Variant, Parker, I won't think any differently of you. Just promise me you'll take care of yourself, and won't end up…like—"

"I promise," she says, not letting him finish, for which he looks grateful.

After that, neither of them really know what to say. Any other time, Parker would feel especially awkward and out of place, but today, after their talk, she feels at peace.

"If you don't mind my asking… what brought you here today?" the General questions. "You've obviously felt this way for a while. What triggered your visit?"

She really wishes he weren't so observant.

"I had a bit of a…training accident this morning. Also, a bit of a falling out with Cale; I think he is angry with me, but I don't know why."

"What kind of accident?"

"Oh, I just stumbled during combatives and hit my head. Dr. Bellamy had to glue me up."

His face hardens but he doesn't respond right away.

"Do I need to have a talk with Prime?" he asks, finally.

"What? No. About what?" she stumbles quickly.

"You said you had a falling out?"

"Oh! Uh, no, I'll handle that on my own, thank you, although there is something you could do for me."

He arches an eyebrow at her.

"Do you think you could possibly be nicer to Cale? He is a good hero, it wouldn't kill you to say 'nice work' once in a while."

"That remains to be seen," the General mumbles. "Oh...all right," he concedes after a withering glare from Parker.

"Thank you."

General Linwood looks down at his watch.

"I don't mean to rush you out, but I have a very important phone conference about to start."

"Oh, no, that's fine," Parker insists, standing up.

"I'm...glad we talked."

"Me too," she smiles sadly.

"I would like, that is, if you would like, to maybe do this again?"

"I'd love that."

Parker gives her father a quick hug and hurries to the door. She is just about out of it when he stops her.

"Parker? I know I haven't told you before, but...I'm very proud of you, for everything."

Not knowing what to say Parker gives him a small smile and leaves the office before she starts crying again.

~

After the training incident, Cale needed to get away. He needed to be alone and think. He tried going to his apartment, but he felt too stifled, too confined by the familiar walls. And he couldn't just take a stroll in the park; Patriot Prime isn't afforded much privacy in public. So, he chose the place where it started, where everyone had finally decided he was a worthy hero...that he was someone to trust and admire. Cale went to the school that had had the partial collapse, the place where he'd saved all those children and marked the beginning of his acceptance by New Edison.

The building is abandoned. Construction of a new school was already underway when this one caved in. Getting in isn't a problem. The door is bolted, but the lock is rusted and it barely takes Cale any effort to break through. Anger and fear radiate off of him as he roams the deserted hallways.

You hurt Parker. She was bleeding. You were out of control.

But I stopped myself.

If you hadn't, she could be dead. You could have killed her.

Cale's shoulder radiates a dull ache now. It's annoying, but nowhere near the lightning shock that had been coursing through it.

She's never going to talk to you again, Cale tells himself. *She's going to demand the Tribunal keep her separate from you.*

A horrifying thought occurs to him.

Has she told them? Has Parker told the Tribunal what happened? She may not understand the significance of this, but they sure will. General Linwood will definitely have me locked in captivity for this. He's always wanted a reason to hide me away, and what better excuse than me attacking his daughter?

Cale shakes his head, disgusted with himself.

Are you really worrying about yourself right now? You should be thinking of Parker.

He stops wandering and leans against one of the bare brick walls, letting himself slowly slide down to the hallway ground. Cale buries his face in his hands and suddenly his meeting with Krista Brandt comes to mind.

"And you, hero… you are a time bomb. I just hope that when your timer hits zero, you're not with someone you love."

He *had* hit zero, he hit bottom and he'd hurt Parker.

That can never happen again.

He traces through his options silently. Cale knows he could, and should, go straight to Bellamy and tell her what happened, but he also knows what will happen when he does. The General will have him packed up and carted off, and who knows what they'll tell Parker. As delusional as he may be, Cale's biggest fear is her finding out that he's been hiding things from her all this time, especially something as big as the disastrous run of the first generation Patriot Guard. Logically, he knows she may never want to talk to him again already, because he snapped on her, but he's holding out hope that he'll be able to gain her forgiveness.

Maybe after we're on good terms again, I'll finally tell her the truth.

He knows doing nothing isn't an option, but honestly, he finds himself terrified of telling the Tribunal that he's losing it like the rest of the Patriot Project First Generation. The only other option isn't *really* an option.

He could contact the Slavers.

They said they had a cure for him. Cale's still not entirely sure what that "cure'" entails, but it's worth checking out.

Isn't it?

He bounces back and forth, unable to make up his mind. The Slavers aren't to be trusted. His life goal the past few weeks has been to hunt them down, and put them behind bars. Is it really safe to accept their offer of help?

Probably not...

Not safe for him, surely, but safer for the city? Safer for Parker? Something needs to be done before Cale loses himself completely and becomes the animal his fellow Project members turned into. He can't risk putting his partner, or the citizens of New Edison in danger. Cale will do anything to keep them safe.

The decision is really quite easy after he removes himself from the equation. It's not about him, he tells himself, it's about protecting others and ensuring that Patriot Prime stays the symbol of justice that he was always meant to be.

Locking all thoughts of himself in the back of his

mind, Cale stands and hurries out of the school. He is mildly surprised to see night has fallen, he didn't realize how long he'd been in the school.

This will make things easier.

Krista had told him to find Benny to get the word out when he made up his mind, and Benny can rarely be found in the daylight hours.

Cale gets in his car and speeds to the red light district. Normally following traffic laws to the letter is important; he now disregards them. As he blows through a stoplight, he thinks of when he told Parker how important it was to obey the laws because they were role models, but remembering that conversation only causes him to press harder on the pedal.

Thinking of Parker makes him even more eager to find Benny… to find his cure.

He has a siren for emergencies, but decides not to use it. Cale really doesn't want attention drawn to what he is about to do. If he causes suspicion among the police, they might take it upon themselves to contact the Tribunal to find out what is going on. Only his fear of this happening causes Cale to slow down a bit, and at least yield at the last stop sign between him and Benny's usual haunt.

Cale pulls up behind the strip club, not bothering to be discreet. He scopes the alley for Benny, but doesn't see him. What he does see is a group of sparkle-dusted strippers on a smoke break.

"Girls," he nods, approaching them.

He suddenly realizes he's still in his training clothes and not in uniform.

"Well, look who's off duty tonight."

"Roxie. Just the girl I was looking for," Cale says, eyeing the blonde warily.

She's wearing a domino mask and cape in addition to her glittery lingerie and heels. She takes a long drag off of her cigarette and winks at him.

"What are you wearing?" he asks, momentarily

distracted.

"What—you don't recognize me, partner? I'm a hero! Your pretty little sidekick has caused a real demand over here."

Cale grimaces.

"Oh, come on! You know you're enjoying the view. And I don't just mean my legs. Everyone knows you've got a thing for the Sentry. It's in your eyes," Roxie insists.

He waves her statement off, not wanting to grace her with a response.

"That's not why I'm here. Where's Benny?" Cale demands.

Roxie tosses her cigarette down, grinds it out roughly, and crosses her arms in a huff.

"Like you don't know!" she pouts.

"I don't. If I did I wouldn't be here."

She gives him a look that clearly says she doesn't believe him.

"Really, Roxie, I don't know where he is. Did something happen?" Cale asks.

"Yeah! He went and got himself arrested. He's down at the city jail now, but they're moving him to county soon."

Cale swears.

"I have to go," he tells her. "…and could you please stop dressing up like Parker?"

"Not on your life, Prime. My tips have tripled."

Cale grimaces again, but doesn't press the issue, instead walking back to his car. He'll have to tell Parker and let her handle this one herself.

Right. Now I need to get Benny out of jail.

Cale thinks quickly, easily coming up with a plan. He opens his trunk and is relieved to find he still has a spare uniform in there. He scoops it up and ducks between his car and the building he'd luckily parked so close to.

After changing, during which he receives a few catcalls from the strippers still in the alley, he sets out for the city jail.

Cale decides the best course of action is to just barge in, pretend he belongs there, and hope the officers on duty will be too flustered to ask any questions. Nobody questions Patriot Prime.

When he arrives at the police station, Cale saunters in, chest puffed out, attempting to be as pompous as possible as he stalks towards the front desk.

The officer on duty is clearly shocked to see Patriot Prime standing before him and has difficulty stuttering out a greeting.

"P-Patriot Prime…sir, what brings you here tonight?"

"I need to see a prisoner of yours," Cale demands. "Benny Johnson."

"Uh, s-sorry, but visiting hours are over."

Cale arches an eyebrow at the man.

"I'm not here for a visit. I'm here on business, and Mr. Johnson will be coming with me."

The officer looks down at his desk and quickly begins flipping through pages of a work log.

"I don't have anything about a, uh, transfer," he says, apologetically.

Damn it.

"Are you questioning me? I am here on official business of the Tribunal, and you are going to stand in my way because we didn't take the time to ensure it was scheduled into your little book?" Cale asks.

"Sorry, t-that's—"

"No, I'm sorry. I'm sorry I didn't take time out of protecting this city from thugs and murderers to file a piece of paperwork."

"Hold on…just…just give me a second," the officer begs.

He turns away from Cale and picks up a telephone.

Shit. If he's calling the Tribunal the jig is up…

"Jerry? Could you get Mr. Johnson and bring him up front? He's being moved."

Thank goodness.

"Yeah, yeah, I know what the schedule says. Just do it," the officer demands, glancing nervously at Cale, "and be quick."

Cale nods a thank you at the man and moves to stand at the far side of the room. He doesn't have to wait long before another officer shows up with Benny in tow.

"Come on, man. I'm not supposed to go to county yet!" Benny whines loudly. "That's not until—"

He falls silent when he sees Cale.

The officer who brought Benny up is so in shock at finding Patriot Prime waiting for him that Cale has to remind him to remove Benny's cuffs.

"I won't need those," he says, nodding towards the shackles.

The officer removes them and Cale grabs Benny firmly by the upper arm and leads him out of the station, nodding at the two still flabbergasted police officers on his way out.

"Prime! Oh my God, thank—" Benny starts.

"Stop. Just be quiet. I don't want to hear it."

Cale drives Benny to the seedier side of town before kicking him out of the car.

"Seriously, Prime, I owe you one. Thank you so much," Benny beams, getting ready to climb out.

"Yes, you do owe me one," Cale agrees. "I need you to get the word out...I'm in."

FIFTEEN

Cale returns to headquarters feeling oddly light. He decides it is out of relief. He may not know what the Slavers' plan is, or how they intend to cure him, but having finally made a decision and chosen a path to follow makes him feel almost content.

Now I just have to patch things up with Parker.

The thought of confronting her sobers him a bit, weighing him back down, and he decides it would be best if he didn't put it off. As soon as he arrives, Cale heads directly upstairs, hoping to find Parker in her room.

As he approaches, he thinks he hears music playing, something light and upbeat.

Well, I know she's here.

Hesitating only a moment, Cale knocks on the door.

"Just a sec!"

The music inside stops, and a few seconds later, the door opens. Parker has a small smile on her face that abruptly disappears when she sees Cale.

"Oh," she says, "hi."

"Do you have a minute to talk?" Cale asks.

"Yeah, I guess…come on in."

She steps out of the way and gestures him to enter, closing the door behind him.

At least she isn't afraid to be alone with me.

Cale stands in the middle of the room and Parker turns to face him. They stare awkwardly at one another for a long pause before they both burst into speech.

"Parker, I—"

"What hap—"

They both stop and she waves him on.

"I am so sorry. I didn't mean to hurt you. Are you okay?" Cale asks, taking a step forward.

"What happened today?" she asks, ignoring his question. "You looked at me like...like you *hated* me. You scared the crap out of me, Cale! Did I do something to make you angry? Was it something I said? Because if it was, I'm sorry."

"No! No, of course not. It was my shoulder. Your last maneuver hit it in the exact wrong way and when the pain hit me...I couldn't think straight. I just reacted, and overreacted by a long shot. When I realized what I'd done, I had to get out of there. I just... couldn't face you. I am so, so, sorry," he pleads, moving closer.

"It was your...shoulder?" she asks, voice small.

"Yes, and I know that is no excuse for my reaction. I promise you, I will never let it happen again. I feel terrible for hurting you. I understand if, uh, you don't forgive me."

"You mean you don't hate me?" she asks him.

Cale looks at her, surprised, and takes her hand.

"Parker, I could never hate you."

To his complete and utter shock, she bursts into tears.

"What? What did I say?" he asks, panicked.

She snorts.

"You ass! I have been worried all day that I did something to make you hate me, and you tell me you turned into a jerkwad because your shoulder has an owie?"

"I—I—" Cale stutters, unsure what the proper response is.

He just wants her to stop crying.

"Parker, I'm sorry. I promise you, I will never let it happen again. I will do everything in my power to prevent it. If you want, we can stop training together... or stop patrolling together," he offers, hesitantly.

Parker wipes her eyes, drying her face with her sleeve.

"You tell me you don't hate me, and then you suggest not working together. Yeah, great job."

"I—"

"I'm joking," she smirks. "Though I will be training alone for a while."

"Understood. I understand you not wanting to put yourself at risk."

"I'll be training *alone* because *you* won't be training at all," she says pointedly. "If your injury is still that bad you can't keep pushing yourself like you have been."

Cale nods slowly.

Even with the relief of putting this morning into perspective, tension hangs around them, seeping into their previously easy friendship. He knows it will take a bit to get back to where they were, and that they eventually will, but Cale feels a pang of sadness for the loss nonetheless.

"So…" Parker draws out, awkwardly. "How was the rest of your day?"

Cale gives her a small smile.

I broke into an abandoned school, freed a criminal from jail by pretending the Tribunal ordered it, and put my life in the hands of the people we are hunting.

"Pretty uneventful," he shrugs. "Just went out for some air to clear my head. How was yours?"

"Well, after Bellamy glued me up, I—"

"Glued you up?"

"Oh, yeah," she points to her head, "I banged my head pretty hard, and she sealed it up with glue."

Cale pulls her over to sit on the edge of her bed, and angles her face away so he can check out the damage. The area is already starting to heal nicely, but his stomach roils with guilt as he looks at the thin line.

"Why didn't you say you practically had to get stitches because of me?" he asks quietly.

"That's why," she answers, turning to face him,

"because I knew you'd get that 'kicked puppy' look on your face. It's only a small cut. You're just lucky she didn't have to shave any of my hair to fix it."

Cale knows the last part was meant as a joke, but he really is grateful no shaving was needed.

"You'd look weird with a bald spot," he remarks. "Okay, so after you were fixed up, what did you do?"

"Had an emotional breakdown."

Cale's mouth pops open and Parker smirks at him.

"There's that puppy look again. Don't blame yourself; my meltdown was an accumulation of things. You don't get all the credit."

Parker starts to tell him about the rest of her day, and how she'd ended up running to the General when everything seemed too much, about how they'd had a heart-to-"place-where-the-General's-heart-should-be" (Cale's words, not hers) and that they decided they were going to finally work on their relationship.

"That's great," he tells her, truly meaning it. "I'm happy for you, and think it is about time you get things in order with him."

"He's actually going to be here any minute," Parker says, glancing at the clock. "We're supposed to go have a late dinner when he finishes up work for the night."

"In that case, I think I should be going. The last thing you need while trying to work out your relationship with the General is for him to find me in your room."

"You don't have to go," Parker tells him. "I explained everything to him, and he knows we aren't a couple. In fact, you could come to dinner with us if you wanted!"

Cale starts laughing, but the look on her face cuts him off.

"Oh…you're serious. Um, that's all right. I think I'll pass this time. I have to, uh—"

Knocking on the door interrupts him from having to think of an excuse.

"That'll be him," Parker says standing up. "Are you

sure you don't want to come?"

"Definitely," Cale answers without hesitation.

She sighs and hurries to answer the door, opening it wide.

"Sorry it took me so long. There was—" the General starts, stopping when he sees Cale sitting on the bed.

Son of a—

"Hello, Prime."

"General."

"Well," General Linwood breathes, "at least you weren't stuck waiting on your own. Are you ready to go?"

"Sure," Parker smiles.

She then gives the General an odd look, tilting her head to the side and giving a small, but noticeable, twitch in Cale's direction.

"I'll leave you two to it then," Cale says loudly, getting up before Parker forces him into joining them for dinner.

He crosses the room and just about makes it past the General when he's stopped.

"Prime, uh, I mean, Cale," the General interrupts. "I just wanted to say… Nice work."

Cale's eyes just about pop out of his head as he studies at General Linwood; the latter looking about as uncomfortable as physically possible.

"I'm sorry?" Cale asks, positive he misheard.

The General clears his throat.

"On the tip line. I know that most of the leads are dead ends, but you have been following all of them diligently, and…I—we, the Tribunal, that is, appreciate all of your hard work. Thank you."

By the time he croaks out the 'thank you', Cale swears the old man is going to have a coronary.

Did he really just thank me?

Cale is in shock, and has a problem forming a coherent reply.

"I, uh…just doing my duty, Sir," he finally manages.

General Linwood gives him a swift nod and Cale hauls out of the room before things get any more awkward.

Not even a full day of reconciliation with Parker and look what she's done to that man.

Cale laughs.

Linwood is so screwed.

Retreating to his room, he feels the full burden of his day hit him. All he wants to do is collapse onto his bed and stop thinking for the next twelve hours. Sighing heavily, he instead forces himself to strip and take a shower. A morning of training, and then roaming in a condemned school building has left him feeling pretty grubby.

When he comes out of the steaming bathroom twenty minutes later, Cale makes it within a foot of his inviting bed when a knock on his door halts him.

Dear Jesus...I just want to sleep.

Opening the door, he half expects to find Parker begging him to come to dinner, or perhaps the General, here to retract any thanks previously given under duress. Instead he finds a short, middle-aged man he's never seen before.

"Yes?" Cale asks.

"Sorry to bother you, Patriot Prime, but this just came for you," the man says, holding out a small envelope. "A courier just dropped it off downstairs."

Cale quickly takes the envelope, recognizing the slanted writing on the front.

"Thank you," he tells the man, closing the door in his face without waiting for a response.

He tears the envelope open, hurriedly removing the note inside. It's longer than any of the others he's received so far.

Cale reads through it as fast as he can, once...twice...three times.

He hadn't expected a response from the Slavers so soon, but after reading their letter, he realizes that they have been ready.

Of course they have been. They knew I would say yes to them, and they have been planning this all along, just waiting for my signal.

Something starts to prickle on the back of his neck, and in his stomach.

Fear.

Cale glances over the note one more time, breathing deeply and trying to control his emotions.

This isn't about you, he reminds himself. *It's about Patriot Prime, New Edison, protecting the people…Parker.*

He once again pushes all thoughts of himself away, letting calm overtake him.

For them… For them, I can do this.

~

When Parker curls up in her bed, she has a stupid grin on her face she can't quite shake. Despite today being one of the worst days she's had in a very long time, she can't help but feel extremely pleased about how it ended.

Cale doesn't hate me, and neither does my father.

She smiles a little more widely into her pillow when she thinks about her dinner earlier. Things went really well. She and her father had talked, actually talked, about a number of random, normal things.

The weather, politics, work, they even talked about a family vacation they once took to Mexico, back before her mother had passed away.

For two people who normally argued, or disagreed nonstop, tonight had been huge for them. They only hit one real snag all evening, when Parker brought up the serial killer while discussing the latest news going through New Edison.

"Speaking of news," Parker started, pausing to sip her lemonade. "Any on that serial killer?"

"Keep your voice down!" The General snapped. "Nobody has confirmed he is a 'serial' killer."

"Then how did you know who I was talking about?" she asked smartly.

"Lucky guess."

"How is he not being classified as a serial killer? He's targeting a specific group of women."

He leaned across the table towards her, keeping his voice low.

"As of now, we are able to keep this quiet while the situation is handled, but as soon as someone straps a label on this guy, calling him a 'serial killer,' word will get out. That's how these things work."

"I don't understand how the media hasn't put it together already," Parker sighed.

The General just shrugged, and waited so long before speaking she had been sure he wouldn't respond.

"It's because of the area of town he's hunting in," he said. "The media has a blind eye for the 'slums.' Not many people care what happens there."

"That's horrible," Parker spat disgusted.

"Yes…but that doesn't mean it isn't true."

After that Parker had changed the subject, not wanting to infect their evening any further with talk of murder and social classes. The rest of dinner had been wonderful.

Things are looking up, she thinks, rolling over in bed. *Now I just need to catch the Slavers and things will be perfect.*

That's not true…I'm still confused over the whole Cale thing.

Parker knows that Cale is sorry for his outburst; she could see it in his eyes, he looked so worried she wouldn't forgive him. She *has* forgiven him…but that doesn't mean she fully understands what happened.

He says he only lashed out because his shoulder hurt, but is that really enough to cause the rage or hatred she had seen on his face?

I stubbed my toe yesterday and nobody saw me smashing up my bed frame, she thinks. *Okay….so a gunshot wound to the shoulder is a little different than a stubbed toe.*

She sighs.

Still though…there has to be something else going on. If he is still in this much pain why hasn't he said anything to Bellamy? I know he hasn't, because if he had, he would be on bed rest if she had to strap him down and force him to recover.

Parker is again getting the feeling that there is something going on she just can't grasp; something just out of sight that she is missing.

Maybe if you thought about yourself a little less…

The thought was meant to be a bit sarcastic, but there is a ring of truth she can't quite ignore. The more she thinks about it, she realizes it *is* true.

Parker has been so caught up with her own drama she's been missing the obvious signs right in front of her. Cale has been distracted for a while, and though she had previously attributed that to his wound, she now thinks there might be even more to it.

What has been happening to Cale? What has him so distracted?

At that moment, she decides that she needs to stop thinking about herself and focus on Cale. He is her best friend and has been there for her every time she's needed him. Sure, she has other friends, or used to, but ever since auditioning for the Patriot Guard and being chosen, Parker hasn't had much time to maintain those friendships. Even when she *had* made time to see old friends, she realized she just couldn't relate to them any longer.

It's hard to have a girl's night out when everyone knows your name, and your metabolism burns up the alcohol before the buzz hits.

Parker realizes, aside from her lunch with Cynthia and Lucy, she hasn't talked to most of her friends for more than a few minutes apiece since she started 'filming.' It hadn't fazed her because she was so busy at the time, but as the truth hits, she feels a tinge of sadness and guilt.

I will not lose Cale, she vows. *I will find out what is going on with him and help him fix it.*

This decision is all it takes to help ease her mind

enough to finally find some sleep. She drifts off peacefully, but her peace is, unfortunately, brief.

It begins with flashes of color, a splash of green, and a hint of brown. Slowly, an image begins to emerge; beautiful green eyes, pale skin, soft brown locks framing a delicate face.

Mom.

As soon as she recognizes the face it starts to change. The eyes turn haunted, and bloodshot, the pale skin becomes hot and flushed, and the softly styled hair turns brittle and displaced.

The image expands and Parker realizes she's in a car. She's in the passenger seat of her mother's car. Shock zaps through her as she turns questioningly to her mother, but before she can ask, the words freeze on her lips.

Her mother is wearing a brand new, blue floral print dress, a gift from Parker's father.

The dress she died in.

Even though she knows it isn't real, that this isn't happening, Parker can't hold back the squeak of fear as she looks out the windshield. They are already on the highway, and the car is veering back and forth in traffic.

"Mom! Please stop the car," she begs.

They keep driving, dodging other vehicles, but only just barely.
"Pull over!"

Her mother merges dangerously into the left lane, cutting off another car, causing the driver to slam their brakes and blare the horn.

"Shove it," her mother mumbles, accelerating.

"Please stop...please, just stop."

Parker's knuckles are white, her hand cramping, as she hangs on to the door handle with all her might, arching back into her seat.

"Stop the damn car!" she screams.

Then she sees it.

The semi.

It's heading straight towards them. Her mother veers the car uncontrollably, jerking them into oncoming traffic. The semi driver slams on his brakes and sounds his horn.

Everything goes blank just before the impact.

"Parker, don't you dare use that language with me," her mother scolds.

Parker is standing...she doesn't know where she's standing. Everything around her is blank. She's just...nowhere.

She turns in a circle trying to find the source of her mother's voice, but sees nothing.

"I'm over here, dear."

She turns towards it again, and this time she sees the outline of a person blurring into existence.

"Mom?" she whispers.

The form becomes more solid, and gradually Parker's mother appears before her, looking so much different from the last time she saw her.

Her eyes are clear, unburdened, her skin and hair are back to their soft perfection, and she almost appears to be glowing.

Ok, *Parker thinks,* this is weird.

Her mother is wearing a long black gown Parker's never seen before, and there is just something *about her.*

She looks older.

She looks how she would if she had never died in the car accident. Small lines crinkle at the corners of her eyes and mouth as she smiles at Parker.

"Parker, you must prepare," her mother says.

"Prepare for what? What is this? Am I dreaming?"

"Prepare yourself. Alone you must find out the truth."

"What the hell are you talking about? The truth about what?"

Her mother only smiles sadly in response.

"He will be saved."

"Who is 'he' and why, if he's going to be saved, do you look so damn depressed?" Parker demands.

"Trust him," is the only offered response.

Before she can ask whom she's supposed to trust, Parker is strapped back into her mother's car just as it collides with the oncoming semi.

Parker jerks awake, and sits straight up in bed. Her heart is pounding, and she's drenched in sweat.

"Just a nightmare," she breathes, trying to reassure

herself. "Only a nightmare."

She's a little surprised at her dream. Parker stopped having dreams of the car accident years ago.

There was something else, she thinks, trying to recall the rest of the dream. *This was different somehow.*

She has a vague vision of a pretty older woman in a black gown, but as soon as she tries to focus on it, it's gone.

Someone said to...to...do something.

The harder she tries to remember, the more quickly the memories slip away, like trying to drink water from a cupped hand.

Sighing, Parker lays back down, unable to remember anything. It doesn't take her long to fall back asleep, and when she gets up the next morning, almost all recollection of the nightmare is gone.

SIXTEEN

Almost two weeks after the "'training incident,'" as they're calling it, things are still feeling tense and awkward between Parker and Cale, and Parker is sick of it. They don't talk like they used to, all banter between them feels forced, and a bit mechanical, and Cale is more distracted than ever.

Granted, he has good reason to be. In fact, maybe you should stop acting like a foolish teenage girl with 'boy troubles' and focus on the real *issues at hand,* Parker chastises herself.

The Slavers have been upping their game, tagging graffiti all over town, calling themselves "The Servants," and trying to recruit members. At least, that's what the Tribunal thinks they are trying to do, though they aren't sure how the Slavers would actually go about getting new members.

I doubt there's an application process or anything, she snorts. *Maybe they have, like, a thug temp agency.*

At first, Parker had been in agreement with the Tribunal's assessment of the Slaver's behavior. They were just calling attention to themselves, trying to draw the public's interest in them, perhaps even trying to rally a riot of some sort.

The Slavers started tagging higher profile areas, like downtown buildings, the bank they robbed, even the police station, much to the police chief's dismay and embarrassment. Their messages got stranger at each destination:

"The Servants will free you"
"TEnergy is draining you"
"Find the truth behind the coal"
"Tesla has the answer"
"The Tribunal LIES while Citizens DIE"

In telling the public to find the truth, that Tesla has the answer, and insisting that the Servants would free them, it sure seemed like the group was shouting "Hey, come talk to us!" That's what the Tribunal was pointing to, but when the last tag was found, luckily (for the Tribunal) by a city employee before the media got wind, Parker started to wonder if there was another motive behind the sudden surge in activity.

To Parker, it makes sense for them to spread charming nonsense talking themselves up and trying to draw favoritism, but it's one thing to bash TEnergy, a company half the population hates, and another to point fingers at the beloved Tribunal, the group singlehandedly responsible for giving the city real life superheroes.

The abrupt surge in activity seems off to Parker, and she has the overwhelming feeling she's missing something obvious.

The local news channels have developed their own take on the Slavers, and the Tribunal is not pleased with it one bit. The reporters haven't gone so far as to suggest innocence of the Slavers, but they have been shining a more sympathetic light on the group.

With the first mention of Tesla's name, the media hounds were eager to dig up a story, and have since been plastering newsstands with opinion pieces of how this is all a plot for Tesla to avenge his great-great-grandfather's name, and take down the company spawned by Nikola Tesla's rival Thomas Edison.

I seriously doubt that's what this is all about.

In addition to the graffiti, the Slavers also blew two more transformers. While there has never been anything normal about the attacks, the latest two were even stranger than before. When she thinks about them, Parker can't help but feel uneasy.

She and Cale arrived at the scene of the first new explosion to find that the Slavers were already long gone, as usual. They inspected the transformer, this time finding no notes, and were just preparing to leave when Parker realized something glaringly obvious.

"What?" she exclaimed.

"What?" Cale asked, turning back to face her.

She gave him a pointed look.

"What?" he repeated.

"I can see you."

"I can see you, too."

"How?" she asked.

Cale sighed, not getting it.

"Because of the...oh my god."

"There it is," she remarked smartly.

There they were, standing near the smoking transformer, the only one in the area, and the whole place was lit up by streetlights. It wasn't possible. The entire neighborhood should be blacked out, but as Parker looked around, it was clear to see that everyone still had power.

They put a call in to the Tribunal, who responded by telling them they must be wrong; there was no way the area could still have power unless every household was running private generators, and if that were the case, they would hear it. Parker argued that, unless the Patriot Guard serum gave her night vision, there was most certainly power on in the area, and the Tribunal agreed to send out a tech team.

Naturally, by the time the tech team arrived, the power had shut down and there was no way for them to track the energy source. After confirming that the power had indeed been on for almost exactly thirty minutes after the explosion, the Tribunal demanded that search efforts to find the Slavers be redoubled.

Like we haven't already been on full alert...chasing every phone call of someone claiming to see a man with long hair that might or might not have been Tesla.

While things have been progressing nicely with her father, going from tolerance to cordialness, to maybe even warmth, Parker can't help but feel frustrated with the lack of useful ideas coming from the Tribunal.

Find the Slavers. Find the Slavers. Find the Slavers.

God forbid they give us any useful information to go on. Nope, 'we just want you to keep up what you've been doing, going to already trashed transformers, and following every phone tip, because that's *panned out so well.'*

"You okay?"

Parker jumps, startled. She had been pacing back and forth outside of the headquarters' call center, waiting impatiently for the next bogus tip.

She turns around to see Cale cautiously eyeing her.

"Yeah, I'm fine. Just...frustrated," she sighs.

"I hear 'ya. This whole thing is a joke. I don't know why they think working hard on our already failed tactic is going to magically help us find the Slavers," he complains, voicing her thoughts.

Parker nods and starts pacing again, while Cale stands off to the side of the hall looking uncomfortable. It only takes a few minutes for the silence to become unbearable.

"Okay!" Parker exclaims, and this time Cale is the one to jump. "What is up? Seriously?"

"What?"

"Don't 'what' me. You know what. You have been distancing yourself from me ever since the training thing. I thought we made up?"

"We did," Cale says. "I haven't been distancing myself from you. We've just been... busy."

"We've always been *busy*," Parker huffs, "but we haven't ever had this weird silence between us. There is usually some sort of talking, or joking, but lately you have been so closed off."

"Sorry, I—"

"You said that the training incident wasn't my fault, but if that were true, you wouldn't be treating me like some sort of leper."

"Parker, it was *not* your fault. I told you what happened," Cale argues. "Look, you're right. I haven't been myself, and maybe…maybe I have been keeping my distance.

"Why?"

"Because I don't want to end up hurting you again, okay? That was one of the most terrifying moments I've ever experienced. Thinking I may have hurt you, and I can't do it again."

"Cale," Parker sighs, "you're not going to hurt me again."

"You can't know that, and I refuse to risk it."

"I'm a big girl, I can take care of myself. If you really think there's that big of a chance you'll slip again, let me promise right here to take full responsibility. Alright?"

"No," he shakes his head. "Not alright."

"You are being so unreasonable! Your shoulder is getting better, maybe a little slower than we'd like, but it is improving. Why are you fighting me on this?"

"I will not put you in jeopardy. I grew up in the system, moving from foster home to foster home. I didn't form attachments, I couldn't afford to," Cale says softly. "The first constant person I had in my life was Dr. Bellamy, and I'm just her twisted experiment. Parker, you are the only one who actually knows me, and cares about me *for me*. To everyone else in the city, I'm just Patriot Prime, and to the Tribunal I'm just a pawn piece in their political games. I can't stand the thought of putting you in danger."

She studies him closely, and sees that he really is worried.

"A couple things," Parker says after a long pause. "First, you are not just some 'twisted experiment' to Bellamy, she really cares about you, and it would break her heart to hear you say something like that. Second, we're still partners. We have to work together, so not talking to me, or not treating me like normal isn't going to make me any safer. I care about you, Cale, and you say you don't want to hurt me, but you are. It hurts when you ignore me. You're my best friend, and I don't want to lose you."

Cale refuses to meet her eyes.

"You can't just ignore me! I'm a part of this too, and it's partly my decision. I'm not—" Parker's tirade is interrupted when the call center door opens.

It's a middle-aged woman wearing a head set.

"Suit up," she says, "the Slavers just broke into TEnergy. Gunshots were fired, and they are still on scene."

Cale and Parker nod, and turn away.

"This conversation isn't over," Parker hisses, as they hurry off to change.

"Trust me, I know."

~

The pressure from the Tribunal, and all of their frustration weighing down on them, urge Cale and Parker to make it to the scene in record time.

The TEnergy power plant sits at the edge of the city. It's a huge company made up of several buildings. In the front are two office buildings, one for all the company bigwigs, and one for the billing and call center; back behind them looms the large power plant itself, and a small security building sits off to the side. The report they received said that the Slavers were in the main offices out front.

Cale has mixed feelings about the call. He's thankful for the timing of it; he really didn't want to continue his discussion with Parker at the moment, but, at the same time, he's not sure he's ready for what's to come. He knows this is it.

The signal.

When he last heard from the Slavers, they said once it came time for his "cure," there would be a big event to signal him. They would need to talk to him in person to set the final details, and since they couldn't risk Cale being seen working with the Slavers, it had to be something where they could interact freely.

Like a big break in at TEnergy…

Cale is still nervous about the whole thing, but he knows it's for the best, especially after the week he's had. While outwardly he'd been chasing down clues about the Slavers, inwardly, he'd been fighting a difficult battle.

Whatever his shoulder injury triggered isn't going away as he heals. Since he snapped on Parker, Cale has been having a hard time keeping his anger at bay. Some of the day, it's pretty dormant, or almost completely absent, but then something will trigger him, like a song he hates, or a snide comment, and he experiences a surge fury he has to wrestle under control.

He's exhausted from fighting it.

Relief hits him, knowing he won't have to fight much longer. It clears his head as he and Parker sneak towards the office entrance, and he signals he'll go in first.

Ironically enough, when he enters the lobby, the power is out.

He sweeps the area, and after finding it empty, signals the "all clear" to Parker. She, like him, has her gun drawn and eyes the lobby warily. On their right is an elevator, on their left a door to the stairwell. In front of them is a glass reception desk centered in the room, and leading away on either side are hallways lined with offices.

Parker signals that she is going to check down the hall to their right, and gestures for him to do the same with the left. He almost stops her, thinking they should stick together, but resists the urge, knowing she is safe from the Slavers.

For now, at least…they wouldn't risk hurting her and causing me to bail on the plan.

Cale gives Parker a stiff nod and turns towards his own hallway, slowly creeping along and trying each office door. Sometimes they open, but more often, they don't. At the locked doors, he places an ear flatly against it, listening and hoping his enhanced hearing will pick up on something.

He's just rounded a corner in the hall and is preparing to check another door when a firm hand clamps down on his arm.

~

Parker is searching her sixth office when she senses someone is following her. Remaining calm, she finishes checking the room before retreating to the hallway. The darkness makes it almost impossible to find her way, let alone see if a figure is hiding in the shadows.

Maybe you're imagining it.

No. I'm not. I know someone is there.

Parker moves to the next office door and tries the handle. It jiggles, but doesn't turn. She could easily break the lock, but doesn't want to make that much noise, so she moves onto the next door.

There! Someone just breathed behind me!

She tries to look as oblivious as possible as she makes her way down the hall. She doesn't want to give her shadow a reason to attack…yet. It wouldn't be wise to start a fight when she doesn't know from where exactly her opponent would be springing.

Parker is trying to decide how best to handle the situation when the next knob she turns twists freely. The door swings open to reveal a large conference room.

Perfect.

The room is softly lit by the moonlight playing through open blinds on the outer most wall. The only obstacle in the large space is an oblong table surrounded by chairs; it is the most ideal place she could hope for under the circumstances.

She tenses as she enters the room, still trying to act unaware that she's being followed. Parker circles the long table, moving to stand in the far corner of the room. She doesn't like being backed against the wall, but her preference for visibility wins out and keeps her from backtracking to the darkened hallway.

Knowing it's time, Parker twists towards the door, drawing her pistol up, and finds she's aiming squarely at the chest of her follower.

Tesla.

She'd been preparing to fire, but seeing who it is catches her mildly off guard and she hesitates.

"Fancy seeing you here," Tesla tells her, casually making his way into the room.

He seems unfazed as she follows his path with the barrel of her gun.

"It's kind of my job," Parker remarks dryly.

"Oh! Before I forget, Aida says 'Hi.' You should really call her, you know. She's worried about you."

"What? When did you talk to my grandmother?"

"Couple of days ago. She was delight   ed to see you, by the way, but jeez, break the poor woman's heart by telling her you're there on business," Tesla says, shaking his head reprovingly.

"*I was* there on business; you may be accustomed to lying through your teeth, but some of us have standards. Besides, if she was that concerned, she could have made a bigger effort to see me sooner! I— wait…why am I telling you this?" Parker wonders out loud.

She raises her gun a bit higher, but Tesla only smirks at her, seeming completely unthreatened.

"Gun shots were fired," she starts, "was anyone...injured?"

"No, the security guards had the sudden urge to lock themselves in a closet and nap. If I'm not mistaken, and I'm usually not, I think a chair managed to find its way over and barricade them in there."

Parker senses he's telling the truth.

Had the urge... is the Criminal Calmer here?

"And the shots?"

"Just wanted to get your attention."

"What? Why?"

"I missed your shining personality," he says, giving her what she assumes to be his most charming smile.

Parker huffs and rolls her eyes.

"I do feel a little bad though," Tesla tells her, growing solemn.

"Why?" she asks warily.

"Last time we were together, I promised our next date would be over dinner."

"Oh, please. This is *not* a date."

"Of course, you're right. I think I saw a vending machine down the hall, though. Would that work? No?"

"I have a better idea," Parker says, giving him a sweet smile. "How about we go somewhere? Actually, they have a pretty stocked pantry back at the Patriot Guard Headquarters. I could whip us something up while you wait to be interrogated."

"You and I have very different concepts of a good time, Sentry. Don't worry, I'm not giving up on you yet."

He winks.

In the time they'd been talking, Tesla had been slowly circling the table, trying to get closer to Parker, but she'd matched him, step for step. She was a little surprised when she realized she was almost back at the entrance of the conference room.

"You're dedicated," she tells him. "Good quality in a man. Unfortunately, breaking the law and being an obnoxious ass counteracts that."

"*You* like it when I'm obnoxious."

"You're coming with me…in handcuffs…now."

Tesla smirks.

"Kinky."

Parker lets out a frustrated yell.

"Enough! Hands up, now! Put them behind your head, or I'll shoot!"

As soon as the words leave her, she realizes her mistake.

Her best bet against Tesla has always been her speed. If she can get close enough to him, she might be able to incapacitate him. Unfortunately there is no way she can reach him on the other end of the table before he could stun her.

And I just told him to raise his hands.

Parker dives out of the door and into the darkened hallway just as a shower of sparks bounces off of the wood she'd been standing in front of. The light from the sparks make it even harder for her to see in the blackness; she keeps seeing bright colored splotches that aren't really there.

Knowing her best chance at this point is to get help from Cale, Parker takes off down the hall, and back the direction she first came. She can hear Tesla stumbling out of the conference room, and pushes herself to move faster.

It's too dark for her to take off at her full speed; she'd end up tripping over a water cooler, or potted plant, and twist her ankle.

Blinding light sizzles past her, and she can feel the static charge of it graze her cheek.

She sucks in a breath, startled at how close his aim was. On the plus side, the orb of energy lights up the path in front of her and she's able to pick up her speed for a few moments before the orb collides with something.

Water cooler, she thinks, trying to dodge the flying plastic debris.

She almost slips in all the water gushing from the smoking cooler, but manages to keep her footing at the last second.

Up ahead, Parker can see light, and knows she's getting close to the lobby. She knows that, if she can make it there, she'll be able to speed up enough to lose Tesla, at least until she can reach Cale.

She's just reached the lobby and pushed towards the opposite hall, when the glass reception desk explodes from another one of Tesla's orbs, and glass showers over her. Parker's arms shoot up to protect her eyes and face, blocking her view. She slips on the glass scattered across the floor and this time can't regain her balance. Parker falls forward and instinctively catches herself, palms out.

She cries out as the shards pierce her hands. The pain causes her to hesitate and suddenly Tesla is in the lobby too.

"Hold still," he says, panting a little. "I only want you unconscious, and it's much easier to be precise with a motionless target."

Parker snorts and struggles to get up without causing further injury to her hands. Tesla approaches and crouches down next to her. When he reaches out to touch her, and most likely zap her, she lashes out with her legs and knocks him over.

She scrambles to get up, but Tesla, groaning on the floor behind her, grabs her ankle and tries to pull her back. She's thankful for her boots, knowing he won't be able to shock her through them. Parker tries to pull herself forward, but just ends up scraping her hands even more.

Needing to catch him off-guard, Parker rolls onto her back, twisting her ankle free of his grasp, and kicks out. It isn't a hard kick, due to her lack of traction, but her boot connects directly with Tesla's face, and when she pulls away, she can see his nose is already bleeding.

He groans, and stops trying to grab her, instead bringing his hands to cup his face.

Parker scrambles to her feet.

"Such a shame to bruise that pretty face," she tosses over her shoulder as she darts from the room.

She launches down the hall Cale went to investigate, and hopes he's okay. The last time he faced down Mother Mayhem, he didn't fare so well, and Parker doesn't doubt for a minute that Krista Brandt is here now.

She has to slow back down after a moment because the hall is so dark. Parker really doesn't want to trip and land on her already damaged palms.

"Cale?" she whispers.

She thinks she hears voices but can't identify them. Parker comes around a corner and sees an open door. She approaches slowly, listening.

"I don't know."

Cale? Who is he talking to?

"Of course you do," a woman replies. "I know you'll be there."

Is that... Mother Mayhem?

"I— yeah. You're right. Of course, I'll be there," Cale sighs.

"Awe, good little hero. Tomorrow night at eleven, don't be late. Also, try to keep your little friend out of this."

What are they talking about? Why is Cale making plans to—?

The wall next to Parker erupts in a shower of sparks, and she jumps out of the way. Tesla is right behind her, and she hurdles into the room with Cale and Mother Mayhem.

As soon as he sees Parker, Cale's gun comes up to aim at Mother Mayhem.

"Watch out, she's armed!" Cale yells.

Parker is briefly wondering who he's warning when she hears a gun go off. At first, she doesn't realize why she's flying backwards, but then the pain hits and she realizes she's been shot.

SEVENTEEN

"Krista! What the hell?" Tesla shouts.

Cale rushes to Parker's side, pulling her into his lap with one arm while the other holds his gun, which is pointing at Krista.

"She'll be fine," Krista scoffs. "It was a rubber bullet, and she's wearing a vest. Let's go!"

Cale touches Parker's side where the bullet hit, and can tell the woman is telling the truth.

"Konstantine!" Krista yells.

Tesla glances down at Parker, who seems to be having trouble catching her breath, and then to Cale.

Cale is glaring daggers at the man, and gives him a look that's trying to tell him to get the hell out. He feels a jolt of satisfaction when he sees the blood on Tesla's face.

Nice work, Parker.

Tesla gives Cale a quick nod and raises his hands, aiming them at the outer wall of the room. A bright light makes Cale look away, but he can hear the wood splintering as the wall gives way. When he looks back up, he just manages to catch a glimpse of Krista and Tesla climbing through a gaping hole in the wall.

When they make it back to headquarters, Cale uses his most demanding voice to tell the Senator and the General to back off.

"I'll answer your questions after I drop her off to Bellamy," he tells them firmly, helping a hobbling Parker along.

She tells him that her side is still in a lot of pain. Cale can tell it's spreading into her abdomen, giving her a hard time standing up straight, but the real issue is her hands. It's hard to see because they are coated in blood, but many of the scrapes she received from the reception desk's glass are healing up already. This would be great normally, but some of the cuts still have shards of glass in them.

The General looks ready to help Cale get Parker downstairs, but Senator Scott intercepts and pulls him aside, whispering furiously.

Cale rolls his eyes angrily and continues helping Parker.

Lousy son-of-a-bitch! *Too preoccupied with how to spin this to the press to even ask if Parker is going to be okay. I just want to wring his—*

Stop. Not now. You have to calm down, Cale tells himself, fighting for control.

He takes a few deep breaths, focusing on the trip to Bellamy.

When he gets there, Dr. Bellamy is waiting, almost as if she'd been prepared for them to come back maimed.

"It's her hands," Cale explains. "They're already healing, but there's still glass in the wound."

Dr. Bellamy grimaces.

"This is going to be unpleasant," she tells Parker, "but I'm going to need to reopen these. I'll get some local anesthetic to numb you, but it'll still sting. Do you have any other injuries?"

"I was shot in the side with a rubber bullet," Parker grinds out. "My vest took most of the impact, but it still hurts like hell."

Dr. Bellamy just nods, and then turns to Cale.

"I'm sure you have two anxious men waiting for you upstairs. Go ahead and deal with them. I'll take care of Parker. She's going to be fine."

Cale nods reluctantly, but quickly heads back upstairs.

He finds Senator Scott and General Linwood easily enough; they are waiting for him in the General's office. They launch into questioning as soon as Cale enters.

"What happened?"

"Were the Slavers there?"

"Is Parker okay?"

Cale holds up his hands to silence them, and slowly walks over to take a seat on a small couch.

"Parker's going to be fine," he reassures the General. "Bellamy's looking after her right now."

"What happened with the Slavers?" Senator Scott demands.

"They were there to steal some files. I think...I'm not entirely sure. I just know when I found Krista Brandt, she was searching through a filing cabinet in somebody's office."

"When *you* found Krista Brandt? Where was the Sentry?" the Senator asks, annoyance clear in his voice.

"We split up to cover more ground. She ran into Tesla on her patrol, and didn't fare the greatest. I think he snuck up on her, and she wasn't able to get close enough to him. She bolted to find me as soon as she could and when she reached the office I was in, it alerted Krista to our presence. She shot Parker, and when I dropped to check on her, Tesla came in, blew the wall open, and he and Krista bailed."

The Senator curses under his breath and starts pacing the office. General Linwood, on the other hand, seems to be in shock.

"Parker...was shot?" he asks. "I didn't see any blood, it didn't—"

"It hit her vest. Worst she'll have is some bruising," Cale says.

"Yeah, you said she'd be fine," Senator Scott interrupts, waving his hand. "You let the Slavers get away. Again!"

Cale has to work to bite back his anger, and from the

look on his face, the General seems about ready to rip the Senator's head off.

"That's it. We can't allow this to continue. Tell him," Senator Scott says to the General.

General Linwood clears his throat, looking uncomfortable.

"The next time we get a tip on the Slavers, we won't be sending you and Parker in."

"What?" Cale asks. "You can't possibly think the police can handle them, do you?"

"No, not the police. We'll be sending in the PGTF, the Patriot Guard Task Force."

"The what?"

"The PGTF is made up of the losing contestants of the Patriot Guard Second Generation. We couldn't just send those people home after giving them super reflexes. It would be a waste, and it's not like there's any way to counteract the serum," General Linwood explains.

Cale tries to ignore the last bit of what Linwood said.

"But they lost. Parker is better than all of them," he argues.

"Maybe better than each individual," Senator Scott says, "but not all of them together. They won't fail at taking down Tesla and Brandt."

"Taking down, or taking in?"

"Whatever it takes," the Senator shrugs.

Something feels off to Cale, and it has for a while. Maybe it's the lack of control that has been growing in him, or maybe he has just reached the limit of crap he'll take. Whatever it is causes Cale to do something he's never done before: question the Tribunal outright.

"What is going on here?" he demands, standing up. "What is your real issue with the Slavers? It's obvious you're hiding something. There's no way you would issue a kill order over some graffiti and damaged property."

The Senator is quick to answer.

"Not that you are owed any explanation, but don't

forget they tried to rob that bank…that they were the ones to shoot you."

"Well, three of them did," Cale counters, "and one is dead, while the other two are in prison. So, why are you so intent to go after Tesla and Brandt?"

"Enough!" the General snaps. "Prime, you are in violation of your oath to this city and to the Tribunal."

"Well, you're in violation of pissing me off! All of your secrets… you send *your daughter* and myself out to risk our lives without even the courtesy of telling us what we're really up against. Grade 'A' parenting there, General," Cale sneers.

Cale and Linwood are chest-to-chest, fists ready to fly, when Senator Scott steps in.

"Alright, Prime. That's enough. Why don't you go tell your girlfriend you two are off the Slaver's case?"

Cale's eyes flash dangerously at the Senator, but he turns and walks away. As he's closing the door behind him, he can hear low talking.

"Well, that's completely out of character for Prime."

~

Dr. Bellamy is just finishing up with Parker's hands when Cale comes storming back into the room. He gives Bellamy an angry look, but she is so focused on Parker that she doesn't notice. The Doctor'd had to go over the sealed cuts with a scalpel to retrieve the glass shards, and is currently resealing the last incision with a butterfly bandage.

"There you go," Bellamy says. "You're all set."

"I need to speak to Parker *alone*," Cale barks, ignoring all formalities.

"Yeah, of course," Bellamy tells him, looking confused at his rough tone.

She looks back and forth between the two before slowly leaving.

"That was a bit rude," Parker insists.

"Well, I don't seem to have much patience for the Tribunal at the moment."

Cale's jaw is clenched tightly, and he looks ready to throw something across the room. Parker can't help but tense up.

"What's going on?" she asks.

Cale sighs and comes to sit next to her, immediately launching into describing his discussion with Senator Scott and the General. Parker is shocked, and furious.

"They're just going to replace us? With the Second Generation castoffs?"

Parker knows she sounds bitter, and a little pompous, but really doesn't care. The people she competed against may have received the same serum as her, but she left them all in the dust.

"What is this going to look like to the public?" she asks. "Super heroes are a morale boost, something special to believe in and inspire hope. But this...this is just another military task force. There's no magic or hope in that. This defeats the whole purpose of the Patriot Guard."

Cale snorts.

"Do you honestly still believe that?"

"Believe what?" Parker asks.

"The party line. That this was ever actually about being a 'morale boost' or to 'inspire hope'? Come on, Parker. This is about power. Plain and simple power."

Cale looks so much different from the man she's used to seeing. He's always seemed to exude peace; she's seen his mere presence steady crowds and calm hysterics, but now...now his face is hard, his eyes are cold, and there is no hint of his usual easy smile.

"What do you mean?" she questions.

"I guess I can't blame you," Cale mumbles, a bit unhinged. "It took *me* forever to see the truth as well. I used to think we were being used as cash cows. You know, lining the Tribunal's wallets from all of the merchandise, while instilling faith in the government. That may still be part of it, but there's more than that. I can see it now."

Cale's eyes are huge, *and a bit deranged,* as he stares at Parker, urging her to understand. When she doesn't say anything, he continues.

"Separately, all the clues don't seem like much, but when you piece everything together, you start to see the bigger picture. When we first went on patrol, I told you how we are supposed to call the Tribunal to check with them before we bring anyone in, and a lot of the times they would tell me to let people go, judges, lawyers, and such. People it would be good to be owed a favor by. There's piece one, the Tribunal collecting favors among high ranking city officials."

Parker bites her lip and nods along.

"Piece two, they constantly lie to us. We're supposed to be beacons of light in this city, and yet we're always kept in the dark. Why are they so hell bent on catching the Slavers? Why won't they let us search for that man killing women in the slums? They say we aren't detectives, yet send us chasing bogus phone line tips. Why? Because the less we know, the easier we are to control. The less they tell us, the more power they have over us."

"Well," Parker suggests, "the General said they are trying to keep the whole serial killer thing low profile so they don't cause a mass panic. If we were looking into it, it would sort of blow the 'low profile' thing. Also, they told us before--they have us checking the phone line tips because, if they do lead to the Slavers, we'd be the only ones able to handle it."

She doesn't know why she's defending the Tribunal. Honestly, she agrees with what Cale is saying.

Maybe I just like playing devil's advocate.

"More lies," Cale answers, waving her off. "Piece three, and this is the crazy one...so, just hear me out."

Parker nods.

"I also think they are faking evidence against the Slavers…pinning crimes on them that don't belong to them."

"What?"

"The bank robbery. It doesn't make sense, you said so yourself. The graffiti tags don't match. Also, I don't know if you've noticed, but every time we actually meet the Slavers, they aren't trying to kill us. But, at the bank, those guys were definitely not pulling punches. I just don't see them as members of the Slavers."

She snorts loudly.

"Okay, then. Maybe they were members of Children of Freedom, Mother Mayhem's militia. She seems a bit unstable. I mean she did just shoot me."

"With a rubber bullet, while you were wearing a vest."

Parker shakes her head.

He's crazy. The Tribunal wouldn't fake evidence. Hide things from us, maybe, use the Patriot Guard to garner favors, probably, but fake the origins of the bank robbery? No way.

"Look, all I'm saying is that there is something big going on here. Something we're not seeing. If you ignore the robbery, all the Slavers are guilty of is a bit of vandalism. Does that really require the need for a secret military task force of super soldiers?"

He does have a…no…don't get sucked into his theory. He's still being weird because of his injury. This isn't really Cale talking; don't encourage him. Tell him he's wrong, try to be gentle about it, but set him straight.

"Cale," Parker starts, not sure what to say.

Luckily, Dr. Bellamy comes striding back into the room. She's holding a clipboard, and looking rather serious.

"We're still talking," Cale snaps at her.

Bellamy does her best to hide the hurt on her face, but Parker catches it and nudges Cale roughly. She doubts the Doctor had anything to do with them being pulled from the case. Parker's seen the way the Senator and the

General treat the woman. Bellamy has about as much control as she and Cale.

"Sorry, but this is important. Parker, I've just received your test results."

Parker feels like all the air has been sucked from her lungs. She stares at the Doctor, wide-eyed and unable to speak.

"It came back positive. You're a Variant."

And just like that, Parker can breathe again.

It isn't that she is happy to be a Variant, but the relief of finally knowing what she is, one way or the other, is satisfying. The stress of not knowing had been weighing down on her even more than she knew, something she is only able to realize now that it is gone.

"Are you alright?" Cale asks, quietly.

"I—yeah. I'm alright."

"Have you been experiencing anything weird lately?" Bellamy questions. "Anything at all out of the ordinary?"

Parker laughs.

"You mean like super speed, or accelerated healing?"

"Point taken," the Doctor smirks.

"Is there any way to tell from the test what kind of Variation she has?" Cale asks.

"Unfortunately not. We don't have that much information about Variations. There haven't been that many volunteers willing to be studied. Perhaps Parker would be willing to let us run some tests though, and maybe give us more insight in the Variation anomalies."

Alarm bells seem to chime in Parker's head, but she ignores them and gives a halfhearted nod.

"I think the only way to find out her Variation," Bellamy continues, "is to wait it out. Maybe do a little self-searching. You might already be experiencing signs that you just attributed to the serum."

Parker starts chewing her lip again, wracking her brain.

Could I have missed something?

"You should go see, Aida," Cale suggests. "Her grandmother," he adds for the benefit of a very confused Bellamy. "She might be able to help you sort things out, or at least explain what you're looking for. It's not like you won't have plenty of free time now."

"What do you mean?" Dr. Bellamy asks.

"Well, since we're no longer on the Slavers case," he says bitterly.

"What? Did you catch them?"

"What? No. We've been booted," Parker explains. "Shouldn't you know that? The Tribunal decided to kick us to the side and pull out the PG Task Force to find the Slavers."

Bellamy's eyes ignite angrily.

"They did what?" she questions furiously.

Without waiting for a response, Dr. Bellamy turns on heel and marches across the room, storming out of the door with a huge bang.

"Told you that you were being rude, she had no idea," Parker tells Cale. "Oh, to be a fly on that wall."

She sighs, imagining the Doctor's glorious fury aimed at the Senator and the General, and smiles.

EIGHTEEN

The next morning, Cale wakes up feeling confused, and a little disappointed in himself. While he's been thinking those things about the Tribunal for a while now, he never meant to bring them up to Parker, especially not when she was just starting to straighten things out with the General.

Not to mention you sounded about as reliable as that "end of the world" nut Jonah. She has got to think you are off the deep end… and maybe you are.

Cale ignores his inner voice, though, intent on having a fun, normal day with Parker that would (hopefully) set things straight between them.

I don't want to leave it like this…broken and unfamiliar.

It only takes him about thirty minutes to gather everything he needs and turn-up in front of Parker's bedroom door.

He has to knock four separate times before she answers. Her squinting eyes and bedraggled hair tell him that she's just drug herself out of bed.

"What is this, Sentry? Eleven in the morning and still in bed? What happened to your perky morning person alter ego?" he teases.

Parker groans and turns back into the room, leaving the door open for him to follow.

"I think she died," she tells him, voice heavy with sarcasm.

He just laughs.

"Maybe we can still revive her. I brought presents!"

Cale holds his arms out, showing her the bags he's laden down with, and the drink carrier that holds streaming coffee.

"Caffeine," she sighs, pouncing on the carrier, "my hero."

"Now, now, don't be greedy. I'm everyone's hero."

Parker snorts into her cup, having already started sipping the hot brew.

"I also brought doughnuts; super unhealthy, chocolate glazed, fresh doughnuts. And—" he stresses, "a pile of cheesy action movies for us to sit around, watch, and make fun of."

She arches an eyebrow at him.

"You brought all of my favorite things. What's the occasion? Am I dying? Is that like my mutation or something?"

"What? Don't be ridiculous. We kind of have the day off after all the crap last night, so I thought it would be nice to do something…normal. No hero stuff, no Tribunal nonsense, no Prime or Sentry—just us. Parker and Cale, hanging out like two normal friends."

"We'll never be *normal* friends," she smiles.

"Well, we can at least pretend. What do you say? Or do you have other plans, like, oh, I don't know…brooding over the confirmation you're a Variant?"

She's quiet for a moment and Cale wonders if he's crossed a line.

"You're right," she says finally. "Let's pretend to be normal."

"That was terrible," Cale groans as the credits start to roll on their fourth action movie of the day.

"What? That was awesome! It was one of the funniest movies I've ever seen," Parker argues.

"It wasn't supposed to be funny."

"You brought it. You knew what you were getting yourself into today."

"Yes, I did…but that was a new level of horrible. Oh, dear lord, the *puns*."

Parker starts laughing.

"What did you expect from something called *Judge Hammer and the Gavel of Justice*?"

Cale smirks, and just shrugs.

"Any more of those dumplings left?"

After exhausting the supply of doughnuts Cale brought, they had ordered an obscene amount of Chinese take-out.

Parker hands him a plate of dumplings, snagging one for herself.

"It's days like these I'm extremely thankful for our increased metabolism."

Cale nods, already stuffing his face.

"So," Parker drawls, "is today your way of getting out of the conversation we started yesterday? Did you decide I was right, and there is no point in avoiding each other?"

No. I still think I'm extremely dangerous, but I don't want to run to the Slavers without us being all right.

That's what Cale wants to tell her. Instead, he says:

"You were right. I shouldn't have been distancing myself from you. I didn't think about how it would look to you. I was only thinking of your safety."

"I appreciate you wanting to look out for me, but I'm still pretty annoyed you think I can't look out for myself," she huffs, crossing her arms.

"Parker…you may be a lot faster than me, but if I had another incident and cornered you like before, I don't think you could beat me. Can't you understand the risk I see?"

"I could take you."

"Could you? Really? Could you exercise deadly force on me if necessary?"

"Deadly? Why deadly?"

"If that was the only way to stop me, could you do it?"

"I don't think it would need to come to that," Parker insists.

"There. That's my point. You would be too distracted by the fact that it's me, you wouldn't be thinking clearly enough to defend yourself properly."

"Would you be able to use deadly force on me if I attacked you?"

"No, of course not," Cale shrugs.

"That's a double standard!"

"Well you aren't the one on the verge of losing your mind!" he snaps.

Parker opens her mouth, but stops, confused.

"I—I just mean," Cale stutters, "you aren't having the same issues as me. You don't have a wound causing you all sorts of problems. Look, I'm sorry. I don't want to fight with you. This whole thing has just been really stressful."

"I can understand that," Parker assures him, "but things have been stressful for a lot of people lately. Don't get all dramatic on me and pretend you have the monopoly on rough times."

"Parker—"

"No, it's okay. Just stop. I don't want to fight either. Let's just drop it, and let things work themselves out, alright?"

Cale nods.

"Alright."

They both sit in awkward silence, looking around the room absently. Cale can't stand the quiet and he frantically tries to think of something to say.

"So…have you given any thought to going to see your grandmother?" he asks.

"A little," Parker admits, "but I just don't know. Maybe if you went with me?"

He gives her a tight smile and nods noncommittally.

"Maybe."

Cale looks to see what time it is and his heart sinks when he finds it's almost ten.

"Hey, uh, I have to go," he tells her.

"Why? It's still early."

"I have to go get something from my apartment," he offers, unconvincingly.

"Do you want me to go with you?" Parker asks.

"No! I mean…we're still under pretty heavy scrutiny from the public. It wouldn't do for you to be seen coming to my apartment this late."

"Ah, good point. How long will you be?"

"I'm not sure," he answers truthfully.

"You are coming back, aren't you?"

Cale suspects she heard him last night talking to Krista, and he's fairly certain they both know her question is asking about more than a trip to his apartment.

"I don't know," he says, not wanting to lie to her.

"Be careful."

"I always am."

Parker walks him to the front door of PG Headquarters, and gives him a big hug before he leaves. He returns it, hanging on a little longer than he normally would, sucking all the comfort he can from the moment.

When he climbs into his car, Cale looks back to see Parker watching him, wishing he didn't have to go yet.

It's for the best.

~

Parker waits until Cale's car is out of sight before making her move. She hurries to the PG parking lot, thankful Simmons is working tonight. He works in the call center, and Parker knows he keeps a magnetic hide-a-key on the underside of his car.

A few weeks ago, he locked himself out of his car and Senator Scott saw him grab the hidden key. Parker had overheard them talking about it in the lobby the next day. The Senator joked that it couldn't be very safe to keep your car key in such an obvious place, but Simmons just countered with "Where would my car ever be safer than at the PG headquarters?"

Sorry to burst your bubble, Simmons...especially if I have to be present for Scott's smug reaction.

Simmons drives a dark blue Aveo, a pretty common car, and Parker feels it will suit her needs just fine.

Cale would spot my car in a heartbeat.

She pulls out of the parking lot, thankful for the quiet engine, but cringing at the squeak coming from the brake pads.

Damn it, Simmons!

Parker catches up to Cale at his apartment building, just in time to see him going inside.

She's pretty sure this is only a pit stop. There is no way he would meet with any of the Slavers in his own apartment.

If he meets them at all, that is.

Parker prays that she is wrong, that she must have misheard what Cale and Mother Mayhem were saying. All possible reasons he could be meeting with the Slavers are bad.

He could be meeting to make a deal with them...very bad. Or, maybe he is working with someone within the Slavers who has info for him...also very bad.

Maybe it's not as bad as actually working with the Slavers, but anything that involves Cale working this case without her seems like a really bad idea.

He's still not fully healed, and Parker fears what will happen to him if he tries to take them on alone, all because he doesn't want her to get hurt.

Doesn't he realize that's kind of a risk that comes with the job?

Forty minutes pass before Cale reappears from inside the apartment building. He's wearing dark clothes and a baseball cap, looking around suspiciously as he walks to the parking lot.

Parker ducks down in her seat and immediately feels ridiculous.

Did we watch so many cheesy action movies that we got sucked into one?

She peeks above the doorframe out the driver side window, trying to ignore the nagging preposterousness of it, as she tracks Cale's progress.

He approaches a black sedan and climbs in after one more wary glance around.

It must be a PG loaner. Cale knew his car would be too noticeable.

She waits until he's a block ahead of her before starting her own engine to follow.

So typically cheesy…I bet he's going to a seedy, abandoned area of town, just to stick with this whole motif.

Parker can't help but groan aloud when Cale leads her straight to the industrial area of town, and when he turns the corner to park in front of an abandoned warehouse, she actually bangs her head on the steering wheel.

She circles around the building before finding an adequate place to park out of sight, hiding the car behind a pair of dumpsters. She quickly pulls a handgun from her purse, hoping she won't need it, but glad she'd remembered to stash it there when Cale took a bathroom break during their movie marathon. By the time she makes it to where Cale's sedan is in view, he is nowhere around.

Damn it.

Parker hurries to the door nearest his car that leads into the warehouse. She's careful to open it slowly, not wanting to give herself away, but when she sees inside, she realizes her efforts are pointless. There is nobody in there.

Son of a…

She steps inside, cursing herself, wondering if Cale went to another building nearby while she was busy parking. Deciding to have a quick look around before searching other buildings, Parker starts edging around the room, her gun drawn and her back to the wall.

The whole warehouse is empty, aside from the garbage. She guesses it must have been used for storage at one point, as a few remnants of broken boxes and packing paper litter the floor. There is nowhere to hide.

Parker sighs and is beginning to holster her weapon when she sees a small glint coming from the wall on the far side of the room. It looks like candlelight, dim and uncertain.

Please, dear lord, tell me I am not crashing a date night between Cale and Mother Mayhem, Parker shudders.

When she gets nearer to the source, she can see the light is coming from a crack in the wall. Upon closer inspection, Parker realizes it isn't a crack, but a hidden door, left open just a sliver. She slides it open to find a flickering, low-watt bulb hanging over a concrete staircase.

Maybe I am *in the right place,* she thinks, starting a slow descent down the stairs.

The stairs let out into a small basement, also littered with debris, and also empty.

Well, that was anticlimactic.

Parker searches around, trying to find a hint of another hidden door. She starts kicking papers and cardboard around, looking at the floor. One piece of newsprint won't budge when she kicks at it, and she stoops down to push it away. When she tries to move it, she finds it seems to be glued down.

Parker tugs at the corner and, though it does lift, it is far heavier than any newspaper page should be. She pulls harder and is astonished when part of the floor starts to pull up too. The paper is stuck to the top of a hidden trap door.

Parker sticks her head down the hole to find a short latter descending into what appears to be a series of tunnels.

Well no freaking wonder we never found the Slavers, she thinks, *they've went full-on super villain and gotten themselves an underground lair!*

Trying not to second-guess her decision to follow Cale, Parker begins climbing down the latter. The metal rungs are damp, and the lower she gets, the more mildew she can smell.

Ugh, they have an underground fortress, but can't spring for a couple dehumidifiers?

Okay, she concedes, reaching the bottom, *this isn't so much a fortress as old drainage tunnels, but still.*

The tunnel she's in T's in front of her, and she tries to find a clue as to which way Cale may have gone. Both ways seem equally dark, and she can't hear any footsteps. Parker crouches down and pulls out her cell phone, using the glow from the screen as a flashlight, and scans the floor for any sort of tracks.

There is a small puddle of water about a foot into the tunnel on her right, and the splatter around it suggests someone recently walked through it.

Right it is…let's hope Cale made the splatter and not some giant rat.

Placing her phone back in her pocket, Parker begins making her way down the tunnel. It's dark, but there is an eerie glow about the place, lighting it just enough that she can see where she's going without tripping.

She's not sure how far she walks before she finds what she's looking for.

The silence surrounds Parker, the only noise coming from the echo of her footsteps on the damp ground. Every six feet or so, there is a door on either side of her, all identical, made of metal and aged by the clammy air. There is a barred gap in each door, and when she looks through, she is just able to make out what seems to be a large chamber.

Parker can't tell if there are more tunnels that lead away from the strange rooms. The farthest areas of them are shrouded by shadows, and when Parker tries to open one of the doors, she finds it rusted shut. She tries a few more and finds the same thing.

She keeps walking, her steps speeding up as she goes.

Everything looks exactly the same down here, she panics, *what if I can't find my way back out?*

If it weren't for the door, she would have completely missed the voices.

Out of nowhere, her scenery changes. In the spot where a rusty metal door should be is a shiny new one.

And it's open.

Parker halts in her tracks. As soon as she does, she can hear voices coming from inside. She recognizes Cale's at once. She tiptoes closer to the door, staying out of sight, wanting to learn what she can before deciding her next step.

"Believe me," she hears.

It's Tesla.

Parker's curiosity gets the better of her and she moves to get a look at the inside of the room, risking compromising her position.

She is surprised at what she finds.

It's a large chamber, much larger than she thought the others looked, and it is surprisingly well decorated.

For a drainage tunnel...

The walls are lined with posters and maps, while the floor is covered in antique-like rugs. She can clearly make out a makeshift kitchen, a dining table, and even what seems to be a mechanical workshop. On the far left side of the room, there are several cots that look well slept in. The whole place appears almost... *homey.*

What really draws Parker's attention, though, is Cale.

He's in the middle of the room on his knees, with two guards dressed in black standing behind him. In front of him is Tesla, holding a gun aimed at Cale's head.

"It's for the best," Tesla says.

Parker draws her own gun and prepares to make her

move.

"Is this where you do your Super Villain monologue and reveal your evil plans?" Cale asks.

Tesla sighs.

"No."

The gun fires.

The shot rings loudly through the stone chamber and the sound reverberates through Parker's chest as biting cold shock makes her numb.

It's Cale's limp body on the ground that wakes her from the shock and drives her through the door. She gives a guttural war cry as she charges, blinded by fury and piercing grief.

Parker barely makes it through the door when she falls to her knees, feeling weak. The gun slips from her fingers, clattering on the hard floor as waves of sorrow crash over her.

Tesla approaches and she forces her heavy-lidded eyes open to glare at him so fiercely, it's amazing he doesn't burst into flames.

In that moment, Parker is glad to be a Variant and urges her body to comply with her mind. She longs for her powers to be unleashed, whatever they may be, and rip Konstantine Tesla apart.

"It's for the best," Tesla says again, just as the Criminal Calmer steps into view.

Parker feels herself losing the battle to stay awake. It's the pain and hatred burning in her chest that gives her the strength to bite out her response.

"You…will…pay," she growls through gritted teeth.

The blackness descends and, unable to fight any longer, Parker is pulled down with it.

NINETEEN

When Parker awakes, she expects to find herself in a small, dank cell, somewhere among the twisting walkways of the drainage tunnels, so, naturally, she is a bit more than surprised to see she is in what must now be considered *her* bed in the PG Headquarters medical center.

She blinks rapidly, trying to be sure her eyes aren't playing tricks on her.

The Tribunal is standing around Parker's bed, and all of them are staring at her. Senator Scott looks bored, Doctor Bellamy appears anxious, and the General looks worried. She feels a slight pressure tighten around her fingers and sees that her father is holding her hand.

"Parker?" he says softly.

"How did I get here?" she asks, looking around.

"We were hoping you could tell us that," Senator Scott drawls. "You were found, unconscious, spread across the front steps of the building."

"Where is Cale?" Doctor Bellamy asks.

At the mention of his name, Parker is reminded of her grief. She wishes they wouldn't ask. To say it makes it real, and she's not yet ready to admit it.

Parker clenches her eyes shut and refuses to look at them, shaking her head.

They misunderstand.

"Sentry?" the Senator pushes.

"She doesn't know," the General says harshly.

"We need to find that boy. Maybe we should send a team out."

"That's overreacting a bit, wouldn't you say?" the General sighs. "He might be on his way here now."

Her heart feels like it is splitting in two. Parker realizes that it is, in fact, much worse to let them go on as if Cale is really out there. It hurts too much to even imagine that he might walk through the door because she knows it will never happen.

She opens her eyes and looks at the tribunal with a teary gaze. Bellamy seems to know what she's going to say. The Doctor clasps her hand over her mouth and starts shaking her head.

"Cale is dead," Parker says, her voice barely a whisper.

Bellamy continues shaking her head.

"What?" Senator Scott asks.

"Cale is dead; he was shot in the head by Konstantine Tesla. I— I saw it happen."

She feels her father's grip tighten, and she looks up at him.

"I couldn't save him," she confesses. "I didn't act fast enough."

And with that, Parker breaks down. Her body shakes with wracking sobs, as the General perches on the edge of her bed. She sees Doctor Bellamy flee from the room as she's pulled into her father's arms.

"Where did this happen?" Senator Scott demands. "We need to get people out there ASAP!"

She feels the General twist to look at the Senator, but he doesn't say anything, and she knows it is because they really do need to know the location. It takes her a few moments to compose herself enough to tell them about the warehouse and the tunnels beneath it.

Parker's barely finished describing the place when the Senator walks out the door, talking on his phone.

Her father stays with her for as long as he can before

he is pulled away.

"I could get somebody else to handle—" he starts.

"No, I'll be fine. They need you," Parker interrupts. "I could use some time alone, anyway."

When she's by herself, she doesn't know what to do. She can't fall asleep, though if she could, she would probably only have nightmares. Parker can't hide from her thoughts.

The scene keeps replaying itself over and over again.

It's for the best," Tesla says.

Parker draws her own gun and prepares to make her move.

"Is this where you do your Super Villain monologue and reveal your evil plans?" Cale asks.

Tesla sighs.

"No."

The gun fires.

Parker pulls her pillow over her face and presses down on it, hard, trying to block out the light, the sound, and her own condemning voice.

Why didn't you move when you saw Tesla was armed? You could have stopped him. You could have saved Cale.

Parker yells into the pillow before chucking it across the room. It hits the glass door of a medical cabinet and shatters it.

"You forget your own strength," a quiet voice says from the doorway.

It's Doctor Bellamy.

The Doctor looks neat and composed; the only sign of her earlier distress is her bloodshot eyes. Parker doesn't know how the woman can hold it together so well.

"Sorry," Parker mumbles.

"Don't be," Bellamy says, approaching the bed. "You should see my office."

Bellamy holds up her hands and Parker notices that the woman is decked out in several small bandages.

Perhaps she isn't as collected as I thought.

Parker doesn't know what to say. Bellamy must hate

her for failing Cale. They were so close.

"They've finished searching the tunnels," Bellamy says.

This gets Parker's attention.

"Already? But it's only been…" she trails off.

How long have I been down here?

"What did they find?"

"Not much. They did find one room with a missing door. Inside, there were traces of blood. We're running it now to see if it's…if it's his. Apparently, those rooms down there used to be for storing alcohol during the prohibition era. They weren't common knowledge and they've been all but forgotten. It's no wonder the Slavers have evaded us so long."

Parker gives a half nod and looks anywhere but at the Doctor, and they settle into an awkward silence.

It doesn't last long; soon, a quiet knock on the door interrupts. It's the General. He looks over at the busted medical cabinet, then back and forth between the two women before him.

"I'll just leave you two," Bellamy offers, hurrying to make her exit.

"Maura," General Linwood says, stopping Bellamy in her tracks. "The test is back. The blood was his. You might want to look at the results."

The Doctor closes her eyes briefly, takes a deep breath, and leaves the room.

"How are you feeling?" the General asks, pulling a chair next to Parker's bed.

"Like I'm living in a nightmare."

"I'm so sorry, Parker. I know I may not have always been on the best of terms with Pr— Cale," she resist the urge to snort, "but he was a good man. I know he was your friend and I am so sorry you have to deal with this."

"Why should you be sorry? It's my fault! I heard him say he was going to meet them! Did I say anything? No! Of course not! 'Oh, I can handle it,' I thought, 'I couldn't possibly be getting in over my head.' Then, what happened? I knew Cale was in danger and I froze—I didn't move when I should have! I hesitated and he is dead. HE'S DEAD!" she screams. "He's dead because I didn't react like I should have. I am no hero."

Again Parker finds herself in tears. She jumps out of the bed and grabs the waist high tray table holding a glass of water and several magazines. She picks it up, knocking the contents off and tosses the table at the already shattered medical cabinet.

"Parker!"

The General is on his feet standing in front of her, his hands on her shoulders.

"It was not your fault! How do you think he would feel if he knew you were beating yourself up like this? Huh? What would Cale say to you?"

She doesn't answer.

"Parker, if Cale could see you right now, what would he say?"

"Stop acting like your father."

The General snorts.

"Yeah, he probably would. What else? Would he want you to blame yourself?"

She shakes her head.

"Say it," he urges.

"No. He would hate if I blamed myself…even if it were true, he would hate it," Parker admits.

"Exactly. Hold onto that. He may be gone, but you are not. You're here, very much alive, and Cale is not the type of man who would want you to live your life hating yourself. Am I right?"

She nods.

The General leads her over to the bed and pulls her to sit beside him.

"Now," he says, "I really hate to ask, but can you tell me what happened down there?"

She bites her lip, positive it is still too soon to talk

about it, but, shockingly, the words come easily. She supposes that, after hours of replaying the scene in her head, the tale doesn't take any consideration to tell. The whole thing just spills out.

Hearing Cale and Mother Mayhem...waiting to follow him...trailing him to the warehouse...searching the tunnels...finding him...and hesitating a moment too long...

"Parker, you couldn't have saved him. You were far too outnumbered. I have complete faith in your abilities, but two armed guards, Krista Brandt, and Tesla? Honey, you would have ended up dead as well."

"Why didn't I?" she asks.

"What?"

"Why am I not dead? The Criminal Calmer put me to sleep. They had me at their complete mercy, and yet, what do they do? Place me on the steps of PG Headquarters for the Tribunal to find. It doesn't make sense."

"I don't know," the General admits. "We had you scanned when you were found. There are no bugs or devices of any kind on you and no traces of drugs or poison in your system. I don't know why they brought you back...but I am more grateful than you can possibly imagine."

Before Parker can respond, the door bangs open loudly, causing her to jump. It's Senator Scott, still on his phone.

"Working on it now," he says, before hanging up.

"What is it?" the General asks.

"I wanted to see how Sentry was doing."

Parker grits her teeth.

I am no hero.

"I'm...doing...a bit better," she says.

"Good, that's good. Look, I really hate to ask, but we need your help," Scott insists.

"With what? Did you find Tesla?" she asks, jumping to her feet.

"No, nothing like that. We are getting ready to make

a public statement about Prime's unfortunate downfall. The studio execs thought it would be best if you were to make the announcement while wearing your hero garb."

Parker's mouth falls open. He couldn't possibly have just said what she thought she heard.

The General must have been having the same thought.

"Did you...just ask her to dress up in a costume on live television to announce the death of her best friend?" he asks.

"Well, when you say it like that, it makes me out to be the bad guy. I just thought it would be good for the public to see that they still have Sentry— er, Parker."

The General stands up and takes Senator Scott by the elbow, leading him towards the door.

"With me, if you please," he all but orders.

They close the door behind them, but she can still hear their voices, and heated tones. From what she can tell, it sounds like the General is really giving it to Senator Scott.

Thanks, Dad.

Parker can't even imagine the next time she would want to look at her hero uniform, let alone wear it.

I am no hero.

The following week is nothing more than a haze to Parker. She spends most of it cloistered away in her private room. She could have gone home, back to her apartment, but she likes feeling close to Cale by being at headquarters. Plus, she really doesn't want to face the public.

On a side note, whatever the General said to Senator Scott in the hallway outside the medical center must have done the trick. She hasn't seen the Senator since then, and she heard he ended up making the announcement himself.

She's glad she didn't have to take part in it, though she has heard the public is starting to wonder about her disappearance. So far, the media is just running the "mourning lover" story, referring back to the pictures of her Cale heading to his place. She doesn't care what they say. Parker is laying down, spread out across her bed, staring at the ceiling, with *Judge Hammer and the Gavel of Justice* playing in the background for the twentieth time this week. She knows she needs to get up and do something, she just doesn't know what. She swore to Tesla he would pay, and she fully intends to make that happen, she just doesn't know where to start.

They completely cleared the tunnels; there isn't the slightest trace of evidence to indicate where they might have gone.

Someone lightly knocks on her door, and she sighs heavily, having to force herself to move and answer it. It's some redheaded girl Parker vaguely recognizes from working somewhere downstairs.

"Yes?" Parker asks.

"They are wanting to clean out Mr. Pearson's room. I thought perhaps you would like to go through it before anyone else. That way you can take what you want…and dispose of anything if you need to."

"Dispose—?" Parker starts to ask, but stops.

She can see from the uncomfortable look girl is giving her, that the messenger is one of those who believes the stories of Parker and Cale being an item. Parker is about to tell her there isn't anything she needs to take care of, when she changes her mind a split second later.

"Thank you," she tells the girl sincerely. "I'll head over there shortly."

Parker actually thinks it is kind of sweet of the girl to give her a warning, and a chance to hide her private life from the public and media, even if there isn't really anything to hide.

"Also, I don't know if you are interested—I imagine it might be hard to watch—but they are showing a tribute to Patriot Prime tonight on television," the girl informs her.

"I didn't know, thanks again…I'm sorry, what is your

name?"

"It's Molly."

"Thank you, Molly."

Molly nods and takes her leave.

Parker closes the door and leans up against it, sighing heavily. She doesn't want to go through Cale's things, but she doesn't want his stuff being thrown away or auctioned off to the highest bidder either. She heard Senator Scott wanted to hold a charity auction for some of Cale's belongings, though Parker wonders how much of the proceeds will go to a real charity and not into the Senator's reelection campaign fund.

Although, he probably doesn't need it, she recalls.

Parker just saw on the news that the serial killer who had been targeting single mothers in the slums had been caught. It turned out that he was the son of Senator Scott's fiercest competitor. With elections only a week away, she doubts Scott will need any more campaign funds with that kind of boost.

Feeling that she needs to mentally prepare to go through Cale's room, Parker decides to take a hot shower. She hopes it will help clear her mind, and give her a break from horrific scene that plays constantly in her head.

It doesn't work.

She still sees Tesla pulling the trigger over and over again, and she still flinches at the imagined gunshot. The only thing that keeps her from cracking up is that she knows *she* has to be the one to make Tesla pay.

After her shower, Parker dresses in normal street clothes, refusing to even look at her hero costume. She doesn't know how she'll ever wear the thing again.

I don't deserve to wear it.

She doesn't see anyone in the hall as she heads to Cale's room, and for that, she is grateful. When she does see them, they either look at her with expressions of deep pity, or questioning glances, wondering when she's going to get her act together and be the hero they need.

When she opens the door and walks into Cale's home away from home, the ache in Parker's chest doubles. It looks like he just stepped outside. His jacket is lying across the foot of the bed, and one of his white capes is hanging from the closet door. The bed is mussed, and he has papers spread all over the bedside table.

She looks around, unsure where to even start. The silence is deafening, and so the first thing she does is turn on the TV. It's set to the local station and she sees they are showing the tribute to Cale now, like Molly had said. They are doing a recap of all the newsfeeds surrounding Cale rescuing those school children shortly after he'd been named hero of New Edison. Parker smiles at the uncomfortable expression Cale wore on camera in the early days of his hero career. He looked so awkward and self-conscious back then, though he had certainly grown into his role over time.

Leaving the program on, Parker turns her attention to the room. She opens the closet and finds a small backpack inside that will fit her needs perfectly. She then starts the hard part… sorting. She doesn't find much she wants to keep in the closet, just a T-shirt Cale loved with the name of his favorite band, *Midnight Wasteland*, on the front, and a thank you card signed by the children he rescued from the collapsed school.

Next, she briefly rifles through his dresser. It's practically empty and she only ends up grabbing a photo of the two of them from back when Parker was still just a contestant on the show. It was a candid shot someone took while she and Cale had been on the sidelines of the training field, and they were both wearing a large grin. Parker thinks it might have been taken during one of their "bash the General" sessions.

She looks through the papers on his bedside table, and almost decides she is done in the room, when she notices the edge of a book peeking out from under one of Cale's pillows. When she pulls it out, Parker sees it is a leather-bound journal. Seeing no point in normal boundaries, she flips to the first page.

So, Doctor Bellamy brought me this. She said it might help pass the time here in solitary if I documented my thoughts. I don't know if that's true or not, mainly because my thoughts are: I'm sick of tests. I'm sick of solitary. I'm fine. I'm sick of solitary. Maybe I can write about something else. I guess I could just start with how I got here in the first place.

I was recruited straight out of basic...

"Parker Linwood..."

Parker's head shoots up, looking around the room.

"There were several promising looking auditions for *Patriot Guard: Next Generation*, but I think we all knew Parker would be a shoo in from the moment they said her name."

It's the TV. The person narrating the tribute to Cale is talking about the process of choosing a sidekick.

"Being the daughter of a Tribunal member made her stand out, but when she got out there, her actions really shone for themselves. We definitely had some disappointed contestants; no one could compete with Parker."

The screen starts flashing with clips from people who auditioned and didn't make the show. Parker almost returns to reading Cale's journal when she sees somebody she thinks she knows on screen.

It's the audition tape of a young man, in his early twenties, with red hair and bright blue eyes. He's pretty good, too— fast. He probably ended up being a runner-up for the show. She watches his video, wracking her brain trying figure out who he is.

He turns to the camera and winks.

"I'd do anything to work for the Patriot Guard," he smiles.

Parker feels as if she's been punched in the gut as recognition hits her.

He's one of the bank robbers!

Suddenly, things start clicking into place, almost more quickly than she can keep up with. For the first time in days, grief isn't her primary emotion.

Anger is.

Parker stuffs the journal into the backpack and swings the strap over her shoulder. Her mind is racing as she storms out of Cale's room, and she has questions she needs answered right now. She runs to the stairs and takes them two at a time, knowing she's faster than any elevator in the building.

When she hits the ground floor, Parker makes a beeline for the General's office. It's pretty late in the day, but she knows she'll find him there. He's been pulling long hours ever since Cale.

The General is sitting at his desk when she sends the door flying open. He looks up sharply, mouth wide open, probably about to reprimand whoever disturbed him so rudely. He manages to restrain himself when he sees it is Parker.

"What's going on?" he asks.

She can tell he is annoyed with her brusque entrance, but he attempts to keep his tone calm, still treading carefully around her because he knows how emotional she's been.

"What ever happened with those bank robbers?" she asks, attempting to reign in her fury, trying for a conversational tone and failing.

"What? Oh, I— they're in jail I suppose. I didn't really track the case."

"See that's the thing," she says, stepping in and closing the door. "No one seems to have tracked the case. It seems like their trial would have been a media frenzy, considering they did almost kill Cale, and yet I don't recall seeing one little segment on it."

The General looks uncomfortable under her watchful gaze.

"Why the sudden interest in this?"

"I was just upstairs watching the tribute to Cale, and you can imagine my shock when, during one of the recap segments on *Patriot Guard: Second Generation*, I see that one of the bank robbers had auditioned. Not only that, but he had made it into one of the final selection processes and is on camera saying he'd 'do anything to work for the Patriot Guard.'"

The whole time she's speaking, her voice is rising to match her temper. The General avoids looking at her and begins shifting papers around his desk.

"I'm not sure where you're going with this. Obviously, we should have done a better background check. The man must have been trying to infiltrate us for the Slavers."

Parker shakes her head.

"You see, I considered that briefly, but then I started remembering other things. Like how the graffiti tag on the bank vault door didn't match the regular Slavers tag. And how, up until the robbery, the worst the Slavers had done was to cut a few power lines. That's a big jump to the attempted murder of a hero!"

His head pops up and he glares at her coldly.

"I think we can both agree that murdering a hero isn't outside of their capabilities."

His words are like a physical blow, but she starts shaking her head.

"Cale said he thought you guys were hiding something. He was starting to think things were inconsistent to what you were actually telling us…that you were misleading us for your own gain." She starts shaking her head. "The Tribunal was behind the bank robbery, weren't you?"

"Parker—"

"WEREN'T YOU?" she screams.

"Yes!" the General snaps. "Yes, damn it we were!"

The admittance still stuns her, even though she knew as much.

"Why?"

"No one was supposed to get hurt, you have to believe me," he begs. "We did it as a demonstration to the people. We wanted to show them you were a hero…a worthy choice for the Patriot Guard."

She snorts in disgust.

"You mean like how Cale wasn't accepted until he proved himself saving that sch— oh my god. You didn't? Oh my god! That was you, too. Wasn't it? When it looked like the public wouldn't trust Cale, you endangered all those kids to make your hero program seem needed."

Parker feels like she's going to be sick.

"They were never in danger. We knew they wouldn't be in that area of the building."

She turns away, refusing to look at him. She never knew she could be so disgusted by her own father.

"Why pin it on the Slavers though? The robbery? I mean, I know now that they have the capability to be…evil…but then, before they really did anything, why pin it on them?" she asks.

He doesn't answer.

"Why?"

"Leave it alone, Parker."

"What else have you guys lied about?" she demands.

Suddenly another memory comes back to her. A conversation she had with Tesla.

"The only reason the killer hasn't been named a priority by now is either to protect someone, or to expose someone, but at the opportune moment. Be careful."

She gasps and turns back to face him.

"The Senator," she whispers. "That serial killer…did you know who it was? Were you keeping us from the case because the timing wasn't right for Senator Scott's campaign?"

"Leave it."

"Tell me."

"Parker, I said *leave it*," his voice is dangerous,

warning her to back off. "You will not mention anything you have learned in this room to anyone," he orders, "or you will be court marshaled and put in prison. In addition, when your bereavement leave is up you will return to work and will not express and dissatisfaction with the Tribunal in the eyes of the public."

"The hell I will," she scoffs. "I quit."

"You what?"

"I quit."

"You can't quit," he insists.

"Just watch me," she mumbles.

Without another word, she flings the office door open loudly and walks out. The General follows her into the hall, sputtering indignantly, and ordering her back. The only response she offers is her middle finger over her shoulder.

Parker doesn't know where she's going as she walks out of PG Headquarters. All she does know is that when she took her oath to become a protector of the city, she never imagined it would come at the cost of constant lies, deceit, and the life of her best friend. She also knows that heroes don't make revenge their greatest stance in life, but currently, her ultimate goal lies in making Konstantine Tesla pay. When she's done with him, the Tribunal better watch its back because she doubts those are the only secrets it's hiding.

Vengeance isn't heroic, she thinks, *but that's okay. I am no hero.*

Stolid Sentry
will return in

THE SERVANTS OF THE PEOPLE

ABOUT THE AUTHOR

Ameythist Moreland is an avid reader, writer, movie enthusiast, and fangirl. She graduated from Western Michigan University in 2013 with her Bachelor of Science, with concentrations in English, Language, and Health (which is a fancy way of saying she jumped majors a lot). When not writing, she is chasing after her toddler son, watching way too much TV, and planning vacations she can't afford. Ameythist lives in Kalamazoo, MI with her husband Kyle, son Nikolai, and their dog and cat, Luna and Norbert. For more information and to stay up to date on all news about *The Patriot Guard Trilogy*, please visit www.ameythistmoreland.com